Love is
a time of enchantment:
in it all days are fair and all fields
green. Youth is blest by it,
old age made benign:
the eyes of love see
roses blooming in December,
and sunshine through rain. Verily
is the time of true-love
a time of enchantment — and
Oh! how eager is woman
to be bewitched!

PRAY, LOVE, REMEMBER

Jane had led a sheltered childhood until the sudden death of her father, and she was ill-prepared for her changing circumstances. Every summer, however, she spent happy weeks with a family of cousins on the Welsh coast. Here she painted, sailed and went fishing with Jim. Then 1939 brought change again. Early in the war Jane met Michael, and they eventually married. But she learned that material success was Michael's only aim. Her despair grew, until through love remembered she found courage to face the unrelenting demands of her life . . .

Books by Margaret Yorke
Published by The House of Ulverscroft:

MARGARET YORKE

PRAY, LOVE, REMEMBER

Complete and Unabridged

ULVERSCROFT
Leicester

This edition published in Great Britain
in 1995 by
Severn House Publishers Limited
Surrey

First Large Print Edition
published 1996
by arrangement with
Severn House Publishers Limited
Surrey

British Library CIP Data

Yorke, Margaret
    Pray, love, remember.—Large print ed.—
    Ulverscroft large print series: romance
    1. English fiction—20th century
    2. Large type books
    I. Title
    823.9'14 [F]

    ISBN 0–7089–3622–9

"There's rosemary,
that's for remembrance;
pray, love, remember:
and there is pansies,
that's for thoughts."

Hamlet

"Oh, the comfort, the inexpressible comfort of feeling safe with a person; having neither to weigh thoughts nor measure words, but to pour them all out, just as they are, chaff and grain together, knowing that a faithful hand will take and sift them, keep what is worth keeping, and then, with the breath of kindness, blow the rest away."

To Shax (sic)

Part One

1

IT was still and calm under the sheltering arms of the weeping willow. Between its green fingers Jane could see glimpses of sky as she lay on her back on the dry dead grass which carpeted the ground under the great tree. This was her special private place, where she brought all the troubles and the joys of her small life. Here she spent hours flat on her stomach on hot summer days, deep in the adventures of Robin Hood or King Arthur's Knights, with the sunlight filtering through the filament branches to cast striped shadows on the book. Here she held meetings with the imaginary companions who adventured beside her through her solitary days. Here, too, under the tree each January, the first shy snowdrops broke the wintry soil.

Today her main thought was that soon the tree would be hers no longer. Out of all proportion in the tragedy that had come so suddenly, the imminent loss of the friendly tree assumed gigantic significance. Where in the new garden would she be able to hide and play her secret games? Perhaps, dreadful thought, there would not be a garden at all. At this, the pale green leaves vanished behind the tears which filled the little girl's eyes, and turning over to bury her face on her arm, she abandoned herself to her grief.

In the house at this very moment Mother was shut in the drawing-room with Uncle Robert and Mr. Pryce. Jane knew they were talking about selling the house, and Mr. Pryce was arranging the details. She did not like him one bit. He was short and stubby, with pince-nez, and a large brief-case full of papers about other people's houses. Jane saw him going through life high-handedly disposing of property against the desires of its owners. He was only the latest in the chain of sombre-suited gentlemen who had seemed to fill the house since that dreadful day three weeks ago. Jane had come home flushed and excited from Helen's party, laden with prizes and a balloon, and bursting to tell her parents all about the wonderful time she had had. Instead of Daddy, Dr. Morris was in the drawing-room with Mother, who was crying. Jane was shocked: she had never before seen a grown-up weeping.

"Why, Mummy, what's the matter? Have you got a pain?" she asked, running to the sofa where her mother sat.

Then Dr. Morris had told her. That afternoon her father had been killed in a motor accident.

At first Jane was stunned; her immediate reaction was to hug her mother and say "Cheer up, Mummy, I'll take care of you." Only later came the finality of realisation, and the tears; remorse, too, that she should have been laughing and gay at a party while her father was already dead, followed. The procession of dark-coated visitors which had begun with Dr. Morris continued. Mysterious men passed through the awful door behind which Jane knew her father lay. Once she was sent to Helen's house for the day. Helen looked at her strangely, and spent the time being as kind and unselfish as she could, lending Jane her most precious toys which normally she could not bear out of her sight, and generally behaving quite out of character. Helen's mother appeared in the nursery, dressed all in black, and enfolded Jane in a scented embrace, saying, "Poor little darling," and with sick horror the child realised she must be going to her father's funeral.

After that the days strung together in a maze. Mother did not cry any more, or at least not for Jane to see. She was very pale, and kept having long talks with Nanny, and with Uncle Robert who had arrived on the day of the funeral. She wrote a great many letters, and Jane and Nanny walked down the road to post them every afternoon. Cook made all Jane's favourite puddings, one after the other, and let her spend hours in the kitchen making cakes and toffee, but otherwise the routine of the days was the same as it had always been, only there was no Daddy, nor ever could be again.

He had been an active, jolly man, happy to join in games of hide-and-seek or Red Indians, always ready to read a story or play 'Beggar my Neighbour.' He was a stockbroker, and travelled to

London every day on the train. He was returning as usual from the station when a lorry had come suddenly out of a side turning and crushed his car and himself to pulp on the same road where he had passed uneventfully so many times before.

It was worst at night; then in the darkness Jane would lie imagining the dreadful accident, horrified that she should have been laughing while her father died. The terror of death appalled her, and she would lie too frightened even to cry, hugging her doll for meagre comfort. Sometimes she was able to visualise her father in Heaven, where everyone assured her he must now be. She saw him riding on a fluffy cloud, dressed in a surplice like the vicar, whilst God, looking rather like His Majesty King George V, whose face was the only bearded one she knew, hovered above. Heaven thus pictured seemed very dull and uncomfortable, and Jane was not convinced that her father would enjoy it.

At last her tears were exhausted, and Jane got up and stood for a moment under her tree. She had pins and needles in her leg, and rubbed it with a damp, grimy hand. Then she went slowly towards the house, avoiding the grim conference in the drawing-room and going upstairs to the nursery.

Here, Nanny had already begun to sort things out for packing. She had a passion for clearing out, from cupboards and bookshelves to syrup of figs. Seeing her charge now appearing with a red, blotched face streaked with dust, dishevelled hair and a dirty, torn dress, she stifled the rebuke which automatically rose to her lips and instead briskly advised a wash.

"Then you can come and help me go through all these books, dearie, and decide what we'll be taking with us," she added.

"But Nanny, I can't spare *any*," Jane protested, looking at her beloved 'Secret Garden' which, tattered by much reading, Nanny now held poised over the rubbish box.

"Well, my duck, there won't be so much room at the new house, you know, and we won't have space for all these books," she said. "Besides, you've read them all, now why not send them to the poor children who haven't any of their own?"

"Well, not that one," insisted Jane. "Perhaps I could spare one or two — but let me do it myself, please Nan," she begged. Her glance fell on a large waste-paper basket which Nanny had already half-filled with battered objects. "Oh no, you can't throw away my paint-box," she wailed, and snatched the shabby black tin from its depths.

"But you've nearly used it all up, Jane," said Nanny in despair. "There's hardly any paint left."

"There's still a bit, and I haven't another, and I don't suppose I ever will have now we're so poor," cried Jane, and once again tears threatened.

"Oh, love, things won't be as bad as all that," said Nanny, giving her a hug. Ruefully she decided to abandon her clearance for the moment, as if Jane was present she would clearly not allow anything to be thrown away.

"Come along, let's find a clean frock, and then we'll go and see if Daisy wants some help with the tea things," she said.

Together they went downstairs ten minutes later, the plump, grey-haired woman who had cared for Jane since her birth, and the sturdy child in her blue gingham dress.

Thank goodness Mr. Pryce did not stay to tea, Jane couldn't have borne that. One pleasant change had come about since her father's death, and that was drawing-room tea for Jane, while Nanny condescended to carry her own small tray upstairs. This reduced the work in the large, pleasant house, where already the staff had been cut down. Mr. Harrison had startled everyone by leaving very little money; and his widow, who had been accustomed since her marriage to modest luxury, now found that there would be little left on which to manage, even after the house was sold and she had moved to a smaller one.

There were fresh scones for tea, and raspberries from the garden for Jane. The silver teapot gleamed, and so did the kettle that stood on its own little stand, with a flame of methylated spirit burning below. Mrs. Harrison poured out. She was a slender woman, pale now, her usual vivacity vanished like a light gone out. Beside her, her brother-in-law seemed by contrast very large and ruddy. Jane liked Uncle Robert, although she did not know him very well. He was a soldier, and was often abroad, but he always remembered her birthday with a suitably exciting present. He had a lot of children, and Jane got a little confused when she tried to recall their names and ages.

He smiled now at Jane, recognising with pity the traces of her recent distress on her round face. What a shame she hadn't a bunch of brothers and sisters; this blow would have seemed much less in the midst of a noisy crowd of youngsters such as his own, where there wasn't time for weeping. That was what she needed, poor little scrap, some young company. Always forthright, the idea was no sooner in his head than uttered.

"Rosamund, what about Jane coming to stay with us whilst you move? The children would be company for her, and wouldn't it make things much easier for you and Nanny?" He picked up his cup and held it poised midway between lap

11

and lip while he waited for a reply.

Mrs. Harrison hesitated, and looked doubtfully at Jane. The little girl paused on a mouthful of raspberry, chewing suspended, her blue eyes large beneath her straight fringe of brown hair.

"We-ell — " Mrs. Harrison began uncertainly. "It would be nice for Jane, thank you, Robert, but — " she paused, torn between the wish for her daughter's company, and the knowledge that the presence of other children might be more important at this time.

"We're off to the sea next month," said Uncle Robert. "At least, Madge and the children are, as soon as they come home from school, and I'll be there whenever I can escape from the War Office."

"The sea!" breathed Jane in an ecstasy, and swallowed her mouthful of raspberries.

"It's very kind of you to suggest it, Robert," said Mrs. Harrison, beginning to weaken, "but will Madge mind? Won't it be too much for her?"

"Not a bit of it, one more makes no difference with all our brood," smiled

12

Uncle Robert. "You let her come, Rosamund."

Mrs. Harrison gave in. "Very well, she shall," she decided.

"Splendid," said Uncle Robert cheerfully. "The sea breezes will soon bring roses to her cheeks."

Jane silently resumed her eating. Perhaps after all life could be endured. Staying with her cousins, she would escape the awful moment when this dear house was stripped of its customary belongings and left empty and abandoned; she would escape also what she dreaded more, walking into the new house and finding in its atmosphere a hostility towards herself. She was half fascinated, half afraid of her cousins, whom she hardly knew, as for years they had been out of England when their father was serving abroad. They were always cheerful and noisy, they thought of exciting games to play, they were hearty and self-confident. But in her secret heart Jane was uncertain of her ability to play the parts demanded of her in their games. However, the blissful prospect of the sea would make up for her inadequacies. Jane had spent holidays on the south coast every year and enjoyed every moment of them; she loved the feeling of space and freedom; above all, last year she had learned at last to swim.

It was 1933, and Jane was ten.

2

IT was hot in London, and there was a lot of traffic which kept holding up the taxi, causing Nanny to lean forward impatiently in her seat and fume at the uncaring cars and buses surrounding them. The driver's back expressed merely calm resignation at the delay.

"Oh, Nanny, we'll miss the train; won't we?" demanded Jane as once again with squeaking brakes they jerked to a halt.

For the hundredth time Nanny consulted the large gold watch which had been presented to her by her previous charges, whose virtues she was for ever citing.

"Well, no dearie, I don't think we will," she admitted, for she had allowed at least twice as long for the journey across London as Uncle Robert had declared necessary. "But still, it's very tiresome to be standing still like this."

The driver suddenly let in his clutch,

and as the taxi sprang forward Nanny was nearly catapulted on to its prickly matting floor. She was an incurable sufferer from train fever, and existed in a ferment until safely in her seat.

By the time they reached Euston she was in a fine state of impatience. She hastened to descend from the cab, impeded by the caging of whalebone and laces that supported her unsupple person. It was a tense business paying off the driver and choosing an honest-looking porter, for another of Nanny's phobias was that most of them would run off with your luggage if you gave them half a chance. They set off at a brisk pace in the wake of the chosen man, Nanny stout and splendid in her grey worsted, with her grey felt hat worn horizontal over her eyes, and her matching grey hair showing in discreet sausage curls at the back. One white-gloved hand firmly grasped Jane's beige one — "Because of the dirty carriages, madam, and what Mrs. Harrison, Aunt Madge that is, will say if we arrive all crumpled and dirty as we generally are I do not like to think," Nanny had breathlessly said to mother when Jane's holiday wardrobe was discussed.

Mother had merely said, "Very well, Nanny, whatever you think best. I don't suppose Mrs. Harrison will even notice what she's wearing."

As well as the beige gloves, Jane wore a flannel coat, and her best printed silk dress that was too short in spite of the false hem, for she had grown so much in the past year. Her white shoes and socks were already scuffed with London grime, and on her head was perched her loathed straw hat which had a wreath of flowers all round its crown. Jane felt very uncomfortable in this attire and thought with longing of the shirts and shorts which, as advised by Aunt Madge, composed most of her luggage.

There was plenty of time before the train was due to move, in spite of the traffic delays. Nanny settled herself into a corner seat facing the engine, for travel with her back to it she dare not, and indicated that Jane should take the opposite one. She looked at her watch again.

"There's just time to buy a paper,

17

dear," she said. "Now don't you dare to move till I get back, I'll only be a minute. Now mind, don't you speak to *anyone*," she warned, ever mindful of white slavers, and with much creaking of her stays she majestically departed in the direction of the bookstall.

Left alone, Jane seized the chance to remove her hated hat, and tossed it up on to the rack. She hoped some more people would come into the compartment, as it would be rather boring with only Nan for company. Still, she was glad she wasn't travelling alone, although she had begged to do so. It would have been rather alarming after all. Nanny was to return on the overnight express, sleeping in it, which sounded very exciting. Jane thought it a pity they weren't both travelling by sleeper, but perhaps it would have been inconvenient for Aunt Madge to meet them in the middle of the night.

She wondered what Rhosarddur Bay was like. Aunt Madge and Uncle Robert had rented a house there for the whole of August. It would be the same as Bognor, she imagined, where last summer she and Nanny had stayed while Mummy and Daddy were in Italy. She turned her thoughts firmly away from the painful direction they had taken, and remembered only poor Mummy, left surrounded by packing-cases in the wreckage of her home, too much harassed now to feel more than relief at Jane's departure. In two days time the vans would come and remove everything to the new house. Jane had seen a photograph of it, and grudgingly allowed that it looked pretty, long and low, built of grey stone, Mother said. It was in a village near where she had lived as a girl, so that in a sense Mother was returning home. There was a small garden too, but no weeping willow. Jane had specially asked.

A train going past with much steam and snorting distracted her thoughts. She could see the people inside it, some still busy reading, some reaching their cases down from the racks, some just gazing with pale faces out of the windows. She wondered what they were all going to do today in London. They all looked much more interesting than Nanny, who now returned, puffing rather like the train after her breathless journey along the platform.

"Phew, dear, what a lot of people," she exclaimed, mountaineering back into the compartment. "We'll shut the door, then perhaps we'll be able to keep this carriage to ourselves," she added, slamming it to, and then sinking exhausted into her seat. She had bought *Rainbow* for Jane, and settled down after much arranging of herself and polishing of her steel-rimmed spectacles to her own *Woman's Life*.

Presently there was the sound of doors banging shut all along the train, and they were off, at first jerkily, and then more steadily, out of the terminus and into the open with its network of lines.

Jane had not travelled many times by train, and she found it very exciting. She watched the grimy buildings passing until at last they were in the open country. She invented stories to herself about the houses she saw and the people who lived in them. Soon it was time for lunch, and they went plodding along to the dining-car, Nanny in some anguish about leaving their luggage unguarded.

Lunch was altogether delightful. There was soup, which swished about with the speed of the train as it hurtled along. There was roast beef and two sorts of potato, and un-cabbage-like cabbage. There was ice cream. There was even fizzy lemonade out of a bottle as a special treat. Afterwards Nanny unskewered her hat and prepared for forty winks. Jane devoured the *Rainbow* and then moved on to *Swallows and Amazons* which Mother had given her for the journey. What lovely adventures those children had! She sighed with envy. They were so brave and resourceful. Perhaps they might go out in a boat at Rhosarddur? She did not know if it was likely, but she and Nanny had been in a rowing boat at Bognor so there was hope.

Time passed. The trip to the dining car for tea was another adventure. This time there were lumps of sugar wrapped in neat little parcels of two, and your own pot of jam, doll size.

Then, looking out of the window, at last Jane saw the sea. Cool and blue, shining in the sunlight, it lay beside the railway line as they hurried along.

"Watch out, now, dearie," urged Nanny. "We'll soon be going into Anglesey."

Sure enough, a little later, before the train plunged into the tunnel bridge, Jane glimpsed for a moment the incredible beauty of the Straits, sloping banks of green-leaved trees slanting down to the blue, blue water.

"We're nearly there," Nanny bustled. "Come along dear, you must put on your hat, and whatever have you done with your gloves? I never knew such a child for getting in a mess." She clucked and tchted as she combed Jane's hair and replaced the hat on her unwilling head.

Aunt Madge and cousin Julia were waiting when the train drew in to the long platform. There was a wonderful smell, partly of train dirt and smoke, blended with the odours of ancient fish, tarred rope and sea water; Jane sniffed in delight this pungent combination as she hopped down from the compartment. Aunt Madge was very pretty and wore a lot of lipstick, much to Nanny's disapproval. Her daughter Julia, who was a year older than Jane, was very like her, a tall, slim child, with golden hair, not at all like square, mousey Jane.

Rhosarddur Bay was only a few miles away, and they soon covered that distance in Aunt Madge's large car. The two girls sat in the back, and Julia chattered away to her cousin while Nanny, erect as a guardsman, talked politely to Aunt Madge, meanwhile mentally thinking in capital letters, "BEACH PYJAMAS WHATEVER NEXT?" for sure enough Aunt Madge was clad in this new fashion and very nice she looked, though not to Nanny's way of thinking.

"Now take Jane upstairs for a wash, Julia," said Aunt Madge when they arrived. "Then you can show her the boat and the bay before bed." She smiled at Jane. "Have you got any rubber shoes, Jane? Good, then I should just slip them on before you go over the rocks."

Boat. Rocks. Jane could hardly believe her ears. She followed Julia up the steep staircase. They rummaged in her case for the canvas shoes, throwing the rest of her clothes untidily about the room in a manner which horrified Nanny when she came to unpack later.

23

"Can we go by ourselves?" Jane asked incredulously as she followed Julia out of the house.

"Of course, silly," said Julia with scorn. "Why, even Nicholas can, though he's only eight."

Jane was awed into silence. At home she had never been allowed to walk alone even as far as the letterbox.

"Idiot! You must make sure there isn't a car coming," cried Julia, as Jane stepped blindly into the road. She blushed with shame at this revelation of her dependence upon others.

"Sorry," she muttered.

They crossed the road and climbed a wall on to a cliff top covered with rough short grass. Below, the sea spread out like blue silk. Julia led the way down a rough sandy track on to the sands of a little cove.

"This is where the babies play," she said with some condescension, indicating where her brother Nicholas and some of his young friends, knee deep in the water, were sailing model yachts. Attendant nurses and mothers sat about chatting gently; a few toddlers pattered round with tiny wooden spades making mud pies at the water's edge, or building castles. Jane, even at her vast age, would have been happy to join them, but instead she followed Julia over the dark rocks which separated this small cove from its neighbour. Here some small boats were moored, and further out on the open water others moved slowly, the almost windless air scarcely filling their sails. They looked like toys.

Jane caught her breath in delight. Aunt Madge had mentioned a boat. Could it be possible that one of these was hers? Jane dared not put such a magical thought into words in case it was shattered at once. She plodded silently on behind her cousin. They climbed up more rocks, slippery with seaweed where the retreating tide had left them bare, and up on to the high headland beyond the cove.

"Our boat's round in the next bay," said Julia. They walked along over the short springy turf of the headland. Now they could see spread below them the wide sweep of the open bay which curved round in a semi-circle, containing within itself a number of smaller coves. Under them, great jagged rocks broke through the surface of the water which sucked at their black sides.

"We go prawning down there when the tide's right out," said Julia. "We catch ever so many in the pools on the rocks."

The path along the headland curved round into still another bay, and now Julia said in some triumph, "There she is," and pointed to where a slender, graceful boat slapped gently at her mooring. She was painted white, and looked bigger than most of the ones Jane had seen so far this afternoon. Gazing eagerly round the bay which was full of anchored craft, Jane began to distinguish several others like her, with their hulls painted different colours.

"The dinghy's moored down here," Julia was saying, clambering over some more rocks. As Jane followed she felt her best dress catch and rip, and her heart sank for a moment until she remembered that she would be away from Nanny's eagle eye for three whole weeks.

"Shall we go for a row?" Julia suggested.

"Are we allowed to?" asked Jane.

"Oh yes, as long as we can swim, and we have to keep inside this bay," said Julia. "You can swim, can't you?"

Jane was thankful that she could.

Without more ado, Julia hauled in the little dinghy, rather pleased to have someone to impress. She climbed aboard, and more clumsily Jane followed, and was bossily instructed where to stow herself. Soon Julia was rowing away with a lordly air and a lot of complaints about the excessive weight of her passenger.

"Could I learn to row?" Jane enquired timidly.

"Yes, rather. You'll have to do your share of the work. Might as well start now," said Julia. She moved one oar and rowlock aft. "Here, you move on to this seat and turn round."

Jane got up to obey. The little boat rocked alarmingly.

"Take care, you'll capsize us," cried Julia.

Jane subsided on to the thwart and took the oar. She began dipping it in the water as she had seen Julia doing and the dinghy started to move in a jerky fashion. Suddenly the blade of her oar met nothing and Julia laughed as Jane lost her balance, nearly falling into the bottom of the boat.

"That was a crab you caught," Julia said without sympathy. "Never mind, you'll soon learn."

Jane was glad her back was turned towards her cousin so that her shamed blushes could not be seen. Clearly there was a lot that she must learn, but it was going to be fun. She had never dreamed that there could be anywhere like this. As for being the same as Bognor, no two places could have been more different. They proceeded in a jerky fashion round the bay, going alongside the sailing-boat *Nymph* to have a look at her, and weaving perilously in and out of the other moored boats. Eventually they arrived back at their own mooring, where Julia made fast the painter, and they walked back to the house.

The day had been a long one, and when at the end of it Jane was in bed in her small, unfamiliar bedroom, she was suddenly overwhelmed. Aunt Madge, coming in to kiss her goodnight, saw some tell-tale tears glistening on her round cheeks.

"What's the matter, pet," she asked, sitting on the bed. "Are you feeling lonely?"

Jane gulped. "Not exactly, Aunt Madge, it's lovely here and so kind of you to have me — " her polite words became an incoherent jumble.

Aunt Madge gathered her into her arms. "You're tired, love," she said. "You're going to have a good sleep now, and tomorrow we'll go for a sailing picnic in *Nymph*, and we'll bathe, and make sand castles, and have a lovely time."

At this Jane sobbed more than before, and mumbled some confused words out of which her aunt caught "Daddy — torn dress — "

"Now what's worrying you, love?" she asked gently, peering down at Jane's hot, red little face. "Have you torn your frock?"

Jane nodded.

"Well, that was my fault for not telling you to change before you went scrambling over the rocks. We'll ask Annie to mend it; she sews beautifully and I'm sure it will

29

never show. Now what's all this about Daddy?"

Jane muttered into Aunt Madge's now damp shoulder something to the effect that she was wicked to have enjoyed herself with Daddy dead.

Aunt Madge was horrified. Where had the child thought of such a notion? "Darling, what a dreadful idea," she exclaimed. "When Daddy was alive he wanted you to be happy, didn't he?"

"Yes," mumbled Jane.

"He played games with you, and if you were sad he tried to cheer you up? Well then, he still wants you to be happy, even though he isn't with you any more. He doesn't want you to go on being sad." She paused and kissed the top of the brown head, desperately searching for the right words, her heart torn with pity. "Of course you miss him terribly," she went on, "we all do, and specially you and Mummy, but you must believe me, Jane, he wants you to be happy, to remember the good times you had together and go on having fun, as if he was still here."

She found a handkerchief and handed it to Jane, who blew her nose hard and then looked up with new hope.

"Are you sure, Aunt Madge?" she asked.

"Of course I'm sure, darling," said Aunt Madge firmly. "Now promise me you'll stop feeling like this. You'll go on missing him, of course you will, but it won't always hurt like it does now, and you've got to live your life, not spend it feeling miserable all the time."

"I didn't think of it like that," said Jane slowly. The awful weight of guilt she had felt whenever she had enjoyed anything in the past weeks began to slip slowly from her. Aunt Madge was grown-up, infallible. She must be right. Jane relaxed, and presently her aunt was able to tiptoe from the room knowing she was soundly sleeping. No one could guess what went on inside a child's head, she thought ruefully. How could one ever conceive of the way they could twist their thoughts about into such unlikely paths? Perhaps after all she should have put Jane to share a room with Julia, whose bold manner would not allow time for morbidity, but she had felt that a child who was used to so much solitude would find the hurly-burly of family life by day company enough, and welcome a certain amount of privacy.

She was right in this, and soon Jane grew fond of her small room, with the huge faded roses on its wallpaper, the hard high bed that sagged in the middle, the small tufted mat on the worn lino floor, and best of all the view across the bay. She would wake up early and jump out of bed to see what the weather was like, and gaze out of the window watching the morning begin. Sometimes there would be one or two hearty bathers going for a swim before breakfast, usually stout red-faced men from the nearby hotel, dressed in bright towelling dressing-gowns. Soon they would return, puffing and looking rather blue, but filled with smug virtue at their spartan achievement.

She quickly learned to row the little dinghy well enough to have the freedom of the cove where it was moored; it was a proud moment when she made her first solo voyage, with the palms of her brown hands covered in plasters because she had worn blisters on them by her strenuous practice.

The sailing picnic on the day after her arrival was only the first of many. As soon as breakfast was over the family walked down to the mooring, laden with picnic hampers, bathing things and shrimping nets. Buckets and spades were considered by Julia and her older brothers to be infra dig, at their ages, and so Jane too pretended to despise them, sometimes taking instead a notebook and pencil, for if she might not dig, perhaps she might have a chance to draw some of the lovely sailing boats they would see. Next to inventing long daydreams, drawing was her passion, and her crude sketches already showed promise of what was to come.

It was blissful skimming along with the sails billowing out before a sharp breeze. You could lean over the gunwale and trail your fingers in the chill water. Sometimes if the breeze was stiff you had to help balance *Nymph* as she heeled over, in case she capsized, and that was terrifically exciting. Sometimes they came upon a school of porpoises, leaping in and out of the water as they dived for little fish.

During that first visit to Rhosarddur a new life unfolded itself before Jane. Her boisterous cousins soon accepted her as one of themselves, and it was novel for them to have in their midst someone who was perfectly content to accept the dullest role in every game. Jane didn't seem to mind how often she was the prisoner, or burnt by Red Indians at the stake; it was altogether delightful to be playing such games, and she never thought of objecting at being cast for the most unpopular parts.

One day she was marooned on a desert island, left to starve by Black Jake and his pirate crew. The island was a massive rock in the middle of the bay where *Nymph* was moored, just within bounds on its landward side of where the children were allowed to go in the dinghy, with its other side facing the open sea. Under Roger's command, the three pirates were looking for Nicholas to make a second victim, but he was not as good-natured as Jane and had made himself scarce.

Jane wandered over the rock, exploring

it, for she had not previously been cast away upon it. She was tanned by the sun and the sea air; her feet squelched inside her sopping wet canvas shoes, squeezing out bubbling water with every step she took. The island was perhaps sixty yards across, steep and sheer in parts, flat in others. Soon Jane found a deep clear pool among the rocks. It was fringed with seaweed, and the floor of it was covered with pebbles. Red sea-anemones and limpets crusted its rocky sides. It vanished under an overhang of rock, and Jane, advancing, found that it continued into a shallow cave. She waded in, fascinated by her discovery, and saw that light shone through from the other side. It must be a passage running right across the island. It was too deep to wade through, and the water soon met the level of the roof, but she clambered out and in high excitement scrambled over the rocks looking for the other end. It took a lot of finding, for the opening was far smaller than the one she had already discovered; when she did find it, it was too narrow to admit her, but even so it was very exciting to find a secret tunnel.

Eagerly she scanned the horizon in true Sinbad style, looking for her captors, but they were nowhere to be seen. However, she sat on a rock, hugging her knees and gloating over her find, inventing a great adventure in which buried in the tunnel there was a huge chest of gold and jewels.

Time passed.

Perhaps the discovery of the tunnel would bring her new prestige in the eyes of her cousins. She hoped they would not leave her here much longer. Out in the open water she could see sailing boats dipping and bending like ballet dancers. She loved watching them. Sometimes they held races, and the children would stand on the headland to cheer Aunt Madge and Uncle Robert in *Nymph*. Often Roger went with them as crew, and afterwards would brag insufferably about any success they had.

Jane began to feel hungry. Several boats passed her island on their way back to anchor, and she began to wonder if she had been forgotten. She saw some friends of her aunt's go by and thought of shouting to them. Then she decided that if the others came back and found she had gone, they would imagine she had been drowned and there would be an awful commotion, so she had better just wait in patience. She inspected her tunnel again, and toured once more round her small domain. She was feeling hungrier and hungrier. The others couldn't possibly care what became of her. They would leave her to starve to death and vultures would peck at her bones. Two tears, the first for a fortnight, fell slowly down her cheeks. She resolved to hail the next boat that came near; but now they were all well out of range, dotted far away on the horizon.

She climbed to the highest point of her island, inspired with the idea of waving her shirt as a distress flag, to be seen from the shore. S O S, dot-dot-dot, dash-dash-dash, dot-dot-dot, three times fast, three times slowly, then fast again. Nothing happened. What a pity she knew no semaphore to describe her plight more graphically. She waved again. Still nothing happened. Then, miraculously, a sail went up far inshore where the smallest dinghies had their moorings.

Had it seen her signal? It was coming towards her, but perhaps that was just its tack. Anyway she would shout at it as it passed. She began clambering down the rocks, still clutching her shirt. Suddenly her wet foot slipped and she slithered a few feet, catching her leg against a sharp point of rock. Blood poured immediately from the wound. Jane dabbed at it with her shirt, for she had lost her handkerchief. It was a big cut, and painful. The sight of so much blood frightened Jane, and she began to cry.

* * *

Jim Fraser had been, like the water-rat, simply messing about in his sailing dinghy, making sure all was ship-shape for tomorrow's race. He was just ready to go up to the house for tea when, glancing seawards, he noticed a figure waving from the rock in the middle of the bay. It looked a small figure from this distance, and its waves were desperate. He remembered seeing the Harrison children splashing round earlier.

Perhaps it was one of them, fooling about. He stowed away the rope he had been neatly coiling, and looked again. The figure was still there.

"Better investigate, I suppose," Jim muttered to himself. "Never know what those kids will be up to next, probably let their boat drift away." This with the condescension of his sixteen years. It was rather good to have an excuse to get the sail up and go out again, but a bit of a waste when he'd just tidied everything up so neatly. He hoisted sail and tacked smoothly out towards the rock. The figure vanished as he approached, and he fumed inwardly. "I'll give them something to think about if they've brought me out on a wild goose chase," he promised.

He tied the boat to a jutting piece of rock and climbed up to the high point where he had seen the child. Below him he saw a huddled, weeping little girl.

Jane, intent on her troubles, did not hear him.

"Hullo! What's up?" Jim asked, jumping down beside her.

"I — I'm shipwrecked and they've

forgotten me, and now I've cut my leg," she sobbed.

"Oh dear. Well, shipwrecked sailors don't cry," said Jim matter-of-factly. "Here have a blow." He handed her a greyish handkerchief. Jane blew her nose hard and achieved a watery smile.

"Well, let's see the damage," Jim continued, looking at her leg. "Hm, you have given yourself a bash, haven't you? How did you do that?"

"I slipped just now, coming down the rocks," she confessed.

"You duffer, just when rescue was in sight," said Jim with a grin. "Well, cheer up. We'll wash it and then it won't seem so bad. Can you stagger to the edge?"

He helped her to the water's edge, and hygienically rinsed his handkerchief in the sea before bathing her cut with the cold water.

"Salt water's a first-class disinfectant," he informed her. "It's a good job I rescued you. I'm going to be a doctor." He tied her leg firmly up with his handkerchief. "Now let's hop aboard and get you home," he said.

"How long had you been out there?"

he asked as the boat gently nosed its way back to land.

"Since about three — it must be seven at least by now, isn't it?" said Jane, beginning to enjoy her martyrdom now that it had ended.

"Good heavens, no, only about half-past four," said Jim, laughing. Then, seeing her look abashed, he added kindly, "But even so, it's a jolly long time to be shipwrecked."

Jane was mollified. She moved into the bow and neatly caught the mooring float as Jim brought the boat round to it.

"I'll come up to your house with you," said Jim, whose parents were friends of Aunt Madge and Uncle Robert.

They walked along together, Jane limping gallantly.

"You're the cousin, aren't you, the one — " Jim stopped; he had been going to say, the one whose father's dead. "The one who's staying there," he amended.

"Yes, I'm Jane," she said.

He smiled down at her. "I'll take you out mackereling one day, if your aunt will let you come," he promised. "Would you like that?"

41

Jane was entranced. "Yes please," she breathed.

Aunt Madge was at home when they arrived.

"Jane darling, what has happened? Where are the others?" she exclaimed, seeing at once the extremely bloodstained handkerchief round Jane's plump leg.

"I don't know where they are," said Jane.

"They left Jane shipwrecked on the Bay Rock," said Jim. "She thought they'd forgotten her, and she cut her leg climbing over the rocks."

"Jim saved me. He saw my morse signals," said Jane.

"How lucky," said Aunt Madge. She smiled at Jim. "Thank you so much, Jim. How naughty of the children to leave her there alone." Characteristically she did not worry about the whereabouts of her own offspring, since experience had proved such anxiety always to be needless.

Jane enjoyed the fuss that was made of her leg. It was nearly bad enough for stitches. If only it had been, how guilty the others would have felt, and how much she would have enjoyed magnanimously forgiving them!

Aunt Madge was very angry with Roger, Hugh and Julia. They had seldom received such a scolding. How could they behave so unkindly and thoughtlessly to their cousin, who was much younger than any of them, as well as being particularly in need of kindness just now? For a punishment they were forbidden to use the boat for three days. As Nicholas had avoided the game, he escaped the sentence, and spent the three days sailing gloatingly about with Jane, who was thriving on her wounded heroine's role.

To celebrate the ending of the boat ban, they decided to hold a midnight feast. Roger and Hugh went shopping in the village for the food, and on the appointed night the children lay in bed pinching themselves to keep awake. Jane lay reading by torchlight, and dozed off several times, waking with a start as her book crashed to the floor.

At twelve o'clock she opened her door and began to creep along the passage to the boys' big room where the feast was to be held. It was pitch dark. Gentle snores, eerie-sounding, came from behind Annie's door. A board creaked. Then, horror! Her outstretched hand touched something warm and fleshy. She stifled a shriek.

"Ssh, silly, it's only me," came a strident whisper from Julia, and in relief Jane drew breath, and followed cautiously along behind her braver cousin.

In the boys' room two candles burned on saucers. Five toothglasses were arranged on the floor, flanked by bars of chocolate, cake and biscuits, and oranges, all that could be obtained in the small village. Roger was busy making a great brew of lemonade powder in a large enamel jug. It fizzed like fruit salts. Jane privately thought it rather beastly, but since it was an essential ingredient for all the best midnight feasts she meekly drank her glass to the last drop.

They talked in giggling whispers, punctuated by tense cries of "Sh, someone's coming." So much cake and chocolate was very filling. As a feast it was disappointing and indigestible, but as an adventure it was a success. The boys regaled the company with tales of their far more daring escapades at school, imagination causing them to describe more and more improbable happenings. Nicholas was going to his prep. school next term, and Julia was to go to boarding school too. Jane felt envious of all the adventures they would have. Well versed in school story books, she could clearly picture Julia as the Madcap of the Lower Fourth. How Jane longed for life and adventure, although when confronted with either her courage dwindled.

Aunt Madge, hearing the creaks and gasps of the girls' passage back to their rooms in the small hours, smiled to herself. The boys' bulging pockets and fantastically innocent expressions that afternoon had not deceived her. Rice pudding for lunch next day, and milk of magnesia all round, she decided, and fell asleep.

3

SIX years later Jane rowed out in the small dinghy to the rock which had been the scene of her shipwreck so long ago. Stowed aboard was her painting equipment — a folding easel, canvas and her paints and brushes. She pulled the little boat through the water with quick, short strokes, moving between the craft which bobbed at anchor in the bay. She reached the island and let the boat drift up to the rocks; then she jumped out and pulled it up out of the water away from the reach of the incoming tide. She carried her things up over the ledges of black rock to a small hollow where she could gaze out over the whole bay. On one side of the mainland the cliffs loomed large and shadowy, and for the rest there was the blue sea dotted with the red and white sails of the boats which skimmed along before the sharp breeze. It was sheltered in this crack between the rocks, and Jane soon had her easel fixed.

She had been planning this expedition ever since she and her mother arrived at Rhosarddur for what was now their annual visit; here she would be free of interruption, and no one would come inquisitively peering at her work. Jane's artistic talent and ability were developing rapidly, but she was too shy to set up her easel where she could be observed.

Soon she was absorbed: the light was perfect, and with skilful strokes she laid her colours. Time flew.

Suddenly a voice behind her said: "Gosh, Jane, that's good."

She nearly jumped off her rock with shock.

"Oh, Jimmy, it's only you! You did make me jump," she gasped, recognising the intruder with relief.

"Sorry," he grinned. "You haven't got yourself shipwrecked again, have you? I didn't see a boat."

"I hauled her up on the rocks over there," said Jane, pointing. "I was afraid I might forget her with the tide coming in."

"Oh, I came the other way, that's why I didn't see her," said Jim. He looked again at her half-finished painting. "That is good, Janey," he repeated. "I didn't know you were an artist."

"I'm not," said Jane with a rueful laugh. "But I hope I might be one day. I've been wanting to do this view for ages, with the rocks and the clouds, and it's a good spot because there aren't any people about snooping around and watching."

"Shall I buzz off?" asked Jimmy. "I don't want to interrupt you. I came here for peace too, to study," he added with a grimace. Jane saw that he held a bundle of books under one arm.

"I didn't mean you were snooping," said Jane. "You aren't people."

Jimmy smiled at the left-handed compliment.

"What have you got to study? Is it for your exams?" she went on.

He nodded, looking suddenly serious.

"I must get on, I can't risk failing," he said gravely. "Doctors are going to be needed."

"Do you really think there will be a war, Jimmy?" Jane asked.

"It's inevitable," he said flatly. "Perhaps

it won't come this year, but it's coming all right."

Jane scratched her ear with the end of her brush, looking at him solemnly. "I suppose there might be another Munich?" she said at last, and then, "but we can't go on sacrificing little nations to save ourselves," she added, with the arrogant ignorance of her youth.

"We can't, Jane," he agreed with a sigh. "But we've had so little time. We'll be fighting with men's flesh, not weapons." The doctor in him shrank from the horrors he knew must come.

"But we've got lots of tanks and things," Jane protested. "Surely it would be over in a few weeks?"

"I doubt it," said Jimmy dryly. "Still, miracles may happen yet, and you want to finish your painting," he added, seeing the look of apprehension on her face. "The light will be changing while we're talking. You'd better get on with it. May I share your island? I won't disturb you."

"Of course, Jimmy," she smiled. "It's your island as much as mine. You rescued me."

He grinned. "I'll go over there, that looks a comfortable perch," he said, and climbed up the rocks to a ledge above and to one side of Jane's position. In a few minutes she was busy again with her work, forgetting him, and he lit his pipe and leaned his back against the rock to begin his own.

Every summer the Harrisons met Jim Fraser. He was too old to share in the children's games, though when they were being pirates he was not above bearing down upon the *Jolly Roger* in his own boat and heartily splashing the dare-devil crew. He owned his own small sailing-boat, the one in which he had rescued Jane so long ago, and every year since then he had taken her out for an hour or two mackerel-fishing. Vaguely he felt that such a quiet creature must get dazed amid the hurly-burly of her noisy cousins; and there was something about her solemn little face that intrigued him. The expeditions had begun with the idea of giving her a treat and a rest from her cousins; they continued because they were a pleasure.

Jim had a round, merry face, with grey

eyes under well-marked brows, and a snub nose. He had a thick mop of brown hair. He laughed often, and his laugh was infectious; he was short, not more than five feet six, and very conscious of his missing inches; even Jane's youngest cousin, Nicholas, now fourteen, was taller than Jim. He was a very kind young man with delightful manners; old ladies and children took to him at once. He would be a very successful doctor, for his heart was as large as his body was small.

At length Jane added the last brushful of colour to her work, and looked at it critically. Now she must be firm with herself and do no more to it, for little dabs and touchings-up would not improve it and might spoil whatever was good about it. She remembered Jimmy's presence, and glanced across at him on his ledge. Pipe in mouth, he sat hunched over his book, one hand against his forehead; his hair stood up untidily where he had rumpled it. Chuckling to herself, Jane picked up her sketch block and pencil, and began rapidly to draw, glancing across at him occasionally. She liked Jimmy. He was always the same, 'never in a bait,' as the cousins sometimes were, and he was always kind.

Presently, with a sigh, he laid down his book and looked at Jane. She sat idle, gazing out over the sea, her arms clasped round her drawn-up knees. A patch of bare brown skin showed where her blue shirt and grey shorts had parted company at her waist.

"Finished?" he asked, getting up and stepping over the rocks towards her.

Jane nodded.

"May I see?"

"If you like," she answered.

Jimmy stood in silence looking intently at the canvas which still rested on the small easel.

"It is good, Jane," he said at last. "You are a clever girl. What a lovely thing to be able to do."

"Do you really like it, Jimmy?" she asked. "You don't have to be polite."

"I think it's wonderful," he said seriously. "The light on the water — the shadows of the rocks — I don't know a thing about painting really, but to me that looks like a little masterpiece." He still gazed at the painting, fascinated by the skill with which Jane had captured the scene before them. "You are clever," he repeated.

"You're much cleverer, and you'll be far more useful, being a doctor," she said practically. "Anyway, it's the only thing I am any good at, and I've got such a tremendous amount to learn."

"Aren't you good at games and lessons?" he asked with a smile at her solemn expression.

Jane shook her head.

"Not much. The only time I played in a tennis match I made such a muck of it that I let everyone else down," she said ruefully. "And I'm never higher than fifth in form."

"Well, that's still much better than me," said Jimmy. "I was usually fifth from the bottom, not the top, and how I'll scrape through my exams I don't know."

"I don't suppose you bothered to work, boys never do," said Jane.

Jimmy laughed. "Touché," he said. "Well, anyway, there's no doubt that you can certainly wield a paint-brush."

He caught sight then of the sketch-block on her knee. "What have you been doing there?" he asked.

Rather tentatively but with the corners of her mouth twitching, Jane held it out for his inspection.

Jimmy looked at it and then burst out laughing.

"Jane, you imp," he said. The sketch was of himself, leaning against the rock reading his book. She had captured and emphasised his likeness very cleverly; his thick hair was just a little longer, his face a little rounder, and his pipe a little larger than life, but there was no malice in the slight caricature she had drawn. Jane took the block from him again and tore off the sheet of paper. She was just going to crumple it in her hand when he stopped her.

"Don't throw it away, Jane. Will you let me keep it? It might be worth a fortune when you're Dame Jane charging hundreds of guineas for portraits."

"Of course you can have it. I thought you might be cross," she said demurely, a dimple showing at the corner of her mouth.

"You didn't at all," he said with a smile.

She gave him back the drawing, and he put it carefully between the pages of his book. Then he squatted down beside her and re-lighted his pipe.

"It would be fun to be a dame," she said musingly. "One would certainly have accomplished something then. But 'Dame Jane' doesn't sound very good. You'd have to be called a grand name like Elizabeth, or Laura — or Caroline — " she sought about for suitable names. "Jane always makes people say 'Plain and no nonsense,'" she ended rather sadly.

"I like Jane," said Jimmy stoutly. "It's a good honest name, short and easy. And anyway, I don't see that you need worry about being called plain." He looked at her critically, for the first time mentally dissecting her features. Hitherto she had been merely a plump, pleasant little girl. "No, you're not in the least plain," he decided. "You've got lovely blue eyes and nice skin, and you'll lose some weight when you leave school, and you seem to have improved your hair. Don't

I remember a fringe?" He visualised the dejected curtain of straight hair that had hung above her eyes, hiding her high forehead.

"Yes, I did have one," she said, rather pleased to be told such nice things about her eyes. Jimmy thought it would be a pity to overdo matters by drawing attention to her short, straight nose and soft, red, perfectly shaped lips. He regarded her with pleasure. In a few years she would be pretty, in fact she was already. He suddenly felt an overwhelming urge to lean forward and kiss her warm, moist, innocent mouth. Sharply he pulled himself together and changed the conversation.

"I need a crew tomorrow," he remarked. "Are you busy? Would you like to come?"

"Oh, Jimmy, how lovely!" she cried, the quick smile lighting up her face. "I'd love it; the others are going in *Nymph* and I was just planning to watch with Mummy and Aunt Madge. What time?"

They arranged to meet at Jimmy's mooring, and then he looked at his watch.

"It's time we got back, or everyone will think we really are wrecked," he said, surprised to see how late it was.

He helped Jane to carry her things back to her boat, and pushed it back into the water for her. Then he went to his own dinghy which was tied to a rock. As he sailed back into the bay he could see the blue shirt bending as she rowed her own way home.

In the night the wind freshened, and the next morning it was squally. Mrs. Harrison expressed grave doubts about the advisability of letting Jane crew. She was not a hardened enough mariner to be nonchalant about the choppy seas she saw through the window. But Aunt Madge saw Jane's anxious face and came to the rescue. She persuaded her sister-in-law that Jimmy was competent and Jane would be safe.

"It isn't as if she couldn't swim," she added reasonably, and made Jane's mother look at her with renewed horror.

It was cold, and Jane wore long trousers and a thick sweater. She carried her fat blue life-jacket over her arm. The bay was full of little boats getting ready for the race; she felt excited. She had crewed several times for other people, and raced in *Nymph* sometimes; it never failed to thrill her.

The stiff wind made the flag on the Yacht Club masthead flap wildly about; a black cone beside it announced a compulsory reef. Jimmy was already aboard his boat, busily tying in the reef. Jane jumped in beside him and began to help. He grinned at her and said, "Hullo," and went on with his task.

Soon they were scudding out, very fast, into the open water.

"It's very squally," he warned.

Jane nodded eagerly.

"Mummy nearly didn't let me come," she told him.

They soon reached the starting line, and Jimmy gave Jane the stop-watch. They practised a few starts in the time left before their race was due to begin. Up on the headland Aunt Madge and Mother could be seen, huddled in the lee of a rock, with a rug over their knees, scarves on their heads and wearing thick overcoats. Jane waved gaily as they sped past below, with the little boat heeling sharply over and the water scudding past the gunwale.

They got off to a good start and beat up towards the first marker buoy, sailing as close-hauled as they could. Jane held the jib-sheet; she wrapped it round her wrist; the wind tugged against her and sought to free it from her grasp, but she held on. Jimmy braced himself at the tiller, both feet against the centreboard casing, holding the mainsheet in one strong, square hand. They sped along. Squalls raced over the water to meet them, casting darker shadows on its already grey surface. At each gust the boat dipped again and Jimmy had to release the sail a little to meet it. He found Jane needed few instructions, trimming her sail to match the wind. Usually he raced the boat alone as she was so small; however in dirty weather like today he needed more ballast, though he had originally asked Jane to come from a wish for her company and not because he anticipated a storm.

They went sharply round the first buoy and were well placed when they took up the new tack. The weather compelled strict attention to their task and there was no time to talk. Several times Jimmy had to bring the boat's nose round as the gusts shook her and the swell took her rolling over the waves. It was exhilarating. Spray blew over them and made their faces wet, and they laughed.

Running before the wind on the last leg of the triangular course was calmer. Jane could let her sheet run out and the sail bellied. They went very fast, borne along, rolling before the wind and the tide. Jimmy rummaged in his pocket and produced a battered bar of chocolate which he broke in half and passed to Jane. It tasted salty and was good.

As they went round the course for the second time a signal was given from the control at the flagstaff to cut short the race after this round, instead of completing the normal three circuits. The wind was stronger and the sky darker. Jane could barely hold the sheet. The tiller shuddered in Jimmy's hand, tugging against him. Side by side, they leaned out over the rushing water, concentrating utterly on their task.

Jimmy judged his last turn very

carefully. He must come up far enough to be certain of getting round the final buoy without having to tack again, yet he must not waste seconds by going too far. At last he judged the moment, and Jane gasped with excitement as they began to rush towards the finish, rapidly overhauling the boat in front which had misjudged the turn. They rolled as the waves caught them; then, coming up behind the other craft they took her wind and sped into the lead. It was a glorious feeling, being propelled along by all the might of the wind. The signal gun fired as they shot over the line, two lengths in front of the next boat, and they grinned at each other in triumph. A flutter of applause broke out from the spectators on the cliff, and Jane's mother relaxed in relief.

Jimmy went about and made for his mooring. The sea was getting angrier every minute, and they shipped a lot of water smacking over the waves. In the harbour bay it seemed very calm after the tumult outside in the open sea, and they eased off to slide back to their anchorage. There was a good deal of water lying in the boat, and Jane baled it out while Jimmy took the sails down; he was going to take them up to the house to dry. Jane crouched on the floorboards, out of his way, busily baling and emptying the bilge over the side. As she worked, Jimmy noticed a long red mark on her wrist.

"Jane!" he exclaimed, and took the baler from her. He sat down on the thwart beside her, and gently took her wrist in his hand, looking at the scar he had seen.

"The sheet did this," he said at last. The skin was raw where the rope had rubbed against it.

"I suppose it did — I didn't notice," she said, colouring faintly. "It doesn't hurt at all, really Jimmy, it doesn't matter. I wound the sheet round my jersey but it must have slipped." She looked at him anxiously, puzzled by the expression on his face. Slowly Jimmy picked up her other hand, where a matching stripe lay across the brown tanned skin.

"Why didn't you say? We could have tied it down," he said. Both her small, dirty brown hands now lay inside his own square capable ones.

"I didn't notice, really Jimmy, it was so exciting," she insisted, and what she said was partly true. She had been aware of the burning friction of the rope, but her mind was detached from it by the concentration and thrill of the race. "They'll soon get better," she added.

"I'm so sorry, Jane," he said seriously. "I had no idea, or I would never have let you hang on to the sheet."

"Please don't think about it, honestly Jimmy, it doesn't matter at all," she assured him, surprised by his concern.

"You are a sport, Jane," was all he could find to say.

★ ★ ★

Some nights later the Yacht Club was to hold its annual dance. Julia and Hugh, being now seventeen and eighteen, were going with their parents. Roger was away with the new Militia, doing his training. It had never occurred to Jane that she should go to the dance; no one would dance with her if she did, she was far too

63

young and dull. She was as astonished as her mother when Jimmy came to ask if he might take her. Immediately she was torn in two; part of her longed to go, part feared to be a wallflower. She had never been to a grown-up dance.

"It's very nice of you, Jimmy," her mother hesitated doubtfully. "But I think she's rather young."

At this hint of opposition Jane made up her mind.

"Oh, Mummy, do let me go," she begged urgently. "Julia went last year when she was sixteen."

Mrs. Harrison looked from her eager face to Jimmy's serious one. At last she gave her consent, and Jimmy, pleased, departed.

Jane was immediately thrown into misery because she had no evening dress, but here Julia came to the rescue, for anticipating much gaiety in her new sophistication she had brought two, and grandly offered to lend the older one, adding realistically, "That is, if you can get into it," with a meaningful glance at her cousin's plump form.

She was much taller than Jane, so

they had to take up a temporary hem; but Aunt Madge had excellent taste and the powder-blue taffeta would have suited any young girl. Jane drew in her breath while she was zipped up the back; she accepted the offer of some of her aunt's face powder; with her bobbed hair newly washed and shining, she looked her best.

Till now, Jane's sole excursion into sophistication had been a Pony Club dance, and tonight was the first time she had worn a long dress. This she artlessly confided to Jimmy as they took the floor.

"It's Julia's," she added. "Wasn't it lucky she brought two? I only just fit into it, I hope I don't burst it."

"It suits you," said Jimmy, smiling at her. Her eyes were bright and her cheeks flushed with excitement. They circled happily round the crowded room. Jimmy danced well; he was light on his feet and moved smoothly, and Jane was small. Too often he had been faced with girls who towered above him, and for that reason he rarely danced at all, but he enjoyed it enormously when he had a partner of the right size. Jane endured dancing lessons at school, loathing them, but this was quite different; Jimmy was easy to follow, and even though she did make a few mistakes it didn't matter with him because he never minded or thought you were silly. But he was by no means her only partner; with many groans of mock dismay her cousin took her round, and so did Uncle Robert, and a number of their friends. Jim dutifully danced with the ladies of his party, and then found he had to wait for his own partner.

Jane thoroughly enjoyed herself; she forgot to be shy as soon as she realised she was not going to be a wallflower. At last Jimmy was able to recapture her; they danced again, and then he got her an orange drink, and some beer for himself, and they went out on to the terrace. The night was warm the sea shimmered under the moon and the air was still, for the gale had blown itself out by now.

"Mm, this is good," said Jane, downing half the glassful at one swallow. "It is hot in there."

"Are you enjoying yourself?" Jimmy asked with a smile.

66

"Oh yes, rather, Jimmy," she said eagerly. "And it was nice of you to ask me. I do love dancing," she discovered in surprise.

"That's good," said Jimmy. He felt tonight as if they were all poised on a precipice, waiting for the crash that must inevitably come, just marking time in the space that was left. He was too uncomplicated in his nature to analyse the motives that had prompted him to invite Jane to come with him tonight. In other years he had simply accompanied his parents without a partner of his own; the girls in the community were all too smart, or too sophisticated, or merely too tall, to appeal to him; but since last week's race he had not been able to forget Jane's gay courage or the freshness of her soft young lips. In a few brief days the holiday would be ended; ahead lay first, examinations, and then horrors undreamed of, as even now Hitler's hordes gathered on the Polish borders; subconsciously Jimmy stored up every moment of happiness against the unknown future.

They leaned on the balustrade, looking

at the sea. A salt tang mixed with the spicy smells coming up from the garden, and behind them the music and voices were loud and gay. Jane's thin hands were lightly clasped in front of her, and a faint scar still showed red on her wrist. She had rather hoped that the Prince Charming for whom she now longed would materialise tonight, but he had not; she had only met the usual members of the Yacht Club. But never mind; she was still only sixteen so there was plenty of time, and he would be sure to appear one day. She sighed, in happy anticipation; she would recognise him at once, and they would both live happily ever after.

Jimmy broke in upon her dreams of romance. With the back of one finger he gently stroked the mark on her skin. Then, abruptly, he said, "We haven't been mackereling yet these holidays. I have to go back to London on Wednesday. Shall we go on Tuesday if it's fine?"

"Oh yes, how lovely," said Jane. "I'm sure that will be all right."

"Let's go for the day," suggested

Jimmy. "I'll bring a picnic. We'll go to Silver Cove. You could bring your painting things."

"What a good idea," said Jane.

"Let's start straight after breakfast," Jimmy went on. "How early can you leave?"

"Oh, about quarter-past eight, I should think," said Jane.

"Good," said Jimmy. "We'll have a lovely long day as it will be the last one. I suppose your mother won't mind you coming out with me all day?" he added on a sudden afterthought.

Jane laughed. "Good gracious, no, why on earth should she?" she said. "Oh, listen, Jimmy, there's the polka! Can we go and do it?"

Permission was duly given for Jane to go to Silver Cove, and Tuesday morning was perfect. The sun rose in a faint mist and the grasses on the headland whispered the hint of a gentle breeze. Jane woke early, and had a bathe before breakfast. Her hair was still damp, curling in wisps round her neck, when she met Jimmy. He arrived at his mooring laden with fishing lines and a big picnic basket.

Jane helped him stow everything on board and hoist the sails. There was no one else about so they had the small harbour to themselves.

They moved silently out of the little bay into the open water beyond, past their Bay Rock Island. The breeze was freshening as the sun got higher, and soon they had enough way on to put out their lines. They sat in the stern of the boat, with Jimmy steering and Jane fishing; soon they ran into some mackerel and she began excitedly hauling them aboard. After they had caught a dozen or so, Jimmy gave Jane the tiller and began tidying the lines; he knew she loved to sail the boat. One or two of the blue-green fish leaped and quivered in after-death devilish dances and Jane shuddered; she could not be calm about their nervous twitchings, though Jimmy assured her they felt nothing. This was an annual joke, and he teased her a little, but his face was tender.

Silver Cove was a small bay lying some miles along the coast from Rhosarddur. It was a little further away than most people went for sailing picnics; as its name suggested, its shore was fringed with fine silver sand. A rocky cliff loomed over the beach and cut it off from easy approach by land. It took some time to get there, but Jane and Jimmy were content. She sailed the boat very happily, and he puffed at his pipe and looked at the view.

"People will think we're the channel steamer, seeing all that smoke," she said mischievously.

Jimmy dipped a hand in the sea and flicked some water at her. "Cheek," he said, and then, "You don't mind it, do you, Jane? I forgot to ask you." He took it from his mouth and looked at her.

"Of course I don't. I rather like the smell," she said. "What a question."

"One should always ask a lady's permission before lighting up," he informed her solemnly.

She laughed. "Well, I'd have jolly soon told you if it made me feel sick," she said. "At least yours doesn't boil and bubble like Uncle Robert's. I don't think he ever cleans it."

They reached Silver Cove and beached

the boat. Jane, always eager for a new scene to paint, found a good vantage point and began to make a sketch of the calm scene in the little bay, where a few rocks stood out of the silver sand, and the small boat lay beached in the foreground. Jimmy had brought some text books and 'Murder at the Monastery.' He browsed through his medical books for a while, and then cast them aside. Jane smiled when she looked up from her painting to see him engrossed in his thriller; but Jimmy was not as deeply immersed in it as he appeared. From time to time he glanced across at her where she sat on a rock, lips pursed, a strand of hair hanging over her forehead, intent. Until this year she had been just one of the Harrison bunch — his favourite, to be sure, and since he had rescued her he could assume a certain proprietary interest towards her, but just a pleasant child. Now Jim prayed that perhaps after all world events would not intervene to interrupt this annual blossoming friendship; if only Jane was two years older: you could not, he supposed, imagine yourself in love with a girl of sixteen, but you could fall in love with the dream of the woman she would become.

The day grew hotter, and presently Jane threw down her brush.

"Phew, I'm roasting. Let's have a swim, Jimmy," she said.

He agreed at once.

They changed behind two of the large rocks that studded the shore, and then raced laughing into the water.

"Race you to that rock out there," Jimmy challenged, and in a flurry of arms and legs they set off to swim out to a rock fifty yards from the shore. To her surprise, Jane won easily; though she was a strong swimmer she was not a very fast one. Jimmy was a safe but unstylish performer in the water. She crowed at her victory as he hauled himself, dripping, on to the rock beside her. A year ago he would have pushed her back into the sea for such behaviour, but now he did not.

The water dried on them as they sat on the rock, basking in the sun.

"Oh, Jimmy, isn't this the most heavenly place in the world?" Jane sighed at last. "I mean, Rhosarddur. I just adore it."

He nodded, scratching at a limpet which was fastened securely to the rock.

"You can do just what you like," she continued, "and not dress up, and not have to be good at things, and everyone's nice, and there are the boats, and swimming, and oh, everything."

"It is a lovely place," Jimmy agreed.

Jane sat up, hugging her knees, and looked at him.

"The war's bound to come, isn't it, Jimmy?" she asked. "I know that now."

"I don't see how it can be avoided this time," he said gravely.

"I wonder if we shall ever come back here," said Jane sadly. "It will be awful for you, the war I mean."

"It will be awful for everyone," he said grimly, "but we've survived other wars, we'll survive this one," he added stoically. "I expect Rhosarddur will still be here when it's over." But he did not say, even if we aren't; and he did not say, if we do come back again we won't be young and lighthearted.

He saw that Jane's eyes were suddenly full of tears.

"I don't know why, but this year has

been the best of all," she said softly. "I shall never forget the fun we've had. You've been a sport to me, Jimmy."

"You've been great company, Janey," he told her. Then, with an effort to bring the conversation back to a lighter plane, he said with a grin, "You'll be able to boast about our grand sailing victory to all the girls at school."

She smiled, as he intended, and he said, "I'll beat you this time, back to the shore and lunch," and dived into the water. Jane plunged in after him, and forgot her sadness as she tried, this time in vain, to catch him.

Dripping and triumphant, Jimmy waited for her to come out of the sea, and they ran together up the sand to where they had left their picnic. There was cold chicken, and ham, hard-boiled eggs, salad, apples and bananas.

"How delicious," said Jane. "I'm starving."

"We ought to have been enterprising and cooked our own fish," said Jim, lying on his back and gnawing a chicken leg in the manner of Henry VIII.

"I can't make a camp fire, can you?"

asked Jane. She rolled on to her stomach and helped herself to a banana out of the basket.

"I was a Boy Scout once," said Jimmy. "I might have managed."

"We'd be too hot if we had to roast over a fire," said Jane, "it's such a glorious, baking day."

And it was hot beneath the summer sun. When they had eaten all they could they basked in it, until they felt too hot. Then they swam again. The water felt very chill against their warm skin.

Jane said, " I must finish my painting. The light's all different now, so I'll have to guess."

Jimmy sat beside her, watching her work, fascinated by her skill. At length she declared it to be done.

"It isn't much good really, I'm not in the mood," she said with a smile. "I ought to have done a polite portrait of you, Jimmy, to make up for the rude one I did before."

"Do you like painting people?" he asked.

"Yes, I do, more than landscapes really, though I love doing them too," said Jane.

"But it isn't very easy to get people to sit, the cousins would think it a great bore. I've done some people at school, and a few odd folk here and there." She wiped her brushes and began to put them away. "Jimmy, shall I tell you a great secret?"

He looked at her. "Yes, if you'd like to," he said. "It'll be safe with me."

"Oh, I know that, and it isn't a complete secret, some people do know about it already. Only you might think I was swanking."

"I promise I won't," Jimmy said solemnly.

"Well, I won a competition in London last term with a portrait," she said boldly.

"Jane, how splendid, well done," said Jimmy warmly. "Who was it of? Tell me all about it."

Blushing slightly, Jane described how in the holidays she had forced her mother's charlady's daughter to pose for her by the fire with a tortoiseshell cat, and how she had taken the finished painting to school, where 'Dabs,' as the art mistress was known, had suggested sending it in for the competition.

"Of course it was only a children's

one," she ended, deprecatingly.

"Never mind, the next one won't be," said Jim. "That's marvellous, Janey."

He was so pleased for her that she almost felt embarrassed. He asked her what she would do when she left school, and she told him of her hopes of the Slade, and then a job which would give her scope and time to paint. "But if the war comes, it'll all have to wait," she ended flatly.

They were back to it again, though Jimmy had tried not to think of the future since their talk in the morning.

"You could still study," he hazarded.

"I couldn't, Jimmy, how could I, when you and Roger and Hugh, and I suppose even Uncle Robert, and everyone else was off fighting. I'd have to be a nurse or something."

Her eyes blazed and she sat up very straight to say this.

"I suppose you couldn't, Janey," he said then. "I wasn't sure if you felt like that."

"It seems such a waste to have to go back to school," she said rather sadly.

"The time will soon go, Jane," he

said. "There will be plenty left for you to do."

"Jimmy, what about you? What sort of a doctor would you have been if there hadn't been a war coming?"

"I don't know," said Jimmy. "I hadn't particularly thought of specialising — I suppose I'd have waited to see how things worked out, really. I hadn't thought of more than general practice and surgery." He looked at her. "I'll have to fill in time too, before I can be any use, finishing my training."

She nodded. "I can't bear to think about it, and yet, in a way, I want it to come," she said. "How awful that must sound, Jimmy. But in a way it would be a relief."

"I understand," he said. "Things are often easier to face when they happen than they are in anticipation. I suppose if that wasn't so no one would ever be brave enough to cope with what they have to do."

They were both silent then, Jim understanding a little of what lay ahead, Jane valiant with the courage of her ignorance. Foolishly, Jim thought oh, if only we could jump into the boat and sail away and away, and escape. Abruptly he got to his feet.

"Come on, Jane, let's explore our cove before tea," he said. He held out his hand to her, and she took it, and he helped her up. They meandered round the little bay, peering in the pools where fat prawns scurried under the fringing seaweed, and looking for shells. There were all sorts of unusual ones lying in the sand.

"We ought to collect them to make those queer boxes people have," said Jane. "You know, like workboxes, satin inside with shells stuck all over the top."

"Shall I make you a necklace of cowries?" Jim suggested. "Then you'd be like a Zulu lady."

"I'd have to have a grass skirt, too," Jane declared.

"You'd be a sensation at a fancy dress ball," said Jimmy.

They both began to laugh, and the shadow passed. After tea, for which they finished up what was left of the picnic, it was time to sail home. The weather had been kind, though Jimmy had kept a wary eye upon it in case it threatened to blow and force them to leave earlier.

Jane took the tiller again, and Jimmy sat on the centre thwart, determinedly not looking at her, for he could not endure the thought that he might never see her again. Jane wondered a little why he was so silent, but she was content. They did not need to talk to be happy together, and she was absorbed in her task of sailing the boat and watching the ever-changing pattern of the light upon the water.

When they had moored the boat, Jimmy divided the mackerel they had caught, and they each took a bundle home, strung on a cord through the gills. Jimmy walked with Jane to her gate; then, with just a brief "Goodnight," they parted.

Jane stood for a moment and watched him walk down the road and round the corner out of sight. He walked quickly, the bundle of fish swinging in his hand, without looking back. She could not understand why there was a lump in her throat as he disappeared.

A week later Hitler invaded Poland.

4

THE black material was hard and stiff in its newness, and Jane's finger was pitted with needlemarks; she was stitching it into curtain linings. A pile of finished work lay on the floor beside her, and at the table sat Nanny, busy whirring with the machine as she stitched up stout heavy green cotton into new curtains for the kitchen thick enough to keep out every ray of light.

"I'd like to get hold of that Hitler," she said grimly, pausing to bite off an end of thread with her teeth. "Making us do all this work, and your poor mother having to spend so much money on this material. Goodness knows what will become of us all." She fixed her glasses more securely on her nose and began turning the handle so furiously that she might have been driving out the German hordes single-handed.

Jane sighed as she sewed; already

Rhosarddur seemed like a distant dream. They had cut short their holiday and travelled home in haste; her last view of it had been shrouded in damp sea fog as the car took them to the station.

This afternoon Mrs. Harrison was meeting the billeting officer, making final arrangements for the reception of the children who would be evacuated from the cities tomorrow. Already Dora, the maid, had left to work in a factory. She explained, with her round face beaming in fervour of patriotism and excitement, "Sorry as I am to leave you, ma'am, but it seems as how it's me duty, like," and Mrs. Harrison had to agree. War was not yet declared, but it could be only a matter of days now; the great metamorphosis had begun.

"I keep thinking of those poor mites, coming tomorrow," said Nanny, with her mouth full of pins as she turned down a hem. "Poor wee lambs, being taken from their families. It's terrible."

"Mm." Jane broke off a length of black cotton and threaded her needle.

"There, that's all ready to machine. Now dear, just slip the hooks on these for me, will you, I'm afraid my poor old eyes can't see where the holes are. I'll go and put the kettle on." She rose creakingly to her feet and went out. Jane put her own work down and fetched the curtain hooks; poor Nanny, she seemed to be ageing very fast. She 'felt her feet,' and suffered from rheumatism in the winter; but she had told Mrs. Harrison not to worry; she would see to the cooking and housekeeping while the younger woman undertook more important work. Jane had begged to be allowed to leave school at once, but her mother was adamant; like Jimmy, she declared there would be plenty of work left for Jane in a year.

Next day, Jane went to help take the evacuated children to their new homes; they came in bus loads from the station to the village hall. All were bewildered. Some laughed and sang in shrill little voices; some wept, with dirty, streaked faces; others, and these were the most pathetic, merely were silent, watching everything with wide, frightened, uncomprehending eyes. Each wore a label bearing its name and address; each carried a gas mask in a cardboard container; each held a small bundle of precious possessions. Brothers and sisters clung together, afraid of being parted; the friendless stood alone. Three nervous, exhausted teachers hovered among their charges, and were revived with cups of tea as they helped parcel out the children to different houses. Jane led little groups round the village to their new homes, handing them over at the various cottages and houses. In almost every case the overworked woman welcomed them with kind gladness into her already overfull home. Jane was profoundly impressed by this display of human goodness, and sadly shaken when Mrs. Cooper at The Grange, a wealthy stockbroker's wife, eyed her allotted trio with suspicion, said coldly, "Well, I suppose we must make the best of it; come along children, haven't you got a handkerchief, boy?" and handed them over to an equally disapproving housemaid with instructions to bath them at once in plenty of Lysol.

During the following week Jane was kept busy on her bicycle delivering clothes which had been given from old hoards or bought by kind benefactors for these ragged victims of an evil they did not understand. The district nurse's telephone rang with ceaseless enquiries from shocked and harassed foster-parents and the chemist's stock of sassafras oil dwindled. Jane felt she was living in tremendous times.

When the Low Countries were over-run, like many other anxious parents, Mrs. Harrison fetched Jane home from school, so that if Britain was invaded at least they would be together.

The lilacs were out, and the early summer days were glorious as the miracle of Dunkirk was wrought. Troop trains with their exhausted passengers thundered through England; Jane helped to cut sandwiches in hundreds and hand them into the trains as they stopped momentarily on their way. She longed to be in one of the little boats which so magnificently made possible the great rescue.

After this there was no more talk of going back to school. The Battle of Britain was won, the expected invasion had not taken place, and by that time Jane had found innumerable small ways to make herself useful. Mrs. Harrison was glad of her help with the evacuees; the first flight had returned home long ago, but now with more bombing came another exodus to be housed, as well as the never-ending shuffle of expectant mothers to hospital, the newly-delivered to fresh homes, and the movement of recalcitrant children. In any time left over from these tasks Mrs. Harrison organised first-aid lectures and sewing parties. She found unexpected satisfaction in all this very necessary work; she was efficient and she was needed; she was busy all day long and every evening.

At home, Nanny did the cooking and an elderly woman came from the village to help with the cleaning. Jane did any task that came her way; she shopped; she went to her mother's office and helped with the paper work; she escorted children on buses and trains; she knitted and she sewed; she went to all the lectures.

In spare moments, mainly at weekends, she helped at the local hospital. It was rather disappointing that all the patients were civilians; Jane would have preferred to have nursed wounded soldiers. In fact, she did no nursing. She washed up, and washed up, and washed up again. She swept floors and scrubbed. She was a glorified, unpaid ward-maid; but she did not complain, and at last, proud day, made contact with the patients when she was allowed to prepare their tea. She grew to know some of them, and was gratified when they recognised her with obvious pleasure.

Soon Jane began to spend more and more time at the hospital. She came home just to sleep, then left again each day at eight o'clock. One day when she was bicycling up the hill to the big grey building she felt a nagging pain in her side; she dismissed it as a stitch, but it persisted all day, and even a hot water bottle at night did nothing to ease it. The next morning it was worse, and the journey to the hospital seemed endless; Jane quailed at the thought of washing-up and polishing.

The day was long; it was very dark in the corner by the sink; there were mounds and mounds of plates to wash, and the remains of rabbit stew clinging to them smelt stale and horrible. Jane longed for six o'clock.

But long before then a young nurse coming to prepare the teas found her crouching on a stool, doubled up with pain, and at six o'clock she was on the operating table having her appendix removed.

★ ★ ★

Jane's illness was a great shock to Mrs. Harrison, who had taken her good health for granted during these last months. Belatedly she realised how little rest the girl had had; an occasional afternoon, an hour or so in the evening, not much.

This was borne out by the doctor; Jane's recovery was very slow, and he said she was in a very run-down condition, besides which they had only just averted peritonitis.

It was pleasant to be pampered, without feeling guilty, and Jane enjoyed her weeks in bed.

One morning Mrs. Harrison came in to say goodbye before going off to her office.

"I think you look better today," she said after surveying her daughter critically.

"Oh, I am, Mummy," Jane hastened to agree, but she knew that she still felt desperately inert and was exhausted by the slightest effort.

"I've had a letter from Aunt Madge this morning," Mrs. Harrison went on. "She's invited you to stay; would you like to go? I think it's an excellent idea, the change is what you need."

"At Rhosarddur?" Jane's cheeks went pink.

"Oh, no, dear. Rhosarddur is full of soldiers now," said her mother. "No, at Moorlands. The air is bracing there, you know, it isn't far from the sea, and she says they have plenty of milk and eggs. I'm sure it would do you good."

Jane adjusted her mind to this new idea. It would be lovely to see Aunt Madge again. Doctor Roberts had said that she could on no account start working for at least another month, so there would be nothing wrong about going.

"When can I go?" she asked.

A week later mother and daughter set out on the long journey to Moorlands. Jane was still too weak to travel alone, and so Mrs. Harrison had taken two days off herself. The train was very slow and crowded. To ensure getting seats they had first-class tickets; Jane sat and looked at the crowded corridor outside their compartment, bulging with soldiers and their kitbags. She had had plenty of time in the weeks since her operation to indulge in day dreams of romance, and now she gazed at her own pale reflection in the window, and imagined a handsome young officer coming into the compartment to fall in love at sight with her interesting, delicate face. But this did not happen. Instead, two stout colonels and an admiral joined them, and at a later stop a very pretty A.T.S. officer, at whom the three gentlemen thereafter cast many a sidelong glance.

Aunt Madge met them at the station. She seemed exactly the same; her pretty blonde hair still curled round her neat head, and she looked charming in her Red Cross uniform.

A very old porter carried their two

cases to the car, and they drove off, with Aunt Madge chattering gaily and telling them all the news. Secretly she was shocked by Jane's white, peaked face, but as all her own family hated being fussed, she made no comment.

When he retired just before the war began, Uncle Robert had bought Moorlands; now he was back in the Army, and so were Roger and Hugh. Julia was in the A.T.S. and Nicholas was in his last year at school. The big house was empty except for brief periods of leave when it echoed to the noise of one or other of the family. Rooms lay dust-sheeted; it was too near the coast for evacuees, and not large enough to be a hospital.

"I hope she won't be dull, Rosamund," said Aunt Madge later that evening over a glass of sherry. Jane, tired beyond measure by the long journey, was upstairs having supper in bed, with the wireless playing and a pile of books by her side.

"I will have to be out quite a bit, but I still have dear old Ethel and Cook, and they never go out so she won't be alone. The air is so good here, and with plenty of food from the farm she'll soon get strong again."

"She won't find it dull," said Mrs. Harrison. "She's so fond of you, Madge, and you've always been good to her. I blame myself very much for what has happened."

"Nonsense, Ros, you couldn't cause an appendicitis," said Aunt Madge robustly.

"No, but if she hadn't been so run-down, she'd have got over it better. And she'd had the pain for two days, without saying anything about it. I should have noticed that she wasn't well. She's been working so hard, with no time off, but I never gave it a thought." Mrs. Harrison looked very dejected as she sipped her drink.

"Youth soon mends," said Aunt Madge with a smile. "And we're all working so hard ourselves these days that it's easy to forget about time off for other people. Don't worry, Ros, in a few weeks she'll be as right as rain."

A few days made a big improvement in Jane. Slowly energy crept back, and when the doctor came to see her after a week he gave permission for her to ride Julia's old pony. The early October days smelled of autumn; it was peaceful wandering round the stubble fields and bridle paths on the fat old pony, with no need to feel guilty because one was so idle. Sometimes, when the wind was in the east, she imagined she could smell the sea far off. She was content. In the evenings she knitted, or played rummy with Aunt Madge, or listened to the wireless, or talked. The two were good friends; slowly her aunt pieced together the picture of Jane's life in the past year; she realised that the nurses at the hospital were the only young company she had, and an occasional visit to the cinema with one of them her only recreation. Comparing this with the gaiety of her own family on their leaves she was appalled.

"What will you do when you go home again, Jane?" she asked one evening as they sat knitting, the one khaki socks for her son, and the other a stout sea-boot stocking.

"Go back to the hospital, I suppose," Jane answered.

"You don't sound very enthusiastic?"

said Aunt Madge interrogatively.

Jane sighed. "I thought of being a V.A.D., but really I'm just as useful as a char," she said.

"You'd work regular hours if you were a V.A.D.," said Aunt Madge mildly. It had not escaped her that Jane spent many hours poring over the recruiting advertisements in the newspapers, and she added, "Have you ever thought of joining one of the Services?" She said it as casually as if it was the most natural thing in the world, as indeed it was to her clear mind.

"Oh, yes, Aunt Madge, I'd love to," Jane burst out. "But how can I? It would mean leaving Mummy all by herself and this other work I've been doing is useful, I do know that."

"I think if you really want to join up your mother would understand," said Aunt Madge gently. "She knows you won't be at home always. One day you'll get married, and you'll have to leave her then. Your mother has plenty of friends, you know, and now her work keeps her busy. She wouldn't want to hold you back."

"Do you think so?" Jane asked wistfully.

"I'm certain of it," said Aunt Madge firmly. "After all, Jane, nearly every woman is alone now, even those who aren't widows like your mother. I am."

This was patently true, but till now it had never occurred to Jane. She brightened. "Perhaps I could," she said slowly. "I can drive. I could be a lorry driver!"

"Of course you could, how splendid," said Aunt Madge. "Julia is coming on leave this weekend, you'd better ask her all about it. Then as soon as the doctor says you're fit you can apply."

She was convinced that unless Jane took an irrevocable step almost at once, she would return home and back into her former rut, which though useful was still a rut. Aunt Madge had no inhibitions about interfering with other people's lives if she was certain it was for their own good. The thought of Jane washing-up for the rest of the war horrified her.

That night Jane went to bed feeling excited. How simple it all seemed as described by Aunt Madge! How reasonable! She would write for all the literature tomorrow.

Late on Friday night Julia arrived, having hitch-hiked from her camp on a series of lorries. She was plumper, owing, she explained to the starchy diet; her cheeks were pink and her eyes shone with good health and enjoyment of life. She consumed an enormous belated supper whilst regaling her mother and cousin with stories of her sergeant and the comic aspects of her life. Jane hung on every word.

"No wonder you're getting fat if that's the amount you always eat," said Aunt Madge as Julia demolished a huge plateful of shepherd's pie.

"Oh, Mum, how can you be so heartless when I'm starving in my country's service," she cried tragically. "This is the first square meal I've had since my last leave." She put another loaded forkful into her mouth and then said, "Oh, by the way, I'm going to a dance in Westmouth tomorrow night; I hope that's all right."

"Of course, dear," said her mother mildly. A well-trained parent, she did not immediately ask the identity of

Julia's partner but waited patiently, and sure enough in a few moments it was revealed. "Philip Fenton's asked me, you remember, Mummy, the one in the Navy, silly ass. But he's jolly nice all the same. Why don't you come too, Jane? Phil could bring a friend."

Jane sat up with a jerk. Her heart leaped; then her self-confidence flagged. She did not know how to answer.

Aunt Madge decided for her. "That's an excellent idea," she said. It would do Jane good to have some fun. "You'd like to go, wouldn't you, Jane?" she assumed. "Where is it, Julia? Jane can borrow one of your dresses."

"Of course she can. It's a posh 'do' at the Grand Hotel," said Julia, laying down her spoon and fork after finishing a huge slice of apple tart. She sighed with satisfaction, then got up. "I'll go and ring up Philip now. He can easily get some more tickets."

"Are you sure it will be all right? Won't it be a lot of trouble?" Jane said hesitantly.

"Phil will do anything for me," stated Julia calmly. "Besides it will be fun and do you good. Poor old dear, how are you?" she asked tardily.

Jane had to laugh; but how she envied Julia's gay life and easy confidence. Perhaps she would be like that too when she joined up, even with a Philip prepared to gratify her every whim. She sighed with hopeful anticipation.

Julia went off to the telephone and embarked on a long conversation which began loudly and ended softly. When she returned to the drawing-room her eyes were brighter than ever. She reported that Philip thought it a splendid idea and would fix everything.

So Jane met Michael Rutherford. He came with Philip in a taxi to take them to the dance. The two young men, both R.N.V.R. Lieutenants, seemed to fill the drawing-room with their tall bodies and deep voices, Jane thought, entering it in Julia's wake and wearing the borrowed cream net dress. Aunt Madge was entertaining them with sherry and chat; Philip was a cheerful young man, with smiling blue eyes and mouse-brown hair, busy telling Aunt Madge that he was thinking of growing a beard to inspire respect from the lower deck. His whole face seemed to light up when Julia came in; he lost the thread of his remarks and simply gazed at her.

Though Philip was tall, Michael topped him by at least two inches. He was very thin; his hair was dark, almost black, sleekly brushed over his head which was long rather than round. He seemed serious, with not much to say at first beyond the politenesses. He had brown eyes, slightly protuberant; Jane thought they looked full of understanding as he said how do you do, bending low to do it. Actually he was long-sighted and had difficulty in focusing at close range.

They piled into the taxi at last and drove the fifteen miles to Westmouth, Philip between the two girls, surreptitiously holding Julia's hand, and Michael in front with the driver. Jane spent the time silently watching the silhouette of his head in front of her; he had neat, well-shaped ears, lying flat against his head. She thought it was very nice of him to take so much trouble to talk to the driver. Philip and Julia spent most of the journey in merry badinage into which they tried to draw Jane, but she was too shy and too much bemused for their efforts to be successful.

They dined at the hotel where the dance was to be held. Julia knew Michael slightly already, and the three had friends in common; the fact that Jane took small part in the conversation was hardly apparent, and she was happy just to listen and to watch. Once or twice Michael turned to her with a remark: was her dinner to her liking? How delightful the weather had been. He looked at her then with those brown eyes, trying to get her in focus, and she thought he seemed to imply that the two of them had much more serious things than these to discuss, more common ground to tread.

They danced, of course, later. It was difficult to talk, for the band was noisy, and Michael's head was far above Jane somewhere up near the ceiling. She concentrated on following his steps, nervously apologising if she stumbled, for she had not danced since her last Saturday hop at school when she had taken the floor with dear Dabs, the art mistress. However, Michael steered her competently round through the crowd appearing not to mind, listening to the band, thinking of very little except that he was having a wasted evening with this schoolgirl. He offered her a drink, and remained calm when she asked for orange squash; while she sipped it, she tried to think of conversation, and when she failed and Michael too was silent, she was convinced they shared the sort of sympathetic silence she had met in novels, where nothing was said but all was understood. She did not notice Michael's constant glances at his watch; when she said she thought of joining up he pulled himself back from thoughts of the gayer parties he had attended and smiled. "Why don't you join the Wrens?" he said. "Then we shall meet again."

5

CLAD in shapeless navy blue cotton overalls, the squad of girls marched briskly up the front. The sun was out, and a sharp wind blew off the sea. The Petty-Officer Wren in charge called out an order, and in ragged fashion the recruits turned about and marched the other way. Up and down they went, turned again, halted, and at last were dismissed. Jane felt self-conscious drilling; she watched the swaying buttocks of the girl in front and knew her own must look just as unattractive; the female form was not designed for the drill square. But, apart from drilling, she liked her new life. A school friend, Molly Green, had joined up with her and they trained together.

There were lectures and drills, but there were long spells of freedom too in which to explore the port, with its bomb-scarred streets and its population of sailors. Jane eyed every tall slim officer with twin wavy gold rings on his sleeve in great anxiety in case he should prove to be Michael. She had met him again, two months ago, when Julia in a mist of white tulle had married her gay Philip. Michael was best man; he had not remembered Jane until she had reminded him of their other meeting, but that had barely dimmed her delight. Now she had, as recommended by him, joined the Wrens, and so would be sure to meet him again. In her single-mindedness Jane took no account of the odds against such a thing happening; she had done her part by joining up, and fate would do the rest, but she must meet fate half-way by being on the watch. Michael had seldom been out of her thoughts since that October dance; every tall, slight young man she saw reminded her of him; all her daydreams now included him. Any young man who had chanced to come along at that particular moment would have had the same effect; Jane's vivid imagination and her loneliness had put her into a state when she was ready to fall in love with the first man she saw.

When their training was over both Jane and Molly were based on Portshead, so that they were able to meet frequently in their spare time. Molly was a placid girl who had been content at school to go for botanical rambles; while Jane had striven for distinction, and found it hard to admit her own mediocrity at games. As they grew older the two had grown closer, drawn together by the fact that they were both lacking in assurance.

The summer passed, and in the autumn Jane was moved to Warehampton. This port had been badly bombed the year before, and there were many wide spaces where once large buildings had stood.

Winter came: it was very cold walking through the dingy streets to the depot every morning. Now Jane missed the small, comfortable quarters where she had lived in Portshead. She missed Molly too, though they sometimes managed to meet for a few hours. She heard from home that Julia was going to have a baby; she had been released from the A.T.S. and was living in digs with Philip who was on a course.

Sometimes, when the weather was coldest and her spirits low, Jane's conviction that she would meet Michael again wavered. Then, with rare realism, she would remind herself that if he had been as much interested in her as she was in him, by now he would have sought her out. But then her other, romantic self would suggest that he only required to meet her a few more times to feel that interest; surely what she felt was strong enough to evoke some response.

Spring came at last; you did not notice it much in the port, but the few trees sprouted green and the sea was less grey. Cabbage began to replace marrowfat peas on the menu.

It was Jane's turn to drive the fuelling officer; this was an unpopular job which involved waiting for endless minutes while he made arrangements for coal or oil with the engineer officers aboard every ship.

Most of the ships in port were armed merchant cruisers or troop ships; there were few genuine men o' war, but sometimes a destroyer or corvette came in for refit. There was a destroyer due in today. When Mr. Smith, Jane's passenger, told her its name the blood sang in her ears. True reward of faith, fate was bringing Michael's ship to dock at Warehampton. Jane almost drove into the sea in her excitement, but she reminded herself warningly that as Philip had left the ship, so perhaps had Michael.

She watched the little ship nose its way against the dock and tie up, a scene that was by now familiar but always held a small thrill. With fast beating and envious heart she saw the fortunate figure of Mr. Smith going up the gangway on to its sacred deck. A bustle of other officials, customs men, and dockers, followed. And then, down the gangway, just like that, came Michael. For one moment Jane thought he was not going to see her where she sat with quaking knees inside her van. But Michael automatically looked at all Wrens with a hopeful eye; he enjoyed a pretty girl as well as anybody. He glanced now at the driver of this van and realised at once that he had seen her before; miraculously his memory told him that she was old Philip's wife's cousin, but what on earth was her name?

"How nice to see you!" he enthused, saluting smartly and racking his brain.

Jane muttered something. Now that this dreamed of, long-imagined scene was actually happening there was a huge lump in her throat and she felt dizzy.

'Plain Jane!' With relief Michael dredged up the information he was seeking. "Come aboard and have a drink," he suggested, deciding he could postpone the phone call to a girl in Portshead which was his reason for going ashore.

Jane had often drunk cups of thick sweet tea aboard the more hospitable vessels; she got out of her van and followed Michael. He was already bored with his idea of inviting her, for he had just remembered how dull she was, however as he had let himself in for it he must be polite and see it through. They scrambled down the steep companionway and into the tiny wardroom. Jane took off her cap, which had suddenly become very tight, and nervously ran her fingers through her short hair. She sat silent, dumb with nerves, only her eyes were very bright, never leaving Michael's face. He, unaware of the electric atmosphere, sought about for something to say and asked perfunctorily about her work.

She found her tongue to answer briefly; then was inspired to break the ensuing silence by telling him the latest news of Philip, Julia, and the baby that was coming.

Perhaps after all she was not so plain, thought Michael in a vague way. The uniform became her; though she was certainly not pretty, the clear skin and shining eyes had a certain charm. He would not be free to go to Portshead before the week-end to see the girl who was attracting him at the moment, but he could meanwhile make use of what was to hand. He invited Jane out to dinner.

And so began the happy time. Jane's stock among her fellow Wrens rose high when they beheld her handsome escort. That first week-end he disappeared, but when he came back he took her out again. She lived in a maze of happiness, for as well as their pre-arranged meetings there was now the added thrill of a chance encounter as she drove around the docks or town. Once she met him coming out of Gieves, and gave him a lift in her rattling old van back to his ship; several times during the refit she delivered stores or technicians and was taken on board to feast on sherry or tea.

Michael had received the brush-off from his girl in Portshead, or rather he had given it to her. He had discovered that he was being used as a second string, and now he was disillusioned. It was convenient to have another ready-made companion and audience in Jane, without having the trouble of finding one. It was clear that she was too simple to be the double-crossing kind; she was a good listener and seemed to enjoy all that he had to say, which was plenty, without trying to interrupt or monopolise the talk herself. They went out to dinner several times, and to the cinema where automatically he held her hand, and to a dance.

Jane relived these evenings over and over again when they were past; it was not until years later that she realised how Michael had dominated them. He told her about his family, who normally lived in London but had rented a house in Berkshire 'for the duration;' he described the major events of his schooldays and hinted at his prowess on the football field; he told her about life at sea. All these things interested her greatly and she hung on every word, but he seldom asked for her opinion or enquired about her life.

Sometimes they discussed the war: when Michael talked about bombings and shellings and U-boat attacks, Jane's vivid imagination more than made up for his lack of descriptive powers. Pity filled her for the horror and the terror he had known, and must face again; the endless days and nights fighting with the cruel weather as well as the foe. He told her too about Number One's wife, who had got bored during her husband's absence and gone to live with a Canadian. He told her about Petty Officer Jones' new son, who could not possibly be his. He told her about the long dark nights in which, watching the traitorous, fluorescent water, the sailor longed for home.

When he left Warehampton at the end of the refit Michael was genuinely sorry to leave Jane; and he told her so as he kissed her in farewell. His lips felt hard against hers, almost like rubber, she thought in shocked surprise, holding her hand against them when he had gone; longed-for and virgin experience, it startled her.

In the quieter moments of his next months at sea, Michael often thought about Jane. He even wrote to her once or twice, and received gay letters back, illustrated with pin-men sketches. He heard that Philip had a son, and envied him. It must be nice to have a son to carry on your name, and someone who belonged. Slowly his thoughts about security became indivisible from thoughts of Jane. She alone of all the girls he knew would not embark upon deceit once your back was turned; her condemnation of the faithless wives of his shipmates was proof of how she felt; besides, she was not the type to attract a lot of notice, she was not pretty, and too shy. Her innocent lips had told him in one kiss that this was the limit of her experience, one that Michael had surprised himself by not giving to her sooner.

After two shattering convoys Michael's

ship crept into Portshead harbour and sank wearily against the dockside. The next evening Michael, still raw from his experiences, was waiting for Jane outside her quarters when she came back from work. For once acting on impulse, he had not even stopped to telephone her but had caught the first train and come; now, in a fever of impatience, he paced up and down on the pavement.

She saw him as she turned the corner at the end of the street, and her heart leaped into her throat. She walked faster, almost running, at the same time thinking in confusion, oh dear, I wish I'd put a clean shirt on this morning, and my hair wants washing; and oh God, thank you for keeping him safe.

He went to meet her, with long scissor strides. Solemnly, because of their uniform, they saluted, and just to see her quite unaltered made him feel calmer. Her face was still smooth and young, her lips were soft, her eyes candid. In the middle of the luckily empty dock road, with slum dwellings on either side, the scene that Jane had so often dreamed of happening in an atmosphere of soft light and romance took place. Michael asked her to marry him.

6

FIVE days after their wedding Michael returned to duty, recalled from leave to take up his new posting as First Lieutenant of another destroyer. Jane was left wondering if it had not all been a dream.

It was an effort to settle back into her own routine, and she was glad when she was posted to a new station away from the places where they had spent so much time together. Her new companions were friendly; the station was in a pleasant place, set among fields on the outskirts of a small seaside village; the work was more varied and interesting. Jane felt more useful here. In her spare time she sometimes went out to the cinema or to supper with the other girls, but more often she stayed in the camp, writing to Michael, or reading. His letters came in batches; weeks would pass without one, and just as Jane felt she could not bear another day without news of him the mail would at last arrive.

The long months passed. Jane lived on her nerves. When the telephone in the Wren drivers' rest room rang to order out a car, there was always in her mind the fear that it might not be a routine call, but a dreadful telegram. Once, when sent for by the Captain, she was nearly sick with apprehension, only to be given a very secret despatch to deliver. The sight of a telegram in the letter-rack would make her heart race in panic. Sometimes at night she would lie awake, hearing the even breathing of the girls who shared her room, and imagining scenes of horror in which he might be involved, floating in the sea with screaming, drowning companions, or being blown skywards in a tremendous explosion. Then she would pray desperately to the God of Whose existence she was uncertain, bargaining with Him by promising that if He spared Michael she would not ask Him another favour for the rest of her life.

Eighteen months went by. Once, she stayed for a week-end with his parents, whom she had only met briefly at the wedding. Colonel Rutherford was as happy as a lark living in the country; he worked busily in the neglected garden of the old manor which they had rented, tore about on A.R.P. work, and gave not a moment's thought to the fact that one day he would have to return to London. He was a slim, spare man, rather whiskery; he had been gassed in the other war and spoke in a hoarse whisper. Jane liked him and found him easy to get on with, while he was pleased that she was not hardboiled and painted. Mrs. Rutherford hated her exile from the city that was her spiritual home. She was tall, and if it had not been for the excellent corsets she still seemed able to obtain, she could have been called stout. She had over-blued grey hair, and a long aquiline nose. She had the same brown, protuberant eyes that Michael had, and she frightened Jane. Her hands were long and elegant, and when she washed up, or helped the elderly cook in the kitchen, she appeared to have an existence remote from those long, capable fingers. They would wipe, rinse, or stir, as if detached, by themselves, held away from their owner's long body, and never guilty of a stray splash or smash. Jane watched them in fascination, tinged with horror, and twice broke cups while doing so. Her mother-in-law cut short her embarrassed apologies with the sort of "Never mind, Jane, it can't be helped," with which one would address a habitually clumsy child. Jane could not feel comfortable at the Manor. When she arrived, in her short uniform coat and tight skirt, she felt herself to be all legs, and feet in heavy shoes, beside the unyielding elegance of Mrs. Rutherford. Later, when she had changed into her only woollen dress, she became all fingers and thumbs, dropping the silver when she laid the table. She thought if only Michael had been there to take care of her she would not feel so strange. In bed, she lay awake till the small hours, afraid and unhappy, hearing the grandfather clock in the hall below chiming away the quarters of the lonely night.

★ ★ ★

It was Jane's turn to drive the salvage van. This was a sordid task; a utility truck had to go all round the camp collecting first, the waste paper for pulping, and then the dustbins. These were transported from the various buildings, emptied in an incinerator and returned whence they came. In charge of operations was Charlie, a seedy civilian who chewed tobacco continuously. He was five feet tall and fond of the horses, ready to place your bets if you wished. He was helped by Ernest, a tall lugubrious man who scorned the van and presided over the incinerator. The pleasantries of these two had begun to irritate Jane.

Driving the van was a dirty job, especially on windy days, when the dust and litter would blow over the driver and get into her hair. Cleaning the van out afterwards was also an unpopular duty.

Today, Jane's gloom was not lightened by the fact that three weeks had passed since she had last heard from Michael. She tried to be calm; no news was good news, and if his ship had been sunk she would have heard, but he might be ill; anything could have happened. Her driving was mechanical and she took no notice of Charlie's artless prattle about tomorrow's big race. At last all the dustbins had been carried back to their rightful places, and Jane began the weary job of cleaning the van. She had almost finished when Alf, the sailor who was in charge of garage maintenance, came whistling into the yard. He was a friend of Jane's; she had sat up with him through one long night duty while he waited for news of his wife who was having a baby.

"How's it going, Jane?" he asked, and stood looking at her, a grin on his face and his cap on the back of his head. "Reverend Mother wants you," he added, referring thus obliquely to the Wren officer-in-charge.

Jane paled. "Oh, Alf!" she gasped.

"What's the matter? Got a guilty conscience?" he asked.

"No, I — it isn't that, it's Michael. I haven't heard from him for ages."

"It's nothing wrong with your better half," said Alf, still grinning. "But show a leg there, you can't keep the old girl waiting. I'll finish the van for you," he said.

"Will you, Alfie? Oh, thank you, you

are a dear," she said gratefully. She paused for a minute, and then added fearfully, "You're sure it isn't bad news?"

"Cross me heart," he told her. "You cut along."

Jane stopped to wash her hands, and pushed her hair up under her cap, then she hurried down the pathway to the Wren officer's office, which was housed in another building. She wore her oldest pair of bell-bottomed trousers, and a thick jersey under her jacket; it was early March and still cold, and you could not combine chic and dustbin duty.

First-Officer Keane's voice bade her enter when she knocked on the door, and still anxious, Jane went into the room. The tall, attractive woman behind the desk was not alone, and seldom were her duties so pleasant, for sitting beside her was Michael.

Jane stared in unbelief.

"It's not a mirage, Rutherford," smiled the older woman, rising to her feet. She gathered up a bundle of paper and moved towards the door. "The Captain wants me, I'll be away ten minutes," she added, but before the door had closed behind her Jane was in her husband's arms and rubbing her head against his jacket.

"Well, aren't you going to kiss me?" he said at last, and she lifted her face. He pushed her cap off to stroke her untidy hair, and she learned between kisses that he had arrived before the telegram he had sent to warn her.

"I've got three weeks leave, and so have you," he said. "It's all arranged. I fixed it with your officer while they fetched you. You'd better go and get into some respectable clothes, Jane. What a sight you look." He held her away from him and looked disapprovingly at her dusty trousers and unpowdered face.

"I've been emptying the dustbins," she explained, trying to stifle the sick feeling his remark gave her.

"You look like it," said Michael. "I'll wait for you here." He looked with approval at First Officer Keane, who now returned, neat and elegant in her well-cut uniform, with her short hair nicely waved, and her face matt.

"Well, Rutherford, run along," she said. "I've seen the Transport Officer and you can go at once. Here are your ration cards and leave chit."

Jane took them and thanked her. She ran back to the hut, fighting back tears of relief and of chagrin. Her fears for Michael's safety were momentarily over, but she had let him down by being so untidy; she could have powdered her face before dashing impetuously to the office. Naturally, since he was an officer, he would expect her to be neat at all times; he had no idea of the squalor involved in the dustbin collection. If a small voice told her that his joy at seeing her should have made him blind to her untidiness she ignored it.

When she rejoined him he looked at her critically for a moment. Then he said, "That's better," in an approving voice. She had found a clean white shirt and he hadn't seen the mended ladder in her last pair of black silk stockings. As they walked off side by side he noticed, looking down on the top of her head, a patch of dust still sticking to her cap.

They spent their leave at the Manor; now at last they were together, but time hung heavily for Jane. Michael slept, read or talked to his mother. She did what she could to help in the house, then retreated to the garden where she helped her father-in-law to dig and plant. Every evening she changed for dinner into her only woollen dress. She broke three plates and two tumblers.

One day Michael had to go up to the Admiralty, and Jane went too. Belatedly she realised that her civilian outfit was far from adequate. She had needed very few clothes before she joined up, owing to her uneventful social life, and fewer still since. Hoarded in her wallet were a few clothing coupons, and she resolved in some excitement to buy a new dress while Michael was closeted with their Lordships. She would wear it for dinner tonight, and surprise him, and at last he would say she was beautiful. Jane still could not admit that when you loved you did not necessarily see beauty in the loved one. To her, Michael was the most handsome man in the world, with his tall slim body, his even features, brown eyes and his shining smooth black hair.

They caught an early train and went in a taxi to the Admiralty, where rows of khaki and brown vans and cars were drawn up outside on the Horse Guards' Parade, behind coils of barbed wire. Jane went on in the taxi feeling gay and excited. Automatically she went to the store her mother had always patronised, famed for the high quality of its merchandise. There were not many dresses from which to choose; there was no choice of material other than wool or crepe. She tried on several dresses, in shades of blue and green, and then a cherry red. She liked this one, it was cut more generously than the other material-saving styles, with a wide flared skirt. The cloth was of high quality too, as the vendeuse said when she saw her unsophisticated customer had taken a liking to it, and she pointed out how the warm glowing colour showed off Jane's fair skin. Jane hesitated; it was expensive, but such good material would last for years; then she plunged. She clutched the precious parcel and went with shining eyes to meet Michael as arranged for lunch.

She was early, so she left her parcel in the cloakroom. Then she went to the mirror and boldly put on a lot of lipstick, since she was beginning to realise that Michael liked it.

They enjoyed their lunch, and Jane, guiltily aware of how pleasant it was to escape from Michael's parents for a brief moment, rejoiced in the fact that except for strangers, they were alone together.

They caught an early afternoon train back to the country. Michael went to sleep in the compartment, and Jane watched him tenderly; he was still exhausted. When they reached the house it was to find the Rutherfords in a great state of excitement; Michael's younger brother, Patrick, was coming unexpectedly on leave from Italy. The telegram had arrived that morning, and he was due on the next train from London.

"What a pity we didn't know, we could have waited and travelled down with him," said Jane when they went upstairs to change for dinner. Mr. Rutherford had gone to the station and Mrs. Rutherford was helping the ancient maid put the finishing touches to the celebration dinner.

"Then we should have had to talk to

him, and it was nicer to be on our own," said Michael, putting his arms round her. Jane did not remind him that he had slept throughout the journey.

It was a good thing she was stock size, she thought, as with fast beating heart she slipped the new red dress over her head. She belted it in; the well-cut skirt made her waist neat, and, the bodice was cut with a high V-neckline and fitted smoothly over her little bosom.

"I'm glad you've found something different from that everlasting blue you're so fond of," said Michael, turning from brushing his hair to look at her.

She waited, looking at him anxiously.

"It's new, I got it today," she told him, when he said no more.

Michael was still looking at her. "Turn round," he said.

Obediently she spun about.

Finally he said, "It doesn't suit you," and went back to brushing his hair.

Jane's eyes filled. She bent and fiddled with her shoes. Six years later, remembering the episode, she still felt that any loving husband would have pretended to like the dress even if he did not, and that such a pretence would have been more honourable than the truth.

He left the room and she pulled herself together. It was no good giving way to tears. For a moment she thought of changing back into the despised blue, but her watch told her there was no time, and so she went downstairs.

Patrick was standing with his family by the fire as she came slowly down the stairs which led into the big hall. He was as tall as Michael, but his features were more rugged and he had sandy hair. Everyone was talking at once, even Colonel Rutherford, and for a moment Jane felt that she could not break into the intimacy of their family group. She hesitated, and it was Patrick who saw her. He glanced for a moment at Michael, and then, seeing that his brother did not move, he put down the glass of sherry he was holding and went straight towards her across the room.

"You're Jane," he said at once, holding out his hand, and as she took it, still standing on the stairs though on the lowest step, he kissed her cheek with brotherly affection.

"I've heard so much about you," he told her, "and I've been longing to meet you. Isn't this grand?" He led her by the arm over to the others, and Jane saw only his kindness and not the shrewd expression in his eyes.

Dinner that evening was a festive meal. To celebrate, Mrs. Rutherford had managed to lure a large chicken from under the butcher's counter, and this was browned to a perfection of tenderness. There were brussels sprouts and roast potatoes; there was a delicious raspberry mousse; there was champagne.

The rest of their leave was transformed for Jane by Patrick. Somehow he infected everyone with his own gaiety. He took her for walks and told her about escapades he and Michael had shared as children; he listened to her dreams of the future when at last the war would be won; and at home he never let her feel out of things, taking care to explain, or to turn the conversation, if it was about things or people with which she was unfamiliar, and encouraging her to contribute remarks of her own. He was surprised by Jane. His mother's letters had led him to expect a dull mouse without a word to say for herself, but he saw charm in her shyness, and when she became animated her blue eyes lost their frightened expression and twinkled with fun. Her adoration of Michael was plain for all to see. Patrick found it harder to observe his brother's feelings.

When Michael had to rejoin his ship the two brothers shook hands in farewell, and Patrick, who had his leave still to finish, kissed Jane once more.

"Goodbye, Jane," he said with his cheerful smile. "It's lovely to have a sister. I hope you'll write to me sometimes." And then he said to Michael, "You're a dashed lucky chap. I wish I'd seen her first."

Jane blushed with pleasure, and laughed. "Goodbye, Patrick," she said.

A month later, just before victory, Patrick stepped on a mine and was killed.

7

MICHAEL spent his last months in the Navy working at the Admiralty, and Jane, demobilised, joined him in London. By good luck they were able to take over the lease of his predecessor's flat, which was in a dingy suburb and at the top of a tall Victorian house. Jane cleaned and polished the shabby apartments all day long; by trial and error she learned to be an efficient cook, though it was difficult to be imaginative whilst so much was rationed. She spent hours devising new ways of disguising corned beef, and took endless trouble stirring sauces. She polished the worn, scratched table in their living-room until it was a mirror; she scrubbed the splintery kitchen floor; she carried coal and wrestled with the ancient gas cooker and the power cuts. She was too busy to wonder if she was also happy. Michael was safe; they were together; that was all she had wanted. If

131

she sometimes felt empty and dissatisfied, she thought it was because she longed to have a child, a living symbol of their union.

Michael had a number of Service friends in London. Often they went out to dine or to dance, and sometimes other young couples visited the flat. All these people and their wives seemed to know each other intimately. Try as she would, Jane could not overcome her shyness. If the conversation lapsed, she would throw desperate, lonely little remarks into the pools of silence, but Michael never helped her by picking them up and rescuing them. Often they were left to drown, hopeless and ignored as someone else captured the attention of the company.

Michael's parents moved back to their London house, mercifully little damaged by the bombing. Colonel Rutherford, miserable again now that he had been uprooted from the country, sought sanctuary in his club with other exiles. Mrs. Rutherford returned thankfully to her Mayfair hairdresser, her tailored suits and her afternoon bridge parties. Sometimes she came to tea with Jane, an ordeal for both since they could find little of common interest to discuss. Mrs. Rutherford senior looked like a bird of paradise among the sparrows amid the dingy furnishings of the flat. She preferred to have Jane sally west to take tea with her, off Rockingham china with wafer thin bread and butter.

It never occurred to Michael to praise the cuisine or even Jane's appearance, though he never failed to draw attention to tough meat or a ladder in her stocking. He had, in the intervals of his work, found himself a promising job with a firm of electrical manufacturers for the time when he was released from the Navy; it was full of opportunity for an industrious man; an elegant, sophisticated wife would be a valuable asset later on. He set about the task of moulding Jane to this requisite. When she saw how important it was to him, she tried hard to be changed and tidy when he came home at night; if she forgot, or he was early, he would look at her appraisingly, head held back to focus, and say, "For God's sake, Jane, can't you get your hair cut?" or "Why on earth haven't you done your face?

You do look a sight." Her eyes would fill then with ready tears, and he would turn away with an exasperated sigh.

He found that she was unbusinesslike about the money he allowed her; she never knew how much she spent at the grocer or remembered what the vegetables had cost. He bought a large double entry cash book, sat her down at the table and as to a child instructed her in the elements of book-keeping. Jane remembered dutifully for the first month, and only had a small deficit at the end of it to explain away; but after that she perpetually forgot to note down what she had spent and had to fake her entries. Michael always caught her out, even though she spent most of the small allowance her mother gave her trying to put things right.

Sometimes Michael feared she would never learn, but after all, this was only an interval; meanwhile she provided him with food and love. Later on, when he was settled into his new job and they could move to a house of their own, she would lose her mouse-like ways and develop into the woman of poise and grace he expected her to become.

Soon, Jane did become pregnant, and though she found the experience filled with disadvantages, for she was very sick and often very tired, the thought of the coming baby helped her to ignore the many ways in which Michael did not measure up to her imagined idea of him.

★ ★ ★

Peter was born at Merton Corner. Michael had been released from the Navy a few weeks earlier and was on long leave. Though he had treated Jane's discomfort of the past nine months merely as the manifestations of nature and so to be ignored, at the last moment he became afraid and anxious for her, so that she felt he did after all need her, and she was happy. He was immensely proud that the baby was a boy. Jane lay against her pillows in exhausted languor, smiling her delight at his pleasure; at last she had achieved something that really made him happy.

But Michael soon tired of the nursery

atmosphere in the house. Nanny and the maternity nurse were busy all day long with small nightgowns and nappies; Mrs. Harrison enthused daily over each ounce gained by the infant; Jane lay in bed, it seemed for ever, feeding the child, an operation that was touching to behold at first but soon grew boring by repetition; and at uncivilised hours the voice of Peter could be heard declaring his wish for this ceremony to take place.

"Would you mind if I went home for a bit?" Michael asked Jane one morning when Peter was nine days old. The March day was warm, and in the garden the thin spring sunlight shone down on Master Rutherford, basking in silent sleep in his pram.

All at once the brightness of the day vanished; the ever-ready tears sprang into Jane's eyes.

"How will you look after yourself?" she said feebly.

"I meant, to mother's, not our home," Michael explained patiently.

"I should have thought you'd rather be in the country just now," Jane foolishly persisted.

Michael sighed. "I could start studying," he said. "I can go to the works and look about. The sooner I begin, the sooner I'll get on."

"Very well, you go, if you want to," said Jane evenly, pleating the sheet in her thin fingers.

"After all, you're tied up here. It isn't as if we could go anywhere or do anything," said Michael, and even to himself he seemed to be making excuses.

"Go, if you want to," Jane repeated, still in a pleasant voice. "We shall be all right here." Go, she silently cried, before these tears spill out.

He left that afternoon, guiltily glad to be free of the atmosphere of baby, and having easily satisfied his conscience that it was his duty to visit his parents and to think about his job.

★ ★ ★

Now that there was a baby, life was completely different. They could not yet contemplate buying a house, and as flats were hard to find they stayed where

137

they were and thought themselves lucky, looking forward to the day when they could move to the country, for in spite of his ambitions Michael saw himself more as a country squire than a Mayfair dandy; he had oddly inherited his father's fondness for the country and not his mother's love of London. Meanwhile he was working very hard at his new job, which had excellent prospects and required all his concentration to learn. He was out all day from half-past eight till six o'clock.

Peter spent the morning in his pram in the small sooty garden behind the house. Every afternoon Jane pushed him through the hot dusty streets till it was time for his orange-juice; if she failed to do this he cried and disturbed the neighbours. She was always busy with his evening feed when Michael came home; there was no time to change her dress. After several scenes, Michael gave up for the moment trying to reform her, for the sight of her tears filled him with disgust. He picked up the paper, holding it at arm's length, for he scorned the disfiguring aid of spectacles, and retired behind it. At week-ends, to her increasing chagrin, he retreated more and more to the golf club where whenever it was fine he played each Saturday and Sunday.

He never thought that Jane might be lonely. He did not realise that the only conversation she had was with the tradesmen. They had no other friends, now that Michael's naval connections had moved away, and though Jane smiled shyly at several other pram pushers on her walks no friendships developed. She realised how true it was that a city can be the loneliest place on earth.

Once, they spent a week-end at Merton Corner. This was a mighty expedition involving quantities of luggage, for the younger you are the more impedimenta you require, but the visit was not a success. Michael was martyred about missing his golf, and found the atmosphere of the House of Women, as he called it, overwhelming, so it was not repeated. It was not surprising that Jane became increasingly dependent on the company of her son.

Quite suddenly, Mrs. Harrison remarried. For years her new husband, Colonel

Forrest, had begged her to marry him, but she had not felt free to do so until Jane was settled. Now that Michael was safely home and doing well she felt able to think of herself.

In theory, Jane was delighted. Her stepfather was a dear, but as her mother had known it would, the fact of her marriage made Jane feel curiously forsaken.

But when Merton Corner was sold, Jane's mother transferred some of the proceeds and most of the furniture to her daughter. Thus at last the long search for the new home could begin.

Nearly every week-end, for months, Jane and Michael set out with high hopes and sheafs of seductive descriptions from house agents, to return weary and disillusioned from inspections of rambling mansions or decrepit hovels. They were agreed that it was worth waiting until they found something they really liked, where they could settle and put down roots, rather than another temporary dwelling, but the search was prolonged as their requirements continued to differ from the desirable residences offered by the agents.

Jane fell in love with Rose House the moment she saw it. They had heard it was for sale, not through an agent, but through a business acquaintance of Michael's who knew the owner. It was a square house of mellowed brick, whose soft pink colour lent its name to that of the house. It was early spring when they found it, and the wild grass under the trees in the garden was full of daffodils, shining bright with promise; across the small lawn, wonder of wonders, a young willow hung its weeping head which bore the yellow wisps of unfolding leaves on every tendril, reminding Jane of the half-forgotten willow that had been her childhood sanctuary.

They rang the front door bell, and stood outside the heavy iron-studded oak door awaiting to be admitted, and Jane's heart beat fast. In the car, Peter, now two years old, sat with a picture book 'reading' to baby Bill, who lay in his carry-cot curling his fingers in the air and chuckling.

The front door opened. Jane steeled

herself to expect inside the house an antiquated kitchen, poky rooms and primitive plumbing, for surely such a perfect outside must conceal some flaws within, but there were none. There were four good bedrooms, and a tiny room that could be the dressing-room for which Michael hankered; there was a bathroom with a gleaming modern bath twice the size of the rust-stained one in the flat, where Michael was compelled to curl up his great length very uncomfortably; there was a dining-room; there was a pleasant drawing-room with french windows that opened into the garden beyond, and there was a tiny study which could be a playroom for the children. The kitchen was light and airy, with a red quarry-tiled floor and a cool larder close at hand. But best of all in Jane's eyes was the staircase. In sharp contrast to the steep sheer flights up and down which she had carried first Peter and now Bill so wearily, these stairs were wide and shallow, broken by turning two corners with little landings before they reached the passage above. Even if a child did tumble down, his fall would be a short one.

Michael asked pertinent questions about drains and the water supply. Jane tried to pretend that they might possibly be persuaded to think about the house seriously, afraid if her excitement showed that the price would leap proportionately.

They drove away, and even Michael enthused.

"It's in wonderful condition, it would hardly need anything done to it," he said, swerving to avoid a dog that ran across the road in front of the car.

"It has a lovely garden, quite a lot of it is wild; we could turn more of it into orchard to save work," suggested Jane.

"We'll make them an offer, subject to survey," decided Michael.

Jane sighed with relief, and looked out of the window at the fields which lay on either side of the road. A herd of black and white Friesian cows munched lazily in the distance, and they passed a flock of sheep with the young lambs white like snowdrops among their grubby mothers. Here, Peter would soon lose his pale London complexion; Bill could have his pram in the garden, and later be imprisoned in his playpen on the lawn.

143

No need to go for walks unless one wanted to; instead she could work in the garden and grow roses and Michaelmas daisies.

Michael glanced sideways at Jane's eager face, and with what was for him a rare gesture patted her hand where it lay on her lap. Her spirits soared. If the house had the effect of inspiring Michael to such a spontaneous act; it could bring their whole marriage alive again from the weary rut of habit it had become.

She was in a fever until the surveyor had safely reported that all was in order at Rose House. No death watch beetle lurked beneath the floor, nor dry rot gnawed behind the beams. New energy came to her as she sewed curtains and cleared out cupboards. She had been very sick during her second pregnancy and had found carrying Peter up and down the stairs and pushing out his pram very wearying. Her recovery had been slow; she had been so certain that this time she would have a daughter that it took her several days after his arrival to digest the fact that she had another son.

What a lot of possessions they had

accumulated, even in the limited space of the flat! She found, packed in a box, the red wool dress she had bought with such high hopes that day so long ago, and worn so few times since. It was still, she thought, a pretty dress, and what a lovely cherry red. She put it back in the box and packed it in the trunk.

Things did not upset her now so easily; her day was too busy. She no longer expected to be praised for her appearance and knew her former belief that people found beauty in those they loved to be a myth. She knew she disappointed Michael in many ways. Now she would make a new start in Rose House. With so much space it would be easy to be tidy; the children would not have to go for walks with a garden in which to play, so there would be time to settle down to the household accounts which Michael insisted upon her keeping and which were the bane of her life. Above all, in the calm of the Hampshire countryside she would not be so tired.

Nanny, who had retired to a bungalow at Clacton when Jane's mother remarried,

took the children away to their grand-
mother's for the move, as she had taken
charge of Peter when Bill was born. She
was well over seventy now, but still a
staunch disciplinarian and Jane was glad
that she was willing to help at such times
of need. The move went smoothly, and
thanks to the Merton Corner furniture
there were no empty rooms.

It was wonderful to have a place that
was really their own. They woke in the
morning to the singing of birds in the
trees; there was no thud of feet clumping
on the pavement outside, no noise of
buses, no sound of nocturnal cisterns
in the flats of neighbours. Michael took
a part of his holiday for the move; he
worked in the garden while Jane hung
curtains and arranged the house, and it
was like a second honeymoon.

Soon Jane began to want the children.
She longed to see Peter's face when
he saw his new cupboard with his toy
soldiers and cars neatly arranged inside;
she wanted to see Bill's cot in the corner
of the cream-painted night nursery. She
pictured the pram standing in the shade
near the little willow tree, with the

cooing birds lulling the baby to sleep. She unwisely said something of this to Michael, two days before they went to fetch the boys.

"I should have thought you'd have liked just being on our own like this," said Michael.

"Oh, I do," she hastened to say. "You know I do, it's been wonderful, darling, only it will be lovely when we're all together in our very own home."

"Well, I'm enjoying the peace, and having you to myself for a bit," he said. "You never have time for me when you're running round after them. Don't forget you've got a husband too."

"I don't, how could I?" Jane wished she had not tried to tell him what was in her mind. How could she tell him that the children needed her in a way he never would? She was in no doubt of their love, when Peter clutched her hand in his own plump little fist, or kissed her wetly when she tucked him into bed, or when Bill's little face creased in a smile of recognition as she bent over his pram. For years Michael had been the centre of her universe, the sun around whom all her thoughts pivoted. When she realised his self-sufficiency, perforce he occupied less of her mind, but she still felt a pang when he left the house each morning, and was bitterly hurt when he failed to show her any understanding.

Now she said aloud, a little hopelessly, "I was just thinking of us all, as a family."

"Well, let's think of you and me for a change," said Michael. "You'll soon have more than enough of the children."

148

Part Two

Part Two

1

TWO years later Michael came home one evening to find the fire almost out. The atmosphere in the train had been one of airless frowst, chilling to the morale if not the body; then the car, which had stood all day at the station, refused to start and he had been forced to spend ten minutes tinkering frostily with it before it could be persuaded to bring him the last five miles of his journey.

There was no sign of Jane; she must be still upstairs putting the children to bed. Michael sighed and rubbed his icy hands together. A faint spiral of smoke rising from the grate indicated that there was still a little life in it; he crouched before it and resignedly began to revive it with the bellows. From overhead, muted bumps and bangs signalled the progress of his sons in their nightly ritual. Judging by their restraint, operations must be nearly complete for their journeyings to and

151

from the bathroom were accompanied by a noise like thunder.

Michael frowned as he worked at the fire; methodically he puffed at judiciously-placed fragments of coal, and soon a comforting warmth began to radiate into the room as the flames shot upwards. Then Jane came in.

"You might have had a decent fire going," he said at once, rubbing his hands on his handkerchief.

"Oh dear, was it out?" she said. "I'm so sorry, Michael, but Bill isn't well and I'm afraid I forgot." She bent and belatedly prodded at it, blackening her hand on the poker.

"As you see, I've dealt with it," said Michael in a frigid voice. "Really, Jane, is it too much to expect that you should have a decent fire going when I get back at night?"

"I'm very sorry, Michael, I just forgot," she repeated, rubbing her hand across her forehead and leaving a smear of coal dust. Her short brown hair stood in untidy wisps round her pale face which now wore a harassed expression.

"You're always forgetting," said Michael

sternly. "It's just a question of a little organisation, that's all. If you made it up before you went upstairs with the children it would be all right."

"I know it would, and I did mean to, but I've told you I forgot," she said again.

"Well, please remember in future," said Michael. "If you spent all day coping with the problems I do you'd expect a good fire when you got home."

"I've said I'm sorry, can't we leave it at that?" asked Jane wearily.

"You always think things can be mended by saying you're sorry, when all that's needed is a little forethought," he said pompously. He had not meant to worry on about the subject, but now launched, he could not draw back.

"I must go and see about supper," said Jane in a tight voice, and she left the room.

Michael followed her as far as the cloakroom, where with exaggerated splashings and scrubbings he removed such traces of his firemaking as had not already been transferred to his handkerchief, and continued by these sounds to remind her of his just grievance.

Jane sighed as she put the fat on for the fish. The evening had not started well, and this morning she had woken up firmly resolved to make a particular effort again. If things went wrong, she had planned that this time it would not be her fault. She would prepare the meal in good time, change into a frock, and be the decorative companion Michael required; but the day had conspired against her. First, Mrs. Barton, who came every morning to help in the house, had not arrived but sent a message to say she had 'flu; then Bill had begun to whine and show signs of a heavy cold. He had been put to bed and promptly been very sick, involving much mess and washing. Next, Peter had fallen off his bicycle on the concrete car-wash and cut his knee quite badly; thereafter he had haunted her round the house, declaring himself too badly damaged to go out and play. At twelve, the plumber, long expected, arrived to do a repair to the hot water system, needing the boiler emptied and countless cups of tea. At half-past three, when comparative quiet reigned with the invalid asleep upstairs and Peter doing his jigsaw on a corner of the kitchen table, Jane was busy baking, trying to catch up on the day, when Mrs. Wilkinshaw from the Manor elected to call. Immaculate in tweed suit and Henry Heath hat, the good lady found Jane with hair standing out in wisps, flour on her nose and a face that had not seen powder since half-past seven that morning. When she left after half an hour, having obtained Jane's promise of help at a charity bazaar, their conversation had twice been interrupted by wails from Bill upstairs and once by an ominous smell of burning pastry from the kitchen. Jane thought Mrs. Wilkinshaw would imagine she had been visiting a lunatic asylum.

This evening poor little Bill was very pathetic, with a flushed face and huge eyes. He lay still against his pillow, very different from his normal busy, chattering self. He began to cry now, and Jane hurried from the kitchen to his room. The little boy was very hot and his hair lay damply on his forehead.

Jane gave him a drink and stayed with him for a few minutes, sponging his face and murmuring to him, wondering if she should call the doctor tonight and not wait till the morning. But presently he was soothed and she left him. Peter, temporarily installed in the spare room, called out to her and she had to go and tell him what she had been doing.

She hurried away from him and back down to her supper preparations, thinking ruefully how the best intentions so often went astray. The road to hell is paved with them, she remembered. Michael was right, she did lack organisation and forethought. It shouldn't be so difficult to mend one's ways, but somehow it was; other things always intervened, hide-and-seek or playing trains, or even simply dreaming.

She bustled to in the kitchen, abandoning the elaborate sauce she had planned and quickly melting some butter. By working at top speed she managed to have dinner on the table only ten minutes late, though typically in her hurry she smashed a tumbler and had to pause to sweep up the pieces.

But Michael was the soul of punctuality when it suited him. Tonight he wanted to listen to a certain programme on the wireless; now it might be missed unless he sank low enough to take his plate into the drawing-room.

"Is your watch losing time again?" he enquired solicitously when Jane put his plate in front of him.

"No, it's going beautifully now," she said in some surprise.

"Oh. You realise, then, that dinner is ten minutes late?"

"I know. I couldn't be any quicker. I was late with the children," she said.

"You must learn to be strict with them," said Michael. "I've heard you go up to them three times since I've been back. I nearly went up to Bill myself to tell him to behave, but I felt too tired."

Jane made a wry face, and stretched one weary leg under the table.

"Poor little Bill, he can't help it," she said. "He's feeling rotten."

"What's the matter with him?" demanded Michael. "You always find excuses."

"I think he's getting 'flu. There's a lot about, and Mrs. Barton's got it. She didn't come today. He's got a temperature of a hundred and two tonight."

"Well, even so, he isn't a baby now," said Michael. "He must learn to control himself even if he isn't feeling well. You spoil those boys, Jane. You let them wear you out, and then you can't even remember a simple thing like making up the fire." He returned in triumph to his original grievance. "Put yourself in my place," he continued, wagging his knife at her like a schoolmaster's pointer. "Just imagine what it's like to come home frozen after a long day dealing with difficult people and problems, and travelling in a dirty crowded train, and then not even find a fire when you get in, and your wife looking like a charwoman."

"I know you come home cold and tired, and I should have had the fire going, as I've admitted," said Jane, with her voice rising, "but put yourself in my place for once and see if you'd feel like a débutante in the evening."

158

Michael said, "Nonsense, Jane, you have nothing to do all day bar cook a few meals. You have the peaceful countryside around you, no vital decisions to make, no policies to plan. Your life is easy."

Jane got up without answering and began to clear away the plates, her own barely touched. Her hands shook with fatigue and angry tears stung her eyes but she did not let them fall. She would not speak, for she could not trust her voice and she would not risk a quarrel.

After dinner she sat furiously knitting until she felt it was late enough to go to bed. Michael sighed and turned the wireless louder to drown the clatter of her needles as she poured her frustration into Peter's new jersey. She could not sit with idle hands and had now turned her very average knitting ability into extreme skill; a stream of garments, jumpers, socks and gloves, poured endlessly from her restless hands; in this way she preserved an element of outward calm, enough to answer briefly Michael's monologues when required, and enough to help her through the more usual silence that prevailed while he read important documents. He seldom seemed now to have a thought that was not connected with his work; his increasing opportunities possessed him completely and the rest of his life mattered only in the way in which it related to his ambition.

In bed at last, Jane wept, sobbing into her pillow until she had no tears left and lay empty, drained of all feeling. Her love, that had been a long time dying, lay in ruins, leaving in place of all her dreams a hollow void.

She lay in the darkness and saw at last that she had brought most of her troubles upon herself. Meeting Michael at a time when her head was stuffed with novelette-ish dreams, she had at once endowed him with all the qualities she admired and without regard for what was real. He could not understand her dreaming nature; to him keeping household accounts was a simple matter of mathematics; raising children a matter of food and discipline; cooking and housework mere mechanics like getting up in the morning. On the other hand in justice Jane knew he was in many ways admirable. He worked hard and was thrifty; she was convinced he was completely faithful. But there was nothing left in their relationship; instead of it deepening into the complete unity she had anticipated they were growing more like strangers every day. For the first time she admitted to herself that she would have been happier if she had never married him, but in the next moment she knew that under the same circumstances she would do it again. Besides, if she had not married Michael, what would she have done? Eventually, she supposed, have married some other man about whom she would have probably also built up a completely false idea in her imagination, and with perhaps unluckier results. She supposed that every couple who was later divorced must have started out with the same high hopes and illusions as hers; probably there was nowhere such a thing as a perfect marriage. The best thing to do was to accept the limitations of her lot and count her blessings. She had two lovely, healthy sons; they made it all worthwhile. She had a lovely home and good friends. It was better not to think of the loneliness ahead; Michael did not come home drunk and beat her, or fritter away his money, so really she was fortunate.

Downstairs, Michael began to thump about as he performed his nightly ritual of locking up. Presently she heard his footsteps on the stairs. Jane pulled the bedclothes up round her face and closed her eyes.

★ ★ ★

The next day Bill still had a high temperature, and lay listless against his pillow. As soon as Michael had left for the station Jane telephoned the doctor. During the two and a half years they had been at Rose House Dr. Brown or his partner, Dr. Gould, had been to see them several times for the usual coughs and colds. The children were fond of both doctors, who were kind and avuncular, the one fat and the other thin. Everyone had been sorry when his wife's poor health had forced Dr. Gould, the thin one, to move away to the more bracing climate of a seaside practice. Jane hoped now that it would be dear old Dr. Brown who would come to see Bill, and not his so far unknown new partner.

She cleared away the breakfast things and washed up. An invoice from the grocer fluttered off the mantelshelf, and Jane rescued it with a sigh. She must try to find time today to balance her accounts, and hoped that there would not be too large a sum to be explained away in the hotch-potch of petty expenses. Michael could not see why she found it impossible to note down the sixpences for sweets or doughnuts before they were forgotten.

Peter was in the nursery, fitting together his railway lines in the warmth of the bright fire. It was another cold, blustery day and the long winter ahead was a dismal prospect. Jane peeped at Bill, who was dozing and muttering to himself, before she put on her boots and her old coat to feed the hens. Her feet and hands were icy when she came back into the house, and she stopped for a moment to warm them and admire Peter's railway lay-out. At nearly five, he was a long, slender child, very much like Michael, with the same dark hair and brown eyes. He was absorbed now, winding the red clockwork engine which was rather battered since the day Bill had inadvertently sat on it. The spring was weak, and the poor thing could barely summon the strength to pull all the coaches that were hooked on behind.

Warm again, Jane went to make the beds. She was tired and heavy-eyed, and her mind kept leaping from worry about Bill to her thoughts of the night. The trouble is, she decided, pulling tight the sheet on the large double bed, people go on changing and developing all their lives, and sometimes they react alike to what happens to them and draw together, but sometimes their paths diverge. Children, instead of being a link, can be a wedge between a couple, if the father cannot accept the fact that his wife is now a mother too. She was aware that the reverse applied also. She felt oppressed by a sense of tragedy and waste; so much ought to be possible and should be natural. She had tried to meet the standard Michael required of her, even to attempting sophistication, but the claims of motherhood were too strong and it was a losing battle. She would fight no more. Michael must accept her as she was, as she did him, or she would lose her own integrity. This above all, to thine own self be true, she thought bitterly. That would be her maxim now; so she would avoid the loss of her own identity.

Bill broke upon her reverie by crying out, and she went into his room. He was sitting up in bed, crying tearlessly, not knowing what was wrong. Jane took him in her arms and nursed him, talking to him softly. He coughed, a hard, dry cough that shook his small body. Jane hoped Dr. Brown would soon come. Presently Bill quietened. She sponged his face and turned his pillow over, and he lay back under the blankets. He felt too bad to look at a book or play with a toy, so she tucked his battered bear in beside him and gave him a kiss. "I'll go and make you a lovely orange drink, pet," she said.

Peter, bored with his trains, demanded to go out in the garden, and looked at his mother in astonishment when for a moment she caught him to her in a wild hug before she dressed him in his warm garden clothes.

* * *

Dr. Fraser rose and opened the door of his consulting room to let his last patient, a rheumaticky old lady, go out. It had been a long surgery today, and now he had a lot of visits to make, for this was the damp season of influenza and bronchitis. He poked his head into the office, where the secretary-cum-dispenser presided among typewriter and mystic bottles, to make sure there were no more calls, then he collected his bag and went out to his car. He was glad he had decided to accept this partnership; he had done locum here once, between appointments, and he liked the country practice with its straightforward, genuine people. He had no regrets because he had not specialised; plenty of people wanted to do that, but G.P.s were still the first essential. Pity they had to waste so much time filling up forms, he thought ruefully, patting his coat pocket to make sure he had a good supply for today.

It was a cold day, and the wind was keen; for once it was not raining. He looked at his list: several chronics for their routine visits, some 'flu victims who should be on the mend, and three new calls. There was old Mrs. Webster with pains in the stomach, Mrs. Rutherford with a child with suspected 'flu and a high temperature, and Mrs. Barton with 'flu. He had better see the new ones first, and then go round the old faithfuls.

The car was cold, and spluttered as it started off down the road. It was four miles to Paxtone, where Mrs. Webster lived in a small grey cottage with three cats. She was just like a witch, Jim thought, as he entered her dark dwelling, and he half expected to see a broomstick parked by the bed. Mrs. Webster was skinny and pale, with a large nose and limp grey hair. Her pains were merely indigestion, and Jim left her a bottle of bismuth mixture which he had circumspectly brought with him.

Monksbourne was two miles from here, and soon Jim was knocking at the door of Mrs. Barton's proud pink council house.

A voice from upstairs called out:

"Come up, Doctor, I'm all alone. Please excuse the muddle."

Everything was neat and bright within the little house.

"There doesn't seem to be any muddle," said Jim with a smile, stepping into the spick front bedroom. "Good morning, Mrs. Barton. I'm the new doctor. Fraser's my name. Now, what's the trouble?" He noted the flushed cheeks of the thin little woman lying neatly between the clean, thick white sheets.

"Very pleased, I'm sure, Doctor," said Mrs. Barton, ever mindful of formalities. "I'm afraid I've got a touch of that there 'flu. My Bert, he would call you, though as I says to him, I'll be over it in a day or two, but it's awkward like, with the children and all, and poor Mrs. Rutherford with such a lot to do; how she'll manage I don't know."

"Mrs. Rutherford? She lives just up the village, doesn't she?" Jim felt the swift pulse in the thin wrist. "I've got to call there to see one of the children."

"Oh, dear, that'll be little Bill. He was a bit irritable the other day and we didn't like the look of him. Oh, poor Mrs. Rutherford."

"You work there, do you?" Jim was always interested in the private lives of his patients. To him they were not merely ailing bodies but very much human beings with their problems.

"Yes, and she is good to me. Such a nice lady," approved Mrs. Barton. "I must get up if she's got Bill in bed, she will be busy," and she sat up in bed as if ready to leap out there and then.

Jim gently pushed her back against the pillow and popped a thermometer into her mouth.

"Let's get you better first," he said. "You'll only be another one for Mrs. Rutherford to look after if you try to move now."

He looked out of the window while he waited for the mercury to rise, and commented on the orderly garden below, and when at length he ungagged her and took the thermometer over to the light to read it, Mrs. Barton purred with pride and told him he should see it in the summer when her roses were a riot, even though she did say so herself.

"I'll make a special trip to see them," Jim promised with a smile, "for I hope you won't need a professional visit then." He bent over her to sound her chest, and at length had to prescribe bed till further notice.

"Will you tell Mrs. Rutherford I'm ever so sorry, Doctor," the woman begged, "and I'll be back as soon as I can."

"I'll tell her," Jim promised. He left medicine and pills on the yellow oak bed-table, and then went back down the steep lino-covered stairs.

He came to Rose House round a bend in the road. Even on this grey blustery day with the tall black elms bending in the wind and the apple trees standing round it bare and leafless, it was an enchanting house. A little boy dressed in a muddy miniature duffle coat and a far muddier pair of corduroy trousers was swinging on the wrought-iron gate that stood open to the drive.

"Hullo. Would you like a ride up the drive?" Jim offered gravely, leaning from his window.

"Yes, please. Who are you?" asked Peter, jumping into the car, mud and all.

They drove slowly up the fifty yards of gravelled drive.

"I'm the doctor. Who's ill? Not you, is it?"

"No, it's Bill, my brother. He's probably dead by now, I should think," said Peter with relish.

"Oh, dear, I hope not," said Jim mildly.

"A funeral would be fun," suggested Peter ghoulishly. "I suppose you're the new doctor instead of Dr. Gould. Mummy will be cross, she said she hoped Dr. Brown would come."

"Oh, did she?" Jim could sympathise with an anxious mother faced by an unknown factor instead of her familiar adviser. "Well, perhaps if you introduce me she'll think it's all right," he suggested with a smile.

"All right. Come in," said Peter. He scrambled out of the car and banged at the front door with his strong young body, for it was too heavy for him to open.

Jim turned the handle, and followed Peter inside.

"It's the doctor, Mummy," yelled the

little boy. "The new one."

He marched, muddy booted, across the square hall with its one rug and polished floor now marked by boots and spaniel paws. A black and white cocker materialised from nowhere and sidled up to Jim, wagging its stumpy tail and craving for love.

"Just coming," called a voice from upstairs. There was a low murmur as Jane spoke to Bill, and then she came running down the stairs. She rounded the last bend and stood upon the last step staring in utter disbelief at the new doctor. Jim, who had taken off his overcoat and laid it on a chair in the hall, was just picking up his bag again. He turned and saw her. It was Peter who broke the incredulous silence of his elders.

"It's all right, Mummy, he's a friend of mine. Bill will like him, you'll see. I had a ride in his car."

At that they both moved, both speaking at once.

"Jane!"

"Jimmy!"

They laughed then, and Jane put out

her hand. Holding it for a moment, Jimmy was carried back eleven years of time.

"You haven't changed, you're just the same," he declared, still looking at her. Her hair was just as untidy as he remembered it, her eyes as blue. The clear skin was still smooth, though little lines of laughter and of something else were beginning to show round her eyes. Automatically his doctor's eyes noted that she looked tired.

"Nor have you changed, Jimmy! I knew it was Dr. Fraser, the new one I mean, but I never even thought of it being you," Jane marvelled ungrammatically. "How lovely!"

Peter watched the grown-ups in amazement. All this fuss!

Jane felt his gaze. "Dr. Fraser and I are old friends, Peter," she explained. "He knows all about boats."

"Oh, do you know about trains, too? Perhaps you could mend my engine?" said Peter hopefully.

"Perhaps, later. Not now, darling," said Jane. "Take your things off if you want to stay indoors now, and go into the nursery while Dr. Fraser comes to see Bill."

Obediently but mutteringly the little boy pulled off his boots.

"I've got a lovely bloody knee you can see afterwards," he told Jim temptingly. "Much more interesting than Bill's old cold."

"I'd like to see it very much," Jim assured him solemnly. "I'll look forward to that when I've been to see Bill." He rumpled the dark hair and looked at Jane, still unbelievingly.

"It's incredible, you and this great boy," he said as he followed her up the stairs.

Jane laughed. "I'm twenty-seven, Jim," she said. "Getting old!"

"Well, you don't look it," he said.

They went in to Bill's room, where the little boy was lying listlessly against his pillows.

"Bill, this is Dr. Fraser, who's come to look after us instead of Dr. Gould. He's an old friend of Mummy's. We used to sail in boats together when we were young," said Jane.

Bill looked at Jim with a small flicker of interest.

"Hullo, Bill. I'm sorry you're feeling ill," said Jim. "What a fine bear you've got. What's his name?"

"He's called Rhubarb," said Bill in a thin little voice, unlike his usual gay tone. "He's feeling bad. He's got a headache and he feels sick."

"Oh dear, poor Rhubarb." Jim sat on the bed and eyed the bear. "Shall I look at him first?" Without waiting for an answer he produced a thermometer from his pocket and popped it under the bear's furry arm. Then he handed the bear to Jane. "Mummy can do him while I do yours," he said, and put a second thermometer under Bill's arm, holding the chubby little limb across the child's chest to keep it in place, and putting his fingers on the pulse.

"You'd be surprised how many I break," he said, glancing at Jane, speaking so quietly that she only just heard him, and with the little smile that was suddenly again so familiar.

Rhubarb was at length duly returned to bed and sounded with the stethoscope, and then it was Bill's turn. Jim was very thorough, and his hands were gentle. At last he tucked the child back into bed and Jane took him to the bathroom to wash.

She sat on the edge of the bath while he ran the tap at the basin.

"Don't worry, Jane," he said. "Poor little chap, children are up one minute and down the next. It's only a nasty dose of 'flu. I'll give you some tablets to bring his temperature down. I've just been to see your good Mrs. Barton. Probably he's caught it from her. There's an awful lot about."

"You're sure? It couldn't be pneumonia or anything?" Jane asked anxiously.

"No, of course not. It might turn into measles but I doubt it, there isn't much about. He hasn't been near it, has he?"

"No, not that I know of. I thought it was 'flu really, but one always expects the worst," said Jane.

Jim looked at her shrewdly. "You mustn't do that, you know," he told her firmly. "It so seldom is, and worry won't lessen it in any case."

Jane laughed. "I know that really,

176

but one can't help flapping a bit," she confessed. "I've been very lucky with the children, Jim. They're hardly ever ill. I'm spoiled."

A door banged downstairs as Peter knocked against it, and she jumped. Jim noticed, but made no comment.

"Here are the tablets. Give him one every four hours; don't wake him for them at night, but if he does wake up, let him have one. He'll probably take them all right if you crush them in some sugar," he said. "I'll come and see him again tomorrow."

"Thank you." Jane took the tablets and put them in the bathroom cupboard, above the reach of questing childish hands.

"Must you go at once? Stay and have a cup of coffee, it's just eleven," she said.

"Oh, Jane, how good that sounds. I shouldn't really, I've a mass of visits, but still, I know none of them are urgent, and this is an occasion." He smiled at her again. "Thank you very much, I'd love it."

On the way downstairs they looked in on Bill again and Jim said goodbye.

He nodded at the pictures of Humpty Dumpty and the other nursery characters that were painted on the bed boards and the furniture.

"Did you do those, Jane?" he asked.

"Yes," she said with a smile.

"I don't suppose you have a lot of time for painting now, do you?" he said as they went downstairs.

"Not a minute. That's all I've done since that last year at Rhosarddur, except for a few sketches of the boys, but they were only rough," she said ruefully. "So much for my aspirations."

"You'll have time later on, when the children are older," Jim said.

"So I shall," said Jane, in surprise. "Peter goes to school next term. Doesn't time fly? It must be how long, eleven years since we were all at Rhosarddur."

She picked up a brown coffee pot and poured its contents into a saucepan.

"I'm afraid it's only the breakfast coffee warmed up," she warned.

"It'll be lovely," he assured her.

"Have you ever been back?" Jane asked, watching the coffee begin to steam.

"Yes, once, just after the war," he said. He could not tell her now that it was nursing a faint flame of hope that he had returned to Rhosarddur in 1946, and there from friends learned that Jane was married. Since then he had tried never to think of her, and thought he had succeeded.

They sat at the kitchen table drinking their coffee and talking. Suddenly she sat up and exclaimed, "Jim, what you must think of me, entertaining you in the kitchen." She half rose, in dismay.

"I like kitchens," said Jimmy. "They're homely and warm, the hub of the house." He remained sitting firmly in his chair, holding his steaming cup of coffee between both hands and smiling at her.

Jane relaxed. "What have you been doing all this time, Jim?" she asked.

"Oh, wandering about a bit, since the war," he said. "Mostly in different hospitals getting myself modernised. I did a locum here three years ago, and when Dr. Gould was planning to leave they wrote and offered me a partnership. It's nice here. I like country people."

"Yes, it's lovely, isn't it?" said Jane eagerly. "Wait till the summer comes, and all the fields are green and fresh, and the gardens full of roses and hollyhocks." Her eyes looked past him into the months ahead when the long winter would be ended.

At last, reluctantly, he rose to go.

"I'll get the sack," he grinned, looking at his watch. "I'll come tomorrow, Janey; keep on with the tablets, and if you're at all worried ring me up. And thanks awfully for the coffee."

"Oh, Jim, I am glad you've come here," she said spontaneously. "Dr. Brown's a dear, but it will be lovely to have you for our doctor." She smiled at him and led the way to the hall where he had left his coat.

Peter, with paint all over his face, came out of the nursery as he heard them approaching. He had been busily occupied colouring a book. Jane unlatched the door and stood to wave Jim out of sight, with the dark, slender little boy standing beside her.

Jim was still smiling as he drove away towards his next patient. Here in this

180

encounter from the past was surely a happy augury for the success of his new appointment. It was not until he arrived back at the surgery at the end of the morning that he realised Jane had never once mentioned her husband.

★ ★ ★

Michael returned in the evening to find the fire blazing cheerily. He stood warming his hands and thinking how simple it was by a timely word to remedy an annoyance. Of course, like all women, Jane always had an excuse for her failures, but he had found that by drawing attention to her faults she often mended them. It had never occurred to him that it might be more fruitful to draw attention to her virtues; those he simply took for granted.

Perversely, she had spent a long time this evening preparing an elaborate meal. After the revelation that had come to her in the night, Michael might no longer be the pivot of her life, but conscience compelled her all the more towards the path of duty. After curry and an omelette, Michael mellowed, and told her in tedious detail about his day. Jane firmly believed that it behoved a wife to take an intelligent interest in her husband's work, but sometimes when he held forth at great length for an entire evening about wiring intricacies, thermostats, coils, insulators and flashing lights on the latest products of his firm, her head would reel and her eyelids droop. The technicalities meant little to her; the business deals seemed to lack integrity; it was hard to simulate interest.

Presently it occurred to Michael to enquire about Bill. He was secretly proud of his two healthy, attractive little sons, and his ideas of perfection extended to them. He was quick to correct them for any naughtiness, but seldom praised an achievement, for those were simply what he expected from them.

Now, in answer to his query, Jane told him that Bill was still feeling very wretched, though the M. and B. had stopped his temperature from rising.

"The new partner came," Jane added, "and isn't it fantastic, he's Jim Fraser, who I used to know years ago at Rhosarddur."

"Is he a decent chap?"

"Oh yes, he's very nice." How inadequate the words were to indicate Jim's warm and friendly personality and the sense of confidence he conveyed. "He's kind," she said, seizing on what seemed to her his outstanding characteristic, and added more quickly, "The boys both liked him."

"Well, that's as well. It would have been awkward if you hadn't liked him since you'd met before," said Michael, not greatly interested. "Do you think he's a good doctor?" This was what really mattered; Michael must always be certain of efficiency.

"I should imagine very good. He examined Bill very thoroughly, much more so than Dr. Gould has ever done, but of course Bill's never been as bad as this before."

"He'll have to get used to it." Michael knew that it was necessary to grow accustomed early to life's trials. "Mrs. Barton back yet?"

"No, she's definitely got 'flu too, and

won't be back for at least a week," said Jane.

"Oh," Michael sighed. That meant a week of disorder in the house and even help with the washing-up at night instead of stacking it till Mrs. Barton came next day as they usually did. "Are you sure she's bad?" he asked.

"Oh yes, she's still in bed. Jim had just been to see her before he came here. He said she was most anxious to get up and come back, especially when she heard about Bill. Besides, she isn't the sort of person to pretend to be ill when she's not." Jane felt indignant on Mrs. Barton's behalf.

"No, I suppose she isn't." Even Michael had to admit that this was not one of Mrs. Barton's imperfections.

The next morning when Jim arrived he found the dining-room chairs stacked in the hall and Jane in the process of 'turning out.' She had not heard his ring above the whine of the vacuum cleaner, and he had not waited for her to come to the door but opened it at once and walked in. A tin of polish stood on the floor of the hall and he nearly stepped in it as he avoided the oak chest which had been moved to allow for sweeping beneath.

"Jane, you chump, what on earth are you doing all this for when you've got Bill in bed and your woman away?" he asked, standing in the doorway of the dining-room and looking at her much as a schoolmaster looks at an incorrigible scamp.

"Oh, I am glad you've come, Jim, now I can stop," said Jane, parking the sweeper which she had switched off at sight of him. "I must do it, though, it didn't get more than a quick flick all last week and Michael will soon notice if it isn't polished up — a legacy from all that cleanliness in the Navy," she added, with false brightness. "Bill's asleep, so it was a good opportunity."

"No wonder you're all on edge, if this is typical of you," said Jim. "I noticed you nearly fell in the bath yesterday when a door banged, so I brought you a tonic, but I'd do better to prescribe no polishing and only licks and promises for the next month." He was still smiling, but his eyes were serious.

Jane looked at him in amazement. It was entirely novel to her to hear her own health being discussed. Unless she had a streaming cold for all to see she was presumed to be in full working order, and considered her own constant fatigue to be natural where there were children to be cared for.

"I mean it, Jane," said Jimmy. He took his overcoat off and laid it carefully on the hall chair. "You must be running up and down stairs all day with Bill as he is, you'll be in bed next yourself and that I'm sure would be difficult. Your husband must realise what a lot you've got to do; of course he won't mind a bit of dust till Mrs. Barton gets back."

Jane looked away from Jim's clear eyes which she felt were capable of seeing right into her head and knowing her thoughts.

"Well, he might bring someone home unexpectedly," she excused her husband, in a loyal attempt to conceal his lack of consideration.

Jimmy recognised the feebleness of this remark; but seeing her discomfort he let the subject drop. Instead, he put a large bottle down on the oak chest.

"Well, here it is, every four hours," he said, "and I shall put Peter in charge of you to see that you don't forget it. How's the patient?"

"Oh, I think he's a little better today," Jane thankfully seized the change of subject. "His temperature is down this morning and he's much more cheerful. But Peter isn't very well, I think he must be starting it. He hasn't got a temperature yet but he didn't want any breakfast. He's in the nursery by the fire."

"Oh dear, poor you, Janey," said Jim, using the old name as easily as he had done eleven years ago. "Still, it was bound to happen. Shall you put them in the same room? They'll be company for each other when they start to feel better."

"Oh, yes, I only moved Peter out when Bill started to sniffle; they do share a room really, but I hoped to stop him catching it."

"Well, if Bill's asleep, shall I look at Peter first?" Jim suggested.

They went into the nursery where

the little boy was sitting listlessly in a chair before the fire that flickered merrily behind a high guard. He held a small post office van in one hand and was idly spinning a wheel of it with his finger. Some other discarded toys littered the floor. Jane put the back of her hand gently against his temple; it felt hot now and she made a wry face at Jim over the top of the child's dark head.

"Hullo, young man," Jim was very cheerful. "You've got a fine collection of cars."

Peter looked at him dumbly; the one he held joined those on the floor with a clatter and he began to cry.

"Poor old Pete, bed for you," said Jane, picking him up and kissing him. "Come on, we'll go up to Bill. He'll be glad to have you for company."

"I don't want to go to bed," Peter wailed, and began to sob noisily.

"Oh, come now, boys of nearly five don't cry," said Jane briskly. She hoisted him up and started off upstairs with her noisy burden. Jim followed behind.

"You stay here and help Dr. Fraser look at Bill's throat while I go and fill you a hot bottle," said Jane, setting him down on his bed in the warm bedroom. "What a treat to have a bottle," she added enticingly.

Bill had been woken up by his brother's roars, and now lay looking at them with bright surprised eyes in a scarlet face.

Peter's yells subsided into sobs. He sat on his bed and sniffed.

"I'll be back in a minute, Jim, I've got a kettle on," Jane said, and went quickly out of the room.

When she returned in a few minutes, carrying the bottle in a fleecy flannel jacket, Peter was arrayed in his blue pyjamas, all ready for bed and smiling a watery smile.

"Ha, we gave you a surprise," he said, with a flash of his normal spirits.

"You did indeed," said Jane. "What a lovely shock." In a minute he was tucked up, bottle to toe, and though he would be the last to admit it, thankful to be in bed.

"Jim, how nice of you to undress him," said Jane gratefully.

"He did most of it himself," said Jim.

189

"He's a big boy. When will you be five, Peter?"

"In March, and I'm going to school after Christmas," said Peter.

"How splendid," said Jim, suitably impressed.

"I want to go to school too," said Bill in a sleepy voice.

"So you shall, darling, when you're bigger," said Jane.

"Goodness, this child's like you, Jane," said Jim, as he rose from examining Peter and came to sit on Bill's bed.

Jane blushed with pleasure. It is always gratifying to a mother to be told her child resembles her, and more so when that child is in her eyes enchanting to behold.

"Do you think so?" she demurred modestly. Jimmy looked at her sharply and saw her smile. He laughed.

"I noticed it at once yesterday. Specially with his hair hanging over his forehead like this, it's just like that awful fringe you used to have, do you remember?"

Jane made a face. "Do I not?" she said, and she laughed, too.

When he had finished looking at the

children they went back downstairs.

"I've got the coffee simmering," Jane suggested.

"You'll be the ruination of me," said Jimmy. "I was hoping you had. If I stay then you'll be forced to sit down for a few minutes, so it's in a good cause."

He followed her into the kitchen, still smiling.

"What a lovely house this is, Jane," he said, when she gave him his cup.

"You haven't seen much of it yet," she told him, "only the more domestic apartments, or whatever they're called. But yes, it is rather lovely. We were lucky to find it."

"Have you lived here ever since you were married?" he asked.

"Oh, no," said Jane. "We've been here about two and a half years. Before that we had a flat on the edge of London."

"That must have been difficult, with two small babies," said Jim.

"It was," she admitted frankly. "To be honest, I hated it. It was horrid having no garden — though there was a tiny plot where we could put the pram out — and having to push for miles

191

every afternoon round the shops. But it couldn't be helped. I suppose we were lucky to have anywhere at all. Where are you living, Jimmy? Have you got a house? What about your wife?"

"I've got very comfortable rooms. Dr. Gould found them for me. It's rather like a flat, with a very nice landlady who does for me," he said. "I'm not married, Jane."

"Oh." Somehow it was no surprise to hear this. "What a pity, Jimmy. Why aren't you? Or shouldn't I ask?" Jane suddenly feared a tragedy.

"Oh, you can ask all right," he said with a grin. "I suppose I just missed the boat. All the best girls got pinched before I could get around to it."

"Oh, dear. Well, I'll have to find a nice wife for you, Jimmy, now isn't that a good idea?" She looked at him impishly.

"You're welcome to try," he told her solemnly, "thank you."

She laughed again. "Oh Jim, you always used to make me laugh," she remembered. "Isn't it nice when you meet someone grown-up that you knew as a child, and you find they're still just

192

as nice as they were long ago? So often people change and you don't like them any more."

"I know," he said gently.

"Wouldn't it have been awkward if that had happened to us?" exclaimed Jane, her eyes wide. "I should have had to ring up Dr. Brown and say I didn't like his new partner and unless he'd guarantee always to come himself we'd have to change our doctor!"

"Yes, and I should have gone back and told him what shocking characters we'd got on our registers," said Jimmy, grinning.

"Perhaps it would have been better to write," said Jane. "' Mrs. Rutherford and family regret that owing to incompatibility they must remove their ailments and maladies to another firm.'"

They both laughed again, and Jane had to wipe her eyes.

"Oh, dear, I haven't laughed as much as this since Molly's last visit," she sighed.

Jimmy did not answer. What a revealing statement. Presently he said, "Who's Molly?"

"She's Bill's godmother. She comes to stay once or twice a year and we giggle together. I was at school with her and we were together in the Wrens," Jane said. "Oh, Jimmy, she'd be such a good wife for you! She's awfully nice and such fun, but plain. Would you mind her being plain?"

"Not at all as long as she can cook," said Jimmy gravely. "I hope she isn't six feet tall?"

Jane laughed. "No, she isn't, she's just the right size, about an inch bigger than me," she said. "What a splendid idea. I must see about causing you to meet."

Jimmy grinned. "Don't expect too much to come of it," he warned, "and now I must fly, Jane."

2

THAT evening Jimmy dined with Dr. and Mrs. Brown, as he did once a week. They were a charming couple, the doctor plump, with thick white hair, and Mrs. Brown a small, wisp of a woman with an enchanting smile.

During the course of the evening Jimmy told them that he had known Jane years ago when they were children.

"How interesting, Jim," said Mrs. Brown. "She's a nice little thing; but dreadfully shy, I always think. Two dear little boys."

"Yes; they've both got 'flu, poor kids, quite badly," said Jim. "I knew she'd married, but I'd no idea what her name was." He was surprised at Mrs. Brown describing Jane as shy; he remembered she had been excessively timid as a child, but there seemed no sign of shyness in her now. She had appeared able to pick up their friendship where it left off eleven years before. Where it left off — the thought reminded Jim of feelings he had supposed forgotten. Aloud he said, "I haven't met her husband." He was curious about Michael, the man abhorred dust, and waited now to see if he would be told about him.

"He seems a good sort," said Dr. Brown. "Very healthy — plays a lot of golf, rather well I believe. I've treated him once for gastritis, and I don't think I've seen him for anything else. We meet sometimes socially."

"He's one of those tall, dark and handsome young men, Jim," said Mrs. Brown with her delightful smile. "I believe he was in the Navy — strong and silent, you know. They married during the war and were parted for quite some time."

"What a lot you know about them, my dear," commented her husband. "And yet you say you never gossip."

She smiled. "I like people, Geoffrey, and I like to know all about them. I think Jim here shares my interest."

Jim looked at her gratefully. She was already his good friend, and had shown him a lot of kindness apart from this weekly dinner invitation.

"How nice for you, Jim, to have found an old friend here," she added now. "Most people seem to find Michael Rutherford very agreeable. I expect you will, too." Jim noticed that she did not mention whether she found him so herself.

For three weeks Jim's visits to Rose House continued, though they decreased from daily down to twice in the last week as the patients improved. By good fortune Jane escaped developing 'flu herself, and boasted to Jimmy that this proved how tough she must be, and that he was wasting public money upon the bottles of medicine he continued to provide; however, she meekly drank the tonic because at every visit he looked to see how far the level had sunk. When the boys were getting up again Michael had to go to Scotland for a week on business, and Jane had a curious holiday feeling of relief whilst he was away. There was no evening meal to cook; no critical eye to notice if the house was rather untidy.

She was sorry when Jim's last

professional visit was concluded.

"But you must come to dinner soon, Jim, and I haven't forgotten about Molly. She'll be coming to stay before long. And you haven't met Michael yet."

Jim agreed that this was so, but somehow he found he was not very much looking forward to this pleasure. A husband who caused his wife to shed ten years and seem seventeen again whilst he was away for a week did not sound like a perfect partner. Michael had been out playing golf during Jim's weekend visits.

"Now, Jane, you must finish that tonic yourself. Do you promise to?" he said sternly before he left.

"Very well, Doctor," said Jane meekly, making a face.

"I mean it, Jane. It will do you good. I think it has already, you don't look so tired."

"I feel fine," she assured him.

"Well, if you do start feeling tired again, let me know and I'll mix you up a powerful booster," he insisted.

"All right, Jimmy, and thank you," she said.

The next few days seemed very

monotonous; but soon Jane settled back to normal life. Christmas came and went, like an avalanche it seemed. The day itself was a mad whirl from stockings to parcels, the stove and church. With Michael at home for four days there was a lot of work, and Jane found herself tending to hover anxiously near the children ready to head them away from naughtiness or other provocation of their father.

Early in the New Year Michael and Jane gave a small cocktail party, since they owed a certain amount of this form of hospitality. To this gathering Jimmy was bidden, and there were about twenty people present altogether. Some of them, though not many, he had already met professionally. They were mostly young or near-young married couples, and Jane was anxious that Jimmy should make as many friends as possible.

Michael was not at all interested in Jimmy except in so far as his medical abilities extended. He was not in the least jealous of a childhood friendship of Jane's; he knew for certain that he was her first and only love, and therefore there was no cause. After his fashion he loved Jane; therefore she must love him still. It was something not to question but to take for granted. Now, meeting Jimmy for the first time, he bent from his great height to greet him with the charm that he spontaneously showed strangers; but mentally he ticketed him for ever as 'that little man,' and when he had given him a drink he moved away and thought no more about him.

Jimmy thought it unlikely that he and his host would find much in common. He watched Michael going round the room with the cocktail shaker, bending his head to talk to his guests, that shining dark head that was so like Peter's. Michael was easily the tallest man in the room; his body was long and muscular, as Peter's would be one day; Jim noticed how effective his smile appeared to be. It was easy to see how the young Jane could have been dazzled by this handsome face and facile charm. Chaps like Michael always had girls swooning in circles round them, Jim thought a little bitterly; they did not swoon so easily over small men — not that he had any particular desire to be swooned over.

Jane would have been surprised to know all that was passing through Jim's mind as he stood near her fireplace chatting pleasantly with the friends to whom she had introduced him. Once or twice he glanced at her across the room. She wore a cherry red dress; her hair was nicely done; her eyes were bright, like Bill's with his fever; she was laughing a lot. She caught his eye across the room and smiled. Jim's heart gave a little lift; he thought she was utterly lovely.

Jane was enjoying her party. She was not, as in the past, busy trying to qualify in her husband's eyes as a perfect hostess. She was no longer just one of his possessions; she was herself, and she had made an amazing discovery. The expression on Victor Farquarson's face told her as clearly as if he had said it with words that he found her altogether attractive and delightful and was thoroughly enjoying their conversation. This astounding revelation was not in the least diminished by the fact that Victor was a known philanderer. Jane had never considered herself attractive to any man, philanderer or not, and six months ago she would never have thought about such a thing, but now, free at last from her long spell of bewitchment she was aware of all sorts of undercurrents in the room that she had never contemplated before.

Michael glanced at her once. He was glad to see she was talking away to their guests; she was improving. In the ultimate result he was confident of transforming her into a poised and elegant woman of the world. With a slight frown he recognised that the red dress she was wearing was none other than the one he had so much disliked years before, but tonight there was no doubt it became her. She was very thin, and now that she was older she seemed able to carry off its sophistication.

Jane moved about the room drunk with her new power of attraction. She saw it reflected in the eyes of dour Archie Fellowes, a silent man who made and lost vast fortunes on the Stock Exchange. She saw it gleaming from behind the earnest spectacles of Charles Hunt, virile father of six young Hunts. She looked at their wives with new perception and curiosity. Soignée Betty Farquarson: had she been wildly and helplessly in love with Victor when she married him, or was she eager for the financial security he offered, the maids, the furs, the model dresses? It was hard to believe her pulses had ever raced at sight of Victor as once Jane's had at every glimpse of Michael. It was sad to think that she would never feel that sharp, sweet pain again.

Maud Fellowes, Archie's wife, was good fun. She loved a joke, preferably coarse, and was a jolly mother to her two young children. What had she in common with the sombre man she had married? Did he perhaps in the privacy of their home also reveal a rumbustious delight in fun, or had he merely offered her an escape from endless shorthand and typing? And Hesther Hunt, poor battered mother of so many, where was the gay and ardent girl she must once have been? Jane almost wished the party would end so that she could think about all these new ideas. She went over to Jimmy who was standing in a corner looking at a painting on the wall, and wondered in an academic way what sort of expression she would see in his eyes. Would it be quiet friendliness, cool politeness, or the admiration that the other men had shown?

When he turned to smile at her, what she did see startled her.

But he only said in a calm voice, "I remember you painting this, Janey."

She nodded, looking quickly away from his clear grey eyes and at the painting on the wall.

"Isn't your husband proud of you?" By talking about Michael Jimmy hoped to remove the feeling of constraint he experienced whenever he thought about him.

"He doesn't know I did it," said Jane. "I told him I enjoyed painting, but he wasn't very interested. He didn't think I meant it seriously, so I just never said who'd done them." She frowned at the blue-black rocks and the blue silk sea in the little picture; it was the first time she had spoken aloud a word of criticism about Michael and she should have felt shocked at her disloyalty, but she didn't.

"It's very immature," she added. "I'd like to do it again."

"You've never been back?" he asked her.

"No. I'd love to go, but Michael's mother has taken a house for us at Milton each year so that's where we've taken the children." She sighed. "It's so entirely different there. But you've been back though, Jim, haven't you, you told me you had."

"Only that one time, immediately after the war. It was rather shabby but still the same. I expect it's all cleaned up again now the Army's gone away," he said.

"I'd love to go back, even if it was only for a day," said Jane dreamily. "It was a magical place to me. I'd like to see it again, but perhaps it would be disillusioning. Perhaps it was one's childish imagination that gave it its charm."

"You will go back one day," Jimmy assured her, "and you'll love it just as much, even if it's a different sort of love."

Jane smiled. "Perhaps," she said, "but all the people would be different, too. The friendliness of everyone was half the fun, and meeting the same people again year after year, picking up your friendship where it had left off the year before. But you can't put the clock back, Jimmy. One must go forward, I suppose." She sighed a little.

"You must go forward and get on to your painting, Jane," said Jimmy. His voice was light, but his face was serious.

"Yes, I've been thinking about it quite a bit lately," she said. "Isn't it funny, I've hardly given it a thought all these years, but ever since we talked about it when Bill was ill I've had it in my mind. I used to wonder what on earth I'd do when the children were both at school, but now I know." She smiled. "I may be Dame Jane yet, Jim."

★ ★ ★

When Peter started school, Jane's life was transformed by the gift from her stepfather of an elderly Ford. She no longer had to make complicated arrangements with Michael if she wanted the car. She and the Hunts and the Fellowes took turns to collect all the scholars in a round trip, thus avoiding a daily journey for everyone, and it became possible for her to go further afield to shop or to meet friends.

It was a grim moment delivering Peter at school on the first morning. He was wildly excited, and Jane dreaded his possible disillusionment. He looked diminutive in his huge navy blue overcoat, bought to be grown into, and his tiny bright blue cap. He disappeared behind the bright matching blue front door of the school, leaving Jane feeling like a murderess. She was on tenterhooks till he returned in the afternoon, chattering like a magpie, having covered his grey shorts and jersey with pastel crayons and particles of lunch. He concluded a lively description of his day with a vivid impersonation of Miss Smithers, his instructress, who lisped, making Jane weep with laughter. After that she worried no longer.

Bill missed him, but he was good by himself, for like all elder children Peter bossed him about and it was pleasant to boss himself for a change. Sometimes he went for the day to play with Anne, the youngest of Hesther Hunt's six children, who was also three, and sometimes Anne came to play with him. One day Jim, passing through Monksbourne with half an hour to spare, dropped in to see Jane, and found her gardening with the help of Bill and Anne. It was a sunny March day, and she was seizing the chance to fork over the rosebeds while the children gleefully caught worms, which, when captured, they added to a horrid slimy collection of writhing bodies in a bucket.

She saw Jim coming towards her over the short damp grass, springy with young growth.

"Hullo!" he called, "I thought I'd just come and see how you all were."

They had not met since the cocktail party, though they had passed each other on the road several times, Jim going to the hospital and Jane on her way with the schoolchildren. Now Jane felt very glad to see him. She rammed her fork into the ground and went to meet him.

"Jimmy, how lovely. How are you?" she cried.

The two children came scampering up to display their horrid hoard of worms, and Jane said, "I've borrowed Anne today," rumpling the little girl's blonde curls. "Isn't she a lamb?" she added, watching the little girl as she seized Bill by the hand and dragged him across the lawn.

"Bill looks well," said Jim. "He's grown."

"Yes, he has. He's very well, and so is Peter, though he's had one or two snuffly colds."

"That always happens when they start school," said Jimmy. "They meet more infection than they do at home. How does he like it?"

"Oh, he loves it," she told him, "and it's done him so much good. He's much tougher."

"He wasn't exactly a shrinking violet before," said Jim.

Jane laughed. "No, but he's a real thug now. I sometimes wonder how I shall cope with two such toughs in a few years," she said. Her eyes followed the plump figures of Anne and Bill as they ran madly about on the grass.

"I'd have loved a daughter, Jim," she confessed.

"You might have one yet," he said gently.

"Michael says we can't afford any more children — he doesn't know how we'll educate these two as it is," said Jane. "It would be nice to have another in a year or two, when Bill goes off to school. I shall be lost without them. Peter will be going to his prep. school before long. Boys are with you such a little time. You do have a daughter for longer." Her eyes were sad for a moment. Then she shrugged. "Still, we might have had another boy and I don't think I could cope with four men," she said. "What about you, Jim? How's life? Have you killed off any patients lately?"

"Only a handful," said Jim. "We have been very busy. I've tried to come and see you several times but always an emergency has prevented me."

"Well, I'm so glad you're here now," said Jane. "Oh, and I heard from Molly today. She's probably coming to stay in May, so you must meet her then."

Jim laughed. "I'd love to meet her,

Jane, but don't be too optimistic. I'm afraid I don't inspire romance."

"Neither does Molly, so perhaps you'll inspire it in each other," said Jane hopefully. But somehow the idea that had seemed originally so good was not now so attractive to her. How strange; what could be more delightful than for two of her oldest friends to marry?

"Jimmy, I've got something to show you, how lucky that you came today," she said then. "It's a painting. Will you come and see it? I know you'll give me an honest opinion without just being polite."

"Of course I'd love to see it, how splendid, Jane," said Jimmy. He followed her indoors and up to the spare bedroom; the furniture was shrouded in dust-sheets, and her easel stood in a corner.

"The light is very good in here, which is a bit of luck," she said, and rather shyly she took the covering off the portrait of Bill which stood on the easel. Mop of brown hair, mischievous blue eyes and dimples, it was Bill and it was Jane who looked out from the canvas.

"You see, I've got some spare time

already, while Peter's at school," she explained hesitantly. "But I'm so out of practice. I've had three goes at this. What do you think of it?"

"There aren't words to describe my reaction," said Jim. He looked at her with admiration. "As far as I can see, it's perfect."

"I haven't done many portraits. There's so much to learn about skin tones and expression," she said, pleased and encouraged by his sincere approval of her work.

"Well, you know I don't know anything about it from a technical angle," said Jim, "but to me it's the image of Bill, and a beautiful thing to look at."

"I'm quite pleased with it myself, considering how long it is since I did any painting," she admitted now with some slight complacence. "But there is a lot wrong with it technically. I wish I could have some lessons."

"You'll be able to later. Those years ahead you speak of, when the boys are away at school; there'll be lots of time then."

"Yes, there will. And I'm lucky really

to have something like this to occupy myself. Otherwise I'd have to take to good works or something dreary like that. The Welfare State doesn't inspire one with a reformative spirit for that sort of thing," she said, pulling a face at such a grim future.

"I find it hard to imagine you in a sacking suit making people sign the pledge, I must admit," said Jim with a grin.

Jane laughed. "I should think not," she said. "But one would have to do something with one's life. One couldn't just sit about with folded hands." The thought of the hours of leisure she would one day have in which to paint as much as she liked was part compensation for the hours of loneliness she foresaw. She began to understand why so many middle-aged women with plenty of money whiled the time away in beauty parlours, bolstering their egos whilst they occupied the hours. She had often envied married couples on the stage, able to share their working life as well as their leisure. Perhaps if Michael worked from home, like a farmer, or a clergyman, or even a doctor like Jim, she would feel closer to him. You could be interested in cows or people; it was hard to stay enthusiastic about washing machines. She sighed.

Jim looked at her sharply. "Why don't you show this to Michael?" he suggested.

"I might. I wonder if he'd think it any good." Jane squinted at the painting with her head on one side, trying to be detached about it and see it from Michael's angle.

"I don't see how he can fail to like it. He'll be very proud of you," said Jim firmly. "In any case, if you really are going to take it up seriously you'll have to tell him. It's a mistake to have those sort of secrets, and if you spend much time at it he's sure to find a paint brush in his soup or something and discover that way." He was smiling at her, but his eyes were grave. Jane had got herself into an awful muddle with her marriage, it was clear. Michael had made her afraid of him; Jim thought he was incapable of warmth and sincerity, but if Jane loved him he must have some good points, hidden though they were.

Jane said lightly, "I'll probably put

214

crimson lake in the anchovy sauce. But I expect you're right, Jimmy. After all, it's nothing to be ashamed of, only I'm afraid of him disapproving."

Jim crossed his fingers. "He'll be thrilled about it," he declared.

Jane was not so sure.

"Well, I hope you're right. Anyhow I'll show it to him," she said. She smiled at Jimmy, and thought how easy it was to explain things to him. He understood at once without a lot of detail, and he made her feel brave. They did not often meet, but when they did she felt as if they had only just parted the day before. In spite of the gap of years that had interrupted their friendship, Jimmy seemed to know just what she was like, quite capable of serving paint instead of sauce, but not to be despised because of that. Now he had made her confident that her painting was good enough to stand up to Michael's criticism.

That evening she propped the canvas against the back of the sofa where he could not fail to see it when he came in, while she put the boys to bed. Deliberately nonchalant, she at last entered the drawing-room herself, but under her calmness she was in a tumult. She discovered that she still minded his opinion after all, and as she could not remember a single occasion when he had given her unqualified praise over anything, it seemed hardly probable that he would begin now.

He was reading the evening paper, holding it at arm's length for he still would not wear spectacles, and frowning. Jane marvelled that he did not get violent headaches.

"Had a good day, Michael?" she asked brightly.

"Oh, the usual grind. Old Norton was on his hobby horse about that new plastic casing." Michael launched into a long description of his tribulations. She tried to listen intelligently and make the appropriate comments. At last it seemed that they had temporarily exhausted the subject, and Jane picked up the canvas.

"Did you see this? What do you think of it?" she said.

Michael had of course seen the portrait as soon as he had entered the room. He had thought it excellent, and had even held it against the wall to see how it would look hanging there, but he was completely astounded by what he felt was Jane's slyness in having it done. It never occurred to him that she could have painted it herself. He had not made up his mind what line to take.

"I noticed it when I came in. Whatever are you thinking of, Jane, wasting money like that?" He lowered his paper and glared at her, brown eyes prominent like pebbles.

"Wasting money?" Jane looked puzzled. "But it didn't cost anything, Michael. I used an old canvas, and I had all the paints. What do you mean?"

Michael regrouped his forces fast. Jane had mentioned that she liked painting; the drawings she did to amuse the children were certainly superior to anything he could attempt himself, but he had supposed this to be a professional piece of work.

"Did you do it? I thought you must have had it done by one of those people who paint from photographs," he said, and added, "It's like him."

Jane knew that he must feel more than

this. If he had assumed the painting to have been done by a professional artist it must at least qualify as 'efficient.' Surely it would have cost him nothing to have been more generous with his praise? She thought of Jimmy's undisguised admiration for her skill, and suddenly she became very angry.

"I'm glad you approve," she said quietly. "I shall do one of Peter in the holidays. I told you I used to paint. I did that, and that, and that." She pointed round the room, where familiar land and seascapes had hung in anonymity for nearly three years. "Now that I have more time I'm taking it up again."

"By all means, Jane, if it amuses you," he said indulgently. "Only don't let me find blobs of paint all over the house. Remember you have a home to keep up. A hobby is all very well as long as it remains as such." He picked up his paper and turned to the financial page. He was a little shaken to discover what a great gift Jane clearly had, and that she had concealed it from him for so long; but it would be foolish to give her too much encouragement, she might get conceited and allow the painting to absorb too much of her time. His policy was always against lavish praise, it only provoked laziness and lack of effort.

Rage filled Jane. She went out, ostensibly to dish up supper, but really because she could not trust herself to keep her temper. Pompous, blown-up ass, she thought furiously. Little tin god in your ivory tower. Angry tears smarted in her eyes, but she would not let them fall. She had vowed to weep no more for Michael. I'll show him, she promised. Hobby, indeed! She stirred the sauce with vicious strokes. She remembered her joke with Jimmy this morning about paint in the sauce and a brush in the soup, and how he had laughed at the thought of such a delicacy. Michael only thought of the time spent on something that excluded him as time frittered away that might have been spent doing something for his ultimate gain.

She would not allow herself to make comparisons, but all the same she could not help contrasting Jimmy's kindness with Michael's humourless frigidity. It was true that Michael had been through dreadful experiences in the war, enough to render cold the warmest heart, whereas though Jim had been an Army surgeon, the scenes he had witnessed were the sort of things with which a doctor was expected to deal in his ordinary life, so that he had not been put to the same test as Michael. Thus loyalty still made Jane attempt to defend Michael to herself, despite her anger.

But even as she did it, the thought was born: how easy it would be to grow to love Jim.

3

THE weeks passed, and in May Molly Green arrived to stay. She had not changed, she never did, except to grow a little plumper. She tolerated Michael, as he did her; each pretended on the surface to like the other, but Jane was always a little apprehensive about these visits, for she knew that Michael thought her friend excessively dull, and she was not so insensitive that she could not guess at Molly's feelings.

Now, Molly was thrilled to find that Jane had begun to paint again, and swift in praise of what had already been done. Peter's portrait was finished; it was not as pleasing as Bill's, but the likeness was good. Jane had done a number of other paintings and sketches, and her brush was growing daily more confident.

Molly already knew from Jane's letters that Jim had arrived in the district, and now she was told she would soon meet him at dinner.

"It's dreadful, he's been here over six months and we haven't had him to a meal yet," said Jane. "The time just seems to fly past and you can't fit things in, yet I often wonder where it all goes. You'll like Jim, Molly, he's great fun."

Inadequate words! Jane had tried not to think too much about Jim, for she realised that it was only since she had met him again that she had begun to understand all that was lacking in her marriage, and it was uncomfortable to think like that. She could be free of her slavish devotion to Michael, yet still be fond of him and happy in her life, but when she was with Jim she was increasingly aware of the kindness, and the understanding, and the friendship that was missing.

Molly said, "It's no good trying to deceive me, Jane, I know what you're up to," and began to laugh.

Jane joined in. "Well, you're quite right, but why not? He's a dear, and so are you. You'll probably click at once and then we'll be neighbours. It would be great fun. Much better than both of you wasting your sweetness on the desert air."

Molly said, "I'm not sure I'm not better off single. After all, if you're a working girl you can always hand in your notice. It isn't so easy if you're married." She spoke lightly, but she meant what she said. Though she was sometimes lonely, she was not convinced that the married state was so entirely enviable.

"Jim would be a wonderful husband, Molly," said Jane firmly. "Just wait and see if you don't agree."

Michael was not too pleased at the thought of the dinner party. He was not too pleased about having Molly to stay for a week either. Jane always become rather foolish and giggly during her visits, and Molly bored him extremely, but perhaps the endless gossip of the two girls would be stilled for an evening if Fraser came to dine. He opened a bottle of wine without too much reluctance, and mentally squared his shoulders to cope with a dull time.

Molly wore a green dress, and Jane sighed, for the colour was all wrong for her sallow complexion. Say what you liked, first impressions were important, though they would not deceive someone like Jim. Jane wore black, for it was to be Molly's evening, and whilst holding no high opinion of her own looks, Jane was aware that she could detract from Molly. She did not realise how pale and clear her skin showed against the fine black wool of her dress, so that Jim could hardly take his eyes away from her. God, how can you be so blind, he thought, when he saw that Michael barely glanced at her all the evening. He was sure that if he had been in Michael's place, even after eight years of marriage, he would still find her lovely.

But he was not here to think like that. He tried very hard to make the most of Molly.

Jane's dinner table held some pinks, an early rose and some columbines arranged in a bowl.

"It's very hard to find anything in the garden just now," she said, "we're all between seasons."

"They smell lovely," said Jimmy.

"Don't they look nice? Molly arranged them," said Jane, coming round the table with his plate. Jim looked at her and his lip twitched. Jane made a face at him

224

over Molly's head.

It seemed that Molly had done a good deal of the cooking, too, as Jane praised her hollandaise sauce and cold soufflé. Jim was not to be allowed to miss her virtues. But he had not yet heard how Michael had reacted to Jane's artistic revelations, and he wanted to know how her painting was progressing. He turned to Michael and said, "You must be very proud of Jane, aren't you? It must be grand to have an artist in the family."

Michael said. "Oh, yes," and Jane interrupted quickly:

"Michael isn't really interested in painting."

Jim glanced sharply at his host. Michael was busy packing salmon and frozen peas into a neat little parcel on his fork.

"I have too many things to think about," he said.

Jim felt like hitting him. By chance he caught Molly's eye across the table, and knew instantly that she felt the same. In that moment a bond was stretched between them, and Jim became reckless.

"Jane was always going to be a great painter, from the time that she was a little girl," he said. "She'll be famous yet."

"Of course you will, Jane," said Molly eagerly. "Do you remember when you won that competition, just before the war? How thrilled poor old Dabs was — what did you do with the picture?"

"Mother's got it, hanging in the hall," said Jane. She looked rather uncomfortable, but Molly and Jim were away now, both determined to draw Michael, though Jim dared not look too closely at Jane in case he saw that she wanted him to stop.

"She used to do the most wonderful sea scenes when we were at Rhosarddur as children," he told Molly enthusiastically. "The ones in the drawing-room, and several others, not to mention cartoons." He patted his breast pocket where his wallet was. "Do you remember, Jane, the one you gave me? I still have it."

Jane blushed.

Molly said, "She used to do them at school and have us all in stitches — usually in a lesson with some frightfully prim mistress."

Michael ate his dinner in silence. It was novel to have Jane the centre of attraction; the idea of her being a riot of fun at school was also new. He could not understand any of it, so he was not interested.

"Has she painted you, yet, Michael?" Molly asked now.

"What? Oh, no, I haven't got time," said Michael abruptly.

"Nonsense, Michael." Molly was bold. "There's all the weekend. Jane, you must begin on Saturday. I'll cook lunch."

"No. I don't think — " Jane began.

"How will you pose him?" Molly asked, sweeping on. "What a pity we don't live two hundred years ago, Michael, you'd look so well in costume."

Jane looked aghast at her friend. She was always wishing Molly would be more lively in company, but she hadn't meant this sort of liveliness. She began to wonder what Michael had put in the cocktail.

"A brocade coat, and breeches, very becoming to a tall man," Molly continued blithely, "or perhaps Elizabethan dress would be better. What do you think, Michael? Doublet and hose?"

Her host looked at her in some doubt.

He was uncertain if she was serious. "Jane shall paint me one day, when I've time," he promised. "I'll wear my naval uniform." He looked complacent. Over the table Jane regarded him for a moment. What could she paint if she tried to do it? Even, regular features; dark skin; lean jaw; hard, expressionless brown eyes; where was the life and animation behind the face? Was there a person there at all, or simply a driving, material ambition? She looked away, and at Jimmy. His round face could by no stretch of imagination be called handsome, but she thought it was one of the nicest faces to look at that she knew. His nose was short and snub; but his mouth curved up so quickly into a generous smile, it was never a thin, hard line. Under his straight, dark brows his eyes were full of compassion and understanding, humour and intelligence. He was eminently paintable; the person behind Jim's face was very real.

After dinner they went into the drawing-room, and Jim showed Molly the sketch that Jane had drawn of him on the Bay Rock so long ago. It was creased now with age, but the pencil lines were still strong and telling, Jim with his pipe and his untidy lock of hair. How clearly the scene came back to Jane as she looked at it again. She remembered how comfortably they had talked together. She looked at Jimmy and said slowly, "Jimmy, light your pipe. Molly doesn't mind, do you, Molly?"

Molly shook her head. She glanced from Jane to Jimmy. He was putting the sketch back into his wallet, folding it very carefully, after politely showing it to Michael, who merely nodded and said, "Very amusing." He put his wallet back into his pocket and looked at Jane. He remembered every minute they had spent together at Rhosarddur; he remembered how, after she had given him the sketch, she had complained about being plain, and how he had reassured her, and how he had suddenly longed to kiss her. For a moment he saw her again, not, as she seemed to him now, an enchanting, mature young woman, but an eager, innocent child in grey shorts and a blue aertex shirt. A whole life could be altered by a single action. What would have happened if he had yielded to impulse on that occasion? Would it have helped to arm her against the Michaels of the world? She met his gaze now, eyes deep blue in her face which had a little colour tonight; she smiled at him, and Jimmy knew that he still wanted to kiss her.

He lit his pipe.

★ ★ ★

Jane did not embark on Michael's portrait that weekend. Molly suggested it again on Saturday, but when Jane made faces at her to desist, and Michael excuses, she gave it up. However, she thought it a singular pity he should not be capable of appreciating Jane's skill.

The summer passed, short and fickle. August at the sea was even colder than other Augusts; it was often wet and windy, with the sea too rough for the children to bathe. Michael played golf every day, while Jane wrapped herself and the children in thick jerseys for chill digging sessions on the beach or brisk walks along the cliff. Everyone was

230

very hungry, and she cooked enormous lunches each day, and firmly felt the ozone did them all good.

Between gales, Peter learned to swim, which was a big thrill and entirely due to Jane's patience in standing waist deep in icy water supporting him during all the previous years. Michael was persuaded to leave his golf briefly to watch while his son puffed and splashed triumphantly for about twelve yards. Then he returned to the clubhouse.

In past years, Jane had bitterly resented all this golf. Her idea of a holiday had been that they should all be together, and happy so, but Michael was reluctant to make sand castles, and did not enjoy swimming, so slowly the golf had won. This year, for the first time, she welcomed it. It removed him for the greater part of the day, and she found it easier to be cheerful and seem pleased to see him when she had not spent all day in his company, but she felt very sad to know this.

One evening they went out to dinner at a hotel, for Jane's mother had come to spend a few days with them, and she insisted that they should go out while she stayed with the children.

"Go along, my dears," she said. "I think it's so hard on you young people nowadays never to go out together. Well, tonight you can. I shall be quite happy."

So they went. Jane took trouble with her dressing; she wore a blue and white print dress that was new this year, and she put plenty of lipstick and powder on her face. They had a huge and splendid dinner; melon and sole, chicken, ice cream and devils on horseback, but through all the meal they scarcely talked, for there was so little to say. They discussed the appearance, odd or otherwise, of some of the people dining, and beyond that they had no ideas. Jane could have talked freely about the children, but Michael only replied in monosyllables, and she knew he was bored by tales of their wit. He talked for a while about golf, and that was all.

How perfectly awful, thought Jane in horror. Here we are, tied to one another for life, out alone together for the first time for months and with nothing to say to each other, both of us utterly bored. She thought of the times during the war before they were married that they had dined together, and began to realise how little conversation they had shared. Michael had talked, oh yes, and she had replied, but he could have been speaking in Arabic for all she cared. It had been enough just to be with him then. She could hardly swallow her ice cream when she thought of the future. How would they ever find mental sympathy now? It wasn't just that she was absorbed by her children, as she had sometimes thought when she found her ideas diametrically opposed to Michael's. It was simply that they had never had that harmony of mind she had deluded herself into thinking they shared.

The next evening her mother made them go to the cinema, and Jane glued her eyes to the adventures of technicolour pirates and allowed no other thoughts to enter her head.

The following morning her mother came down to the beach; she was leaving after lunch, and already thinking with pleasure of seeing her husband again, assured of his joy at her return. She was not so confident of Jane's happiness. The thought came to her that though she herself had been widowed for the greater part of her adult life, she had known more married contentment than her daughter could expect in a lifetime. She and Jane's father had adored one another and the child they had created; though they were not alike in temperament, they had been perfect foils for one another. Now her second husband, quite different in himself from the first, cared for her with tenderness, made her laugh and was her greatest friend. But it did not seem as though there was much friendliness between Jane and Michael. They had spent the few days of her visit talking busily to her, but seldom to each other, and neither had appeared very animated after their evenings out. Mrs. Forrest was fond of her son-in-law in a mild way, but he was the sort of tall, polished young man who tended to intimidate her. She saw clearly that he was bored by domesticity, while Jane, for all her artistic nature, was a somewhat anxious and over-devoted mother. Perhaps if Michael had more interest in the children, Jane would have less, and they would have met one another half-way. As it was, the boys would soon be off to their prep. school. Michael might then be able to bring himself to think more of his wife, and Jane, without the boys, would be forced to seek his companionship. Mrs. Forrest sighed. Michael had a sound job with excellent prospects, but she would have felt happier about Jane if he was a starving writer provided he had a sense of humour.

She and Jane crouched in the lee of a hut out of the wind, with coats over their knees, while the little boys began vast irrigational activities with some other children. Jane had enjoyed having her mother to stay, but she was frightened in case Mrs. Forrest, who was by no means dull, observed the apathy into which she and Michael had sunk, so in a way it was a relief that the visit was ending.

"Brr, it is cold," she said. "It surely was never as cold as this at Rhosarddur, was it, Mummy?"

Mrs. Forrest laughed. "Often colder, darling, and very wet. I don't suppose

235

children notice that like we do."

"Funny. I can remember bad days, of course. Being made to go for dreary walks round the shore in sou'westers and gum boots, but I remember so many glorious days, too," said Jane.

"Our memories are kind to us," said her mother. "They store up, the better things and veil the ones that aren't so happy."

"Perhaps." Jane sighed. "All the same, it would be lovely to go back there, especially now the boys are getting bigger. Peter would enjoy the rocks, instead of all this bleak sand." She waved a hand at the grey, windswept scene around them.

"I expect it's pretty dismal at Rhosarddur today," said her mother practically.

"I'm sure it is," Jane laughed. "But it's altogether different."

"Wouldn't Michael like to go there?" said Mrs. Forrest. "Maybe he'd like a change next year?"

"Well, it's a bit tricky," said Jane. "His mother takes this house every year, and I suppose it would seem ungrateful to say we'd rather go somewhere else. Anyway Michael loves it here, and he has lots of buddies at the Golf Club. He doesn't like the sound of Rhosarddur. Too rocky." She sighed. Then, with more animation, she said, "Wasn't it funny Jim Fraser turning up again? I told you he's our doctor now, didn't I?"

"Yes. What an extraordinary thing." Mrs. Forrest remembered that Jane had told her this news in a letter during the winter when the boys had 'flu.

Jane said, "I'm busy match-making between him and Molly. Wouldn't it be fun? And Bill could be a page."

"He isn't married, then?"

"Not yet. He came to dinner when Molly was staying in May. They seemed to get on very well."

"I always liked Molly," said Mrs. Forrest. "It's a pity she hasn't married. Well, perhaps she will now."

"I hope so," said Jane, "but actually I think she's quite happy as she is. I sometimes think all this pity for spinsters is overdone. They often have much happier lives than lots of married women, even if they haven't any children."

"They're lonely, though, surely?" suggested her mother.

"They usually have lots of friends," said Jane. She did not add that married people were often lonelier. At that moment Bill poured a bucket of water over Peter and she had to separate their fighting forms.

4

SEPTEMBER and October were flighty months, sandwiching their sunbursts between storms and fog. November came, and with it jolly Maud Fellowes' annual invitation to a bonfire party at half-past five on Guy Fawkes' night. Every year they made an enormous bonfire in one of their fields, and asked all the families in the district to share it. Everyone brought a contribution of fireworks, and the fathers collaborated to set them off. Michael surprisingly was willing to attend this function, for it gave him an opportunity to be efficient, which he always enjoyed. There was usually a fine display since so many people were involved and pooled all their resources.

The morning was grey and a fine drizzle fell. Peter was gloomy going to school.

"I'm sure it will rain tonight," he said, with a long face.

"Well, darling, if it does I expect we'll

put it off till tomorrow," said Jane. "Now come along, we must hurry or you'll be late."

She bustled him into the car, complete with large satchel filled with more Dinky cars than schoolbooks. Bill, in his duffle coat, sat beside her, and they set off to fetch the other children, for it was Jane's turn to be the school bus today. The two Fellowes children were full of excitement, bragging about the height of the bonfire and the excellence of the guy their mother had made.

"The bonfire is a hundred feet high," declared small Jackie.

"And the guy is eight yards tall," boasted his sister.

"Don't be silly, it couldn't be," said Peter in a superior voice. "Your Mummy couldn't carry such a big one, could she, Mum?"

Jane preferred hearing rather than taking part in the children's arguments, but thus appealed to she had to answer.

"I expect Judy meant eight feet high, not yards," she said mildly. Peter was getting very dogmatic: he often thoroughly squashed the younger children with some crushing remark, and the annoying part was he was usually right. He's very like Michael, she thought.

"We've got lots of whizz-bangs, jumping jacks, and smashing catherine wheels," said Jackie. "And we're having supper afterwards, Mummy says, soup and sausage rolls, and drinks for the grown-ups."

"How simply smashing," said Peter. Jane hid a smile; this was the latest superlative. School slang now included daring expletives like "Golly" and "Gosh," uttered with bated breath and heard by the younger children with awe.

They picked up the three middle Hunts, who went to school with them. By now the car was very full, and as the last miles were covered thoughts of arithmetic began to take the place of explosives. Jane delivered the scholars, and then she and Bill went on into town to do some shopping. Jane liked Wolverstoke at this early hour. As you arrived it was busy with cycling shop assistants, and schoolchildren hastening to be at their places by nine o'clock. There was no crowd, and you were served quickly without waste of time. There were minutes in hand for pleasantries with the fishmonger about the weather, and leisurely choice in the sweet shop. At home, Mrs. Barton would have arrived and be dealing with the chaos of breakfast; there were hours before thoughts of lunch must force one to the stove. She and Bill wandered round Woolworth's, yielding to its temptations to the extent of buying a new box of crayons each for him and Peter, and two new pencil sharpeners, for the lives of both these essentials seemed to grow ever shorter. They paused at W. H. Smith's counter to gaze at the new shiny magazines piled upon it, and Jane wondered if there really were women who lived as they advised, with all that creaming and massaging of the face, and worry about the waistline. All was to help in the pursuit of romance, whether illusory or not. Jane sighed, thought more prosaically of milk of magnesia and dragged Bill out again into the mizzling rain.

In the chemist's shop she marvelled at how quickly you could spend a pound, for she also needed soap and tooth brushes and a tin of band-aids. She must remember to make a note of what they had all cost as soon as she got home. Her accounts for last month were still in a state of fog, and Michael was sure to insist on seeing them this weekend. Thus thinking, she opened the door of the shop and pushed Bill out in front of her on to the pavement; then, extricating herself and her basket from the doorway she bumped into someone who was trying to enter the shop.

"Oh, I'm so sorry," she exclaimed, looking anxiously after Bill to make sure he had not run into the road.

"Why, Jane, you do look worried," said Jim, still holding her arm, for she had nearly sent them both flying.

"Jim!" Jane had not seen him since they returned from the seaside, and the unexpectedness of the meeting caught her by surprise. Her heart jumped and swift colour filled her face. "Why aren't you in your surgery?" she asked, saying the first matter-of-fact thing that came into her head.

"It's not my day today," said Jim.

"I've run out of hypo needles and I'm just going to see if Mr. Gregson has any. Well, Bill," to that young man, who had appeared now on his other side, "you look very well. Did you enjoy the sea?"

"Oh, yes," said Bill, "and Peter can swim. I'm going to next year."

"That's right," said Jimmy, "you do that." He smiled at Jane. "You're still brown. How did you do it, Janey, with no sun?"

"The wind would have tanned a rhinoceros," said Jane. "Did you go away, Jimmy?"

He shook his head.

"I had a long weekend in Scotland," he said.

"But that's no holiday. You should have a proper one," she scolded.

Jimmy laughed. "It was all I wanted," he said. "I'm thinking of going to Italy next summer."

"How lovely," said Jane.

"That's what you and Michael should do," said Jimmy. "Park the children with your mother and go off and see the lakes and the Leonardos."

"What a hope," said Jane. "We might

if we won the football pools, I don't see how otherwise. Besides, Michael says he saw enough of the world in the war, and he sometimes goes abroad on business." She thought a little sadly of what fun it would be to adventure abroad with Jim.

"We're going to a bonfire tonight," interrupted Bill. "Are you coming, Dr. Fraser?"

Jim said, "I am, Bill. Won't it be fun?"

"There'll be whizz-bangs," promised Bill.

"Good," said Jim, with proper appreciation of the importance of this.

"Are you really coming, Jim?" asked Jane in surprise.

"Yes. I had dinner with the Fellowes' the other night and they asked me. I'll be a bit late, I expect, as I've got to take evening surgery," said Jimmy. "I'll see you tonight then, Jane."

"Yes," said Jane happily. She took Bill's hand. "Goodbye, Jimmy."

Jimmy smiled. He said goodbye, and turned away, but he stood with his hand on the doorlatch of the shop watching till the two figures had vanished round the corner by the Cosy Neuk Café.

Jane and Bill sang songs at the tops of their voices as they drove home. Their repertoire ranged through 'Jack and Jill,' 'Good King Wenceslas,' 'Drink Puppy Drink,' and 'London's Burning.' Jane still sang when she got home, and Mrs. Barton thought how nice it was to work in such a happy house. At intervals Jane looked out of the window at the sky, and saw the clouds gradually breaking. It would be fine after all, and tonight she would see Jim. She looked ahead no further.

Bill was put to bed after lunch for a good rest, as he was going to stay up late. It was only the second time he had been to a firework party, and last year he had been, though by no means frightened, rather too young to enjoy it to the full. Whilst he slept in rosy abandonment Jane practised drawing hands, which she found difficult. Presently she began to draw faces, and after that the faces began to look like Jim.

At a quarter to four the blissful children were released from school. They surged out of the big blue door on to the pavement. Jane seized the ones she was to collect. They all looked so alike in their school clothes that she had nightmares of taking the wrong ones home. The journey was like travelling with a zoo, so noisy were the passengers, freed from the firm hand of their schoolmistress.

After tea, Peter and Bill put on thick jerseys and long corduroy trousers and their duffle coats. Jane put on her only tweed suit, her warm camel coat and her boots. She tied a scarf over her head as it was very windy, and made sure everyone had gloves. Then she piled the little boys into the car and they set off for the Fellowes'. Michael was to go straight there from the station if he caught an early enough train.

The field where the big bonfire stood was already sprinkled with children and their parents. Everyone stamped their feet and said, "Isn't it windy?" Jane saw in the light of her headlamps that Jim's green car was not here yet, so she did not look for him among the shadowy figures. Everyone seemed very pleased to see her; she no longer felt shy or reluctant to join them. A year ago it would have been an effort to her to have broken into the scene; now she had enough confidence in herself to know when she was welcome.

Soon most of the invited guests had arrived, and there was a good number of uninvited from the village, who annually gate-crashed the party, but were welcomed as long as they behaved. It ended as an uproariously democratic gathering.

Archie Fellowes, silent and grim as ever, lit the bonfire. It was well laced with paraffin, and in spite of the morning's rain it went up with a roar of flame. A gasp ran round the crowd, and turned into cries of delight. The guy, who wore a distinct resemblance to a certain politician, toppled in his chair on the top of the fire, and was engulfed in flames.

Now, at the other end of the field, Archie and his friends were busy letting off rockets, whizz-bangs and the rest. There was no sign of Michael, but Jane had forgotten about him and had not noticed his absence. She enjoyed the fireworks as much as any of the children, and she knew the other mothers did the same. The bonfire's light showed up all their happy faces, the laughing or awestruck children, and their elders released briefly from the demands of life. Superb, lavish catherine wheels of such excellence that only the rich Farquarsons could possibly have contributed them spun round in a spiral of brilliants. Rockets shot skywards with a whroosh, and exploded in a shower of coloured stars. The children had sparklers to hold, and ran about waving them gaily, scattering sparks, or more timorously stood and held them very still and watched their silver cascades.

Presently all the fireworks were gone, but the bonfire still burned on, red and glowing, and now someone from the village began to walk round the field playing a piano accordion. "I've got a luvverly bunch of coconuts," he sang loudly, a short fat red-faced man who often entertained the company in the Crown and Anchor, and everyone joined in. They linked hands and began to walk round the bonfire, all singing, with the musician inside their circle, Jane between Hesther Hunt and Bill, with Peter very grown-up further on beside Jackie Fellowes; and as they sang, and walked around the slowly fading bonfire, Jane's hand that held Hesther's was gently detached, and Jimmy joined the circle between them, smiling at Hesther, pressing Jane's fingers gently, and cheerfully singing 'Ten green bottles.' Someone threw another bundle of brushwood on to the fire, and it crackled up again. The flickering light revealed the laughing, sometimes sleepy, faces of the children, and the relaxed, unselfconscious faces of their elders. There was not a person present who was not at that moment completely happy. Maud Fellowes knew that as always her venture was its annual success; her husband was pleased to think that his hedge trimmings had been destroyed. Hesther Hunt forgot that her varicose veins ached and that the boys needed new walking shoes; her husband saw in the firelight's glow the relaxed lines of her face and remembered what a lovely girl she had been. Even elegant Betty Farquarson, well wrapped up in a sheepskin coat with her face protected from the wind by heavy layers of different creams, was enjoying tramping round, while her husband got pleasure from knowing that his expensive fireworks had lent the caviare touch to the display.

Jane did not think at all. She held Bill tightly with her left hand, and did not worry about Peter who was old enough to look after himself. Her fur-gloved right hand was firmly held by Jim. He smiled at her sometimes in the light of the fire, and she laughed with him as they sang, songs that were appropriate and songs of the utmost unsuitability, according to the whim and ability of their leader on his accordion.

"If you were the only girl in the world," sang Jim, and the surging of their circle cast her up against his shoulder like a boat swaying on its anchor. She leaned against him briefly; her scarf had fallen back and her hair, blown by the wind, tickled his nose.

"There would be such wonderful things to do," sang Jane blithely, and was borne away from him to arm's length again by the eddying movement of the patrol around the dying bonfire.

At last the fire was reduced to a pile

of glowing embers, and Maud summoned everyone to the house. Jim picked up Bill, whose small legs must now be tired, hoisted him to his shoulder and carried him over the bumpy field. Peter ran on with Jackie.

Bill urged Jim forward with clicking noises, pretending to be riding a horse, and soon they reached the house, where with sanguine disregard for muddy feet Maud was busy handing round cups of soup and plates of sausage rolls. Jimmy lowered Bill to the ground and went to help. Jane, drinking soup, watched him. He seemed to smile at everyone, and everyone was glad to see him. He's so *nice*, she thought, a little hazily, and sighed. Presently he was beside her again, and Maud was giving them both cocktails; then Jim was smiling at her, and Jane suddenly knew without any doubt at all that he loved her very much.

5

MICHAEL stood before the
bathroom mirror lathering his
lean face. Then he began to
use his razor, neatly, methodically, round
his jaw, across the lip, down the neck.
Slowly his smoothed skin reappeared, pale
and tight over the bones. He watched his
reflection with complacence, well pleased
with what he saw, unmindful of the fact
that he was pulling his face into ridiculous
grimaces to meet the blade. Today was his
thirty-fifth birthday, but he would defy
anyone to guess him as much. To reach
the centre of life's expected span was a
milestone, certainly, though not such a
one as must be faced at forty. However,
he was well pleased with his situation as it
was. He turned his head from side to side:
not a sign of grey, and by skilful brushing
over the crown the thin place was easy to
mask. He grinned unsmilingly at himself;
his teeth were white and perfect, barely
filled. He was seldom ill; the war had

been kind and left him no legacy of malaria or lameness. He rarely thought about it now; it was as though all his experiences had befallen another person, and so they had, for Michael was by now another person.

He got into the bath and stretched out in, the steaming water, looking down his long, lean body as he did every day for signs of extra flesh. He pinched his stomach anxiously, but all was well; no superfluous inch had been added overnight. He began to wash.

At breakfast the little boys were very excited because it was his birthday.

"You don't know what I'm giving you, do you, Daddy?" said Bill, hugging himself delightedly.

"That's my present," said Peter, pointing to something bulgy on top of the pile in front of his father's plate.

"Hurry up with your breakfast, Peter, you'll be late for school," said Michael, spearing bacon and egg with his fork; but because he felt benign he spoke more gently than usual.

"I expect Granny's present will come by the postman when you've gone,

Daddy," said Bill sadly.

"I'll open my parcels tonight," said Michael.

"But we'll be in bed," Peter protested.

"Well, whose birthday is it, yours or mine, I wonder?" said Michael, but without sarcasm. The boys smiled happily. Daddy's moments of *bonhomie* at breakfast time were rare.

"Hurry up, Daddy, you've time to open some before you go, anyway," said Peter.

Michael unwrapped socks and some strange pieces of wood nailed together from Peter, and handkerchiefs and surrealist drawings from Bill; then he left for the station. Jane tidied up the scattered wrapping paper after he had gone, and bundled Peter down the drive to wait for the school car. She had bought Michael what she thought was rather a gaudy waistcoat, but he had admired one like it that Victor Farquarson wore, so she thought it would please him. Nearly forty, nearly middle-aged, and what had happened to his youth?

At the station Michael walked up and down the platform waiting for the train. It was cold and draughty, as it always is on stations, they seem to catch every prevailing wind. He pictured to himself what he must look like, long and thin, very spruce in his navy blue overcoat, striding up and down, a rising young industrialist, someone who was destined to do well for himself. Yes, things were working out well. He had recently been promoted to the board; he was well paid now and would be still better rewarded soon. Of course, it was only what he deserved, for he worked hard enough, goodness knew; seldom an evening passed when he did not open his brief case at home. There was no doubt he would go far.

At home, things were nearly as satisfactory. Jane was improving fast now that the boys were out of the nursery. She seemed to have grown quite pretty, certainly she was better-looking than she had ever been as a girl. She had acquired poise of late, was seldom ruffled or dismayed, and at last seemed able to organise her day with efficiency. Even her accounts had balanced last month. Meals were punctual and good, and she seemed to have lost her tendency to weep at the slightest hitch. His chairman, Mr. Norton, and his wife, had come to dinner last week, and everything had passed off most successfully; there had been an excellent dinner, piping hot, and Jane had been chatty and attractive in crimson velvet. In fact, old Norton had, over the port, complimented him on his wife, though naturally he wouldn't have dreamed of repeating this to Jane, for it would only make her grow careless and self-satisfied. Really things had worked out very well. Marrying in the war had been a gamble; at that time he had looked only for the safety and affection that Jane offered; now, she had proved able to provide the well-run home he required, and was learning to entertain his business friends with efficiency. In a few years' time she would have developed more and be capable of undertaking the ambitious schemes he planned. She would learn to be a gracious hostess, and eventually be a big asset. Over Christmas a small rash of cocktail parties had broken out, and instead of staying by his side like a limpet as she had formerly done, Jane had been quite happy circling round without him. In fact they rarely met from the time they arrived until it was time to leave, and if he glanced at her it was to see her always talking away as if she had never been the shy mouse who had captured him by that very reticence. Yes, as always, he had acted wisely in marrying Jane. She was incapable of deceit; he could read her like a book and rely upon her utterly.

That painting was a funny business, though. There was no doubt that she was really good at that. How odd of her to have kept it dark so long, but of course it was not as though she had been painting away secretly in an attic all those years. He realised that her skill might well be capitalised. 'Mrs. Michael Rutherford, wife of the prominent industrialist, who is well known for her portraits,' — he imagined, years hence, in the glossy magazines.

The train whistled in the distance and came rapidly into the station. When it stopped, there was a first-class compartment facing him, as it was every morning. He opened the door, stepped over a pair of slender nylon-covered legs, took a seat in the corner and prepared to absorb himself in the difficulties of selling washing machines in Nicaragua. The owner of the slim legs looked at him for a moment. Then she said, "Do you think we might have the window closed? I've struggled with it, but it's much too stiff." Her voice was deep. She had long, blonde hair framing an oval face. She was smiling at him helplessly, revealing beautiful, even white teeth.

Michael rose and swiftly dealt with the window. Then he closed his brief-case and offered her a cigarette.

★ ★ ★

An air of relaxed relief descended upon Rose House after its two working men had departed. Bill went out into the garden and Jane made the beds and got out the Hoover. Downstairs, Mrs. Barton washed up to the strains of 'Housewives' Choice.'

Jane looked out of the window occasionally to see what Bill was doing; he seemed occupied with a major construction in the sandpit and was quite happy. He was always content to play on his own, absorbing himself in games with his toy cars if she was drawing, and tolerant of abstracted conversation. Jane was working hard whenever there was time with exercises she had imposed on herself to improve her painting. Since she could not have lessons, she was seizing upon her weakest points, finding out how other people overcame the same difficulties, and setting to work to do it herself. She had been to several exhibitions and she had borrowed books from the Public Library, and very few days passed when she did not spend at least two hours experimenting with colour and line.

This morning she was wondering if Peter would catch chickenpox, which was currently raging at school. If he did, it would mean visits from Jim. Deliberately Jane allowed herself this thought. After the bonfire party she had known, "Tonight I am really happy," and it was rare that such occasions registered themselves so consciously. She could look back and number the times when she remembered thinking "Now, this minute, I am happy." There was the day she had won the painting competition at school; the time she was engaged to Michael; her wedding-day; the day that Peter was born. On those occasions there had been awareness of her joy. But most happiness came when you weren't thinking about it, it was only later that you knew it had been there; those were the times like days spent as a child reading tales of adventure under the weeping willow; days spent painting; picnics with Peter and Bill; days spent sailing at Rhosarddur, days of sunshine, catching mackerel. Perhaps her longing to revisit Rhosarddur was simply because she had only happy memories of it.

Happiness was a negative thing in the main. If you were not unhappy, then you were happy. If you were busy all day long you were happy, for you had no time to be anything else. In fact, you were content, and then there came an isolated moment of such radiance that you were reminded of what it was possible to feel. Such a day had been November the Fifth. But Jane always enjoyed the firework parties, it wasn't just because Jim had been there, she told herself firmly. It was foolish to think that his presence had made it seem better than ever. There was nothing remarkable in the fact that he loved her; indeed, she loved him. She also loved Molly, her greatest friend, apart, she knew, from Jim. Because he was a man and she was a woman did not mean that as old friends they could not love each other in just the same way that they would love a friend of their own sex. So Jane attempted to dispose reasonably of her feelings, and felt quite reassured that if chickenpox struck there was nothing to make her feel guilty about being pleased to have an excuse to see Jim.

Chickenpox did strike. Three weeks after Peter began it, not only Bill but Michael too succumbed.

Jane, telephoning Jim to report the newest pimples, had to fight an attack of the giggles.

"Poor Michael, it is bad luck, but it does sound so funny," she explained, "I'm sure he feels wretched."

"He'll be worse yet," said Jim, chuckling

unsympathetically.

Jane said, "I can manage, Jim, don't come if you're busy. I'll ring up if either of them is bad. Bill seems very chirpy and he's only got a few spots so far."

"I'll come, though," said Jim. He knew very well that Michael would think him negligent if he did not call to confirm that the spots were genuine, even if he could offer no particular advice.

Michael had it badly. He burned all over and itched unbearably, and when he saw his face in the mirror he groaned. He could not shave properly between the spots and he looked awful. Jane felt very sorry for him, she had had it badly at school and had been old enough to remember now the intense irritation. She patiently dabbed him with calamine and cooked him tempting food. He was in bed for ten days, and walking about, pale and blotched, for another fortnight before he was pronounced by Jim fit to go back to work. To get chickenpox at his age: what a fun-provoking calamity.

Jim thought it funny, though he too was sorry for the victim; but he was sorrier for Jane who had to look after him. He would not have been human, disliking Michael as he did, if he had not enjoyed standing, for once towering, over him, reminding him not to scratch and to keep his bowels open.

Jane, coming into the bedroom with a spoon for Jim to peer down the invalid's throat, tried not to laugh at Michael who looked like a clown beneath his daubs of calamine, and thought once again how unfair it was to compare them, especially when poor Michael was hardly showing to advantage.

Jim tried to keep his mind on his bad-tempered patient, and did not glance at the vacant space in the big bed where Jane must spend her nights.

Michael was cured in time for Easter, but it took him weeks to live down the laughter at the office.

★ ★ ★

As the better weather began and it was possible for Bill to spend more time in the garden, Jane started work on a painting of Mrs. Barton, posed at her work, saucepan in hand, by the sink.

She had long wanted to do this, for the little woman had an interesting face with a gentle expression, and Jane had often caught her standing in the perfect position with the light from the window highlighting her hair and the pan she held. She had made some preliminary sketches, and from the start the picture went well; she had no difficulty in catching the likeness, and the discipline she had used in her practice during the winter now bore fruit. At the end, she achieved exactly the effect she had aimed at, and with Mrs. Barton's proudly blushing permission she submitted the picture to the Royal Academy.

She took it to London herself on the train, wrapped in brown paper. Then she walked blindly away from the back of Burlington House and into the Burlington Arcade. She stood glowering at chessmen in a window, trying to regain her composure. It would be sure to be turned down; how mad she had been to try. Even well-known artists had their work rejected. She accepted the certainty of failure and started rapidly off up the Arcade again with the intention of buying herself a hat for the school sports next term.

"Jane, if you run in the Burlington Arcade you'll be had up," said a voice behind her, and there was Jim, rather smart in a new grey suit.

Jane felt again the lovely, agonising catch in her heart that the sight of him always caused her now, and that once she had thought herself too old to feel.

"Jim, what are you doing here?" she exclaimed, halting in her rapid flight.

"I might say the same to you," Jim said, smiling at her. They were islanded amid the passers-by, Jane in her high heels as tall as he, both slightly dumbfounded by the unexpected miracle of their meeting. Then she clasped her hands urgently and said, "Oh Jim, I've done something awful!"

"How awful? Laddered your stocking, run away from home or bought a new hat?" asked Jim.

She laughed. "None of those, though as a matter of fact I'm just going to buy a hat. No, it's a picture, the one of Mrs. Barton. I've just taken it to the Academy!"

"Jane, how splendid! That isn't awful, it's a marvellous idea," said Jim with enthusiasm. "I thought it was shaping very well the last time I saw it."

"I nearly asked you to come and see it when it was finished, but I thought it might be a bore," said Jane.

"It wouldn't have been, but now I'll be able to see it when it's hanging on the line," said Jim with confidence.

Jane gave a happy little sigh. "Oh Jim, I am glad I met you, you do my ego good," she said artlessly. "You make me feel sure they'll accept it, even if no one wants to buy it, and even though I really know they won't."

"Well, if they don't they're a lot of asses," said Jim dismissingly. "Now what else are you up to besides an orgy of hats?"

"Nothing really. I was going to get a silly toy for the boys and some paint, and catch the four-thirty home."

"Is Michael meeting you for lunch?"

"No." Jane blushed. "He hasn't time to come up from the works," she excused. It was true that she had not given him much encouragement, pretending to have a lot of shopping and that she would have a quick meal at Lyons.

"Well, have lunch with me then," said Jimmy. "I've finished my shopping, which was of a sinister medical nature. I've got to go to a conference this afternoon at half-past two. If it's over in time I'll catch the four-thirty too and we can travel back together."

There was no discussion. It was all arranged.

Jimmy said, "Now, let's go and get your hat. Can I come too?"

"Won't you be frightened?" asked Jane, laughing.

"I'm a doctor, I've seen grimmer sights," said Jimmy. "Besides, it will be an experience." He grinned. "Now let us proceed more sedately through this illustrious Arcade."

"Do they really have you up for running in it?" asked Jane.

"Indeed they do," said Jimmy. "I believe there are all sorts of other rules about it too, but I know that one because my aunt was once warned, though not actually prosecuted."

"What a dreadful crime," said Jane, chuckling.

They walked up Bond Street together, looking in all the windows, and deciding what they would buy if they were millionaires.

In the hat shop Jim sat on the edge of a tall thin chair and watched while a pleasant salesgirl brought Jane dozens of hats to try. She turned down several that were made wholly of flowers, and that he thought charming, on the grounds that Michael would think them too young.

"But Jane, old dowager duchesses wear flowery hats," said Jim, protesting. "And anyway, you are, young. Now, try that one, go on, it looks just your very hat."

Obediently Jane popped the small white shape on her head and pretended she was wearing her best grey silk dress. It did look nice, but not nearly matronly enough for a parent who was so much afraid of her son's tall headmistress that she felt like putting herself in the corner.

Jim laughed when she explained this.

"If you buy that hat she'll think how lucky she is to have such a glamorous mamma among her parents," he said.

The salesgirl added her persuasion to Jim's. She was fascinated by this couple. Reluctantly, for she was a romantic at heart, she concluded that they were probably just brother and sister.

"Very well, then, I'll have it," said Jane boldly. "And I'll wear it now," she added. "It will be an excuse as you're giving me lunch, Jimmy," she added.

The salesgirl went off to fetch the receipt and arrange for Jane's old navy blue hat to be posted home. Jim watched while Jane combed her hair again before replacing the little cap. Looking at her reflection in the mirror he saw suddenly that her short brown hair was clearly streaked with grey above each little ear.

"What's the matter, Jimmy? Have I got a smut on my nose or is it just my grey hairs you've seen?" she asked with a smile.

"Your grey hairs," said Jimmy, recovering himself. "I'd never noticed them before."

"They seem to have come all at once," said Jane. "I'll be white before I'm forty."

"Then you'll be prettier than ever,"

said Jimmy. "I love white-haired ladies."

Jane met his eyes in the mirror. Though he spoke lightly, she knew he was sincere. Jim thought her pretty! A lovely wave of colour flooded her pale cheeks. She began to bustle about with her handbag till the blush ebbed, and turned away from the mirror.

"What nonsense you talk, Jimmy," she said, getting up, and beginning to laugh. The girl came back with her receipt and watched the two of them leave the shop, both laughing. She found that she was smiling too.

He took her to lunch at the Dorchester, because she looked so nice in her new hat, and when she protested that it would cost him the earth he said he was a rich bachelor gay with no one to spend his fat National Health pay upon, and must be allowed to have his fling. They had a delicious lunch, and Jane made Jimmy choose all the food because to see the prices on the menu made her feel faint. He ordered some wine in a grand way, and asked where she would have lunched if they had not met.

She told him.

"It's fun there," said Jimmy seriously. "One is dazzled by the choice and there's no time for reflection."

"Do you go there?" asked Jane in surprise.

"Of course I do, I know every Lyons and A.B.C. in town," said Jimmy.

Jane was silent. Michael would not call a cafeteria fun. If he could not afford the sort of meal they were having now he would prefer not to eat. It was true that he did a certain amount of entertaining in the course of his work, and was accustomed to the best, but clearly Jimmy was no stranger to it either.

They had such a lunch that Jane said she wouldn't be able to rise from the table.

"I'll be ringing you up tomorrow for bismuth medicine," she warned with a twinkle.

"Do you good to have something you haven't had to cook yourself," said Jimmy. "How long since you went out to a meal, Jane?" He was curious, for he knew little of Jane's life beyond the cares of house and children.

272

"Oh, not long," said Jane swiftly. "We sometimes have to dine with business friends, or have them to us. I'm getting quite good at producing effortless party meals."

Jim said, "I meant, not business, just you and Michael."

Jane said, "We haven't been out on our own since we were at the sea last August. Mummy came to stay then and made us go out."

She remembered again the dreary dullness of that evening. How utterly different was this meal today with Jim. They never had enough time to talk, there was always so much for them to say. She could not imagine that a day would ever come, however often they met, when they would be at a loss for conversation. You could say just whatever came into your head to Jimmy, and it never mattered if it was trivial or foolish. Being with Jim made her feel so safe; there was no need to be afraid of anything when he was there. Dear Jimmy, darling love! She smiled at him across the table. Then she remembered what they had been talking about. "But I hardly ever think about it," she added hastily, "Michael goes away sometimes so I have a rest from cooking then, I have boiled eggs for supper."

Jim said seriously, "All the same, it's good for you to go out on your own sometimes. You can get Mrs. Barton to sit in, can't you?"

"Oh yes, but Michael prefers home food," said Jane quickly.

"It's because you're such a good cook," said Jimmy with a smile.

Jane said, "I often think of hiring myself out for dinner parties by the evening. Table laid, dinner cooked, served and washed-up, a guinea a night."

"Too cheap," said Jimmy. "You'd be worth five guineas at least."

Jane said, "I'm sure there's a fortune to be made. When I'm having a grand dinner party — Michael's boss, for instance — I'd gladly pay well to be rid of the worry — and get Michael to put it down to his expenses too. I think I shall advertise."

"I'll come as butler," said Jimmy. "We'll need our dinner and a glass of sherry too, as well as the five guineas."

"For an extra pound I'd do the

flowers," Jane said.

"And thumbnail sketches of the guests, ten bob apiece," said Jimmy.

Jane began to laugh weakly as they talked. "We'd be so good we'd be well worth the money," she said.

"We'd be booked up weeks ahead," he agreed.

Jane dabbed her eyes. "Oh, Jimmy, I've got a pain from laughing so much," she said. "We must think about something solemn."

"All right. What shall it be?" said Jimmy. "The way your feet will ache after pounding the pavement today in unaccustomed high heels?"

Jane giggled again. "Jimmy, it's the wine, I believe I must be just the slightest bit drunk," she said.

Jimmy thought with great tenderness, yes, you are, but not with wine, you're drunk with being made a fuss of for a change.

"Have a walk in the park afterwards, and make your feet even worse," he advised aloud. "That'll sober you up."

Jane made a prim face. "Let's think about the selection committee at the

Academy looking at the pictures," she said. "That's sobering enough. 'Ha, what's this?' says the President. 'We don't want pictures of charladies in our exhibition, what next, I should like to know? Who has had the cheek to send this one in? It would be a good advertisement for Tide. An excellent likeness of the saucepan, I confess.'"

"'Sir, with respect I must join swords with you,'" Jim took her up at once. "'See the rosy glow in the charlady's cheeks, and the tendrils of her hair? Even dukes are thankful to have charladies nowadays; such a painting is in the best democratic tradition. I think we should hang it in the middle of the first gallery beside your portrait of the Queen.'" He grinned at Jane, and then went on, "'And now, what is this?' goes on the President, 'Who can have sent in this squashed banana and a bicycle, what is it called, "A Ship at Sunset"? Good gracious me, but it has been painted by Sir Willoughby Knickerbocker so I suppose we must hang it, but let us put it in a dark corner.'"

Jane smiled dreamily, watching him over the table. His clear grey eyes were twinkling at her while he made up more nonsense. "Oh, Jimmy, this is such fun," she said happily.

After lunch Jimmy had to hurry away to his conference.

"I'll look out for you on the four-thirty," Jane promised. "I can't wait for the next one as I promised Mrs. Barton I'd come on that."

"I'll catch it if I possibly can," said Jimmy.

"In case you don't, thanks awfully for the lunch," said Jane.

But he caught it. With two minutes to spare, he came walking quickly along the platform and saw Jane standing waving at him, small and slight in her best navy-blue coat, hatless now and with her hair blowing a little in the draught. Doors were slamming all along the platform; Jimmy got in to the train after her.

They spent the journey having tea.

"Though really after so much lunch it seems extremely greedy," Jane said. "I love train meals, though, don't you?"

"Yes, especially when the train jerks

and makes me spill my tea," said Jimmy with a grin.

Jane made a face at him across their little table.

"Eating on the train was always one of the best parts of the journey to Rhosarddur," she remembered. "Tiny individual pots of jam for tea."

"And sugar wrapped in packets of two lumps," said Jimmy.

"I remember during the war someone we knew who didn't take sugar used always to put his two lumps in his pocket and take them home. He must have collected several ounces a week — he went up every day. I used to think it very dishonest," said Jane.

"It's one of those fine points," said Jimmy. "He was entitled to put it in his tea, so it was his really."

"Yes, I know. I'm not so sure about the ethics of it now," said Jane. "But when you're young you seem to see everything in rigid shades of black or white, when really most things are grey." She was silent for a moment. "What a prig one is when one is young," she said at last. "One thinks one knows it all." She sighed a little, then said briskly, "Have some more tea, Jimmy," and began pouring out of the dribbly little pot.

The train arrived on time, and Jimmy in his green Austin drove down the hill away from the station behind Jane's shabby Ford. Where their roads diverged they blew a farewell on their horns and went their different ways. Jimmy wished he could follow her to make sure she arrived safely. He drove on rather unhappily.

In the evening he dined with his senior partner to discuss the conference which he had attended that day, but he found it hard to attend to what he was saying. He kept seeing Jane in her flowery cap smiling at him over the luncheon table and hearing her say, "Oh Jimmy, this is such fun."

He did not go to bed at once when he got back to his rooms. After he had put the car away he went for a walk. He walked for three hours, till his body was exhausted. It was such a sordid situation. Now he knew why people did murder for love. The obvious course was to resign his position here, move away, and never see Jane again, but that would let down Dr. Brown who had been so kind, and it would mean giving Jane a reason. If Michael was a nicer chap it would seem even uglier; as Jimmy could find no good word to say about him or the way he cherished his wife he left him out of his thoughts. Jimmy privately thought of Michael as a whited sepulchre: who but Michael, having the fantastic good fortune to be married to Jane, could let her come to London for the day and not seize the chance of taking her to lunch? No business that Michael was occupied with could be more pressing than that, thought Jim unreasonably. He deserves to lose her, he went on angrily to himself, and knew he would cast all scruples aside if it were not for the little boys, and do his best to steal her.

But Jane seemed content. She must be fond of Michael to put up with him. She had a delightful home and two lovely children. Michael earned a good deal more money than Jim did or ever would. Later on when she had not the solace of her sons she would have money enough to oil the machinery of life. Her painting would come to take a larger place, and Jimmy was confident that she would in time achieve recognition. She looked well now, not so thin and not jumping with nerves at the slightest sound as she had when he had first come here. If he stayed, he could at least see her sometimes, watch her health, encourage her painting, and perhaps even give her lunch again, for of one thing Jimmy was sure, that Michael would never be jealous for he was too conceited to think that she could ever look away from himself; and if he ever thought another man might want her the last person he would suspect would be Jimmy, for to men like Michael Don Juan never dwelt in a small and humble body.

Jimmy had no reason to suppose that Jane felt any more for him than simply the revival of her childhood affection. All other thoughts must be on his side; provided they stayed that way and were kept concealed, no harm could result.

He finished his walk resolved to remain; at least he would be near if Jane should ever need him, even if it was only to assuage an attack of mumps.

★ ★ ★

One day a letter came from the Royal Academy to say that Jane's picture, 'The Helping Hand,' had been accepted for the Summer Exhibition. Jane could hardly take it in at first. She read it several times, then dashed into the kitchen, waved it at Mrs. Barton who had just arrived, and whirled her round the room.

"Oh, Mrs. Barton, isn't it marvellous? I can't believe it," she exclaimed.

"There now, I always knew they'd take it," said Mrs. Barton complacently. "My, fancy my picture looking down at all them famous people! Well, I never!"

"You must come and see it hanging, Mrs. Barton," said Jane. "Oh, what a wonderful thing to happen! We'll have a jaunt to town and see it hanging in state," she said. "Oh, what an excitement!" She danced out of the kitchen. She must ring up her mother tonight, and write to Molly, but first of all she must ring up Jimmy.

He was thrilled by the news. He was in his consulting room pummelling the obese stomach of the local butcher when the telephone rang, but thought nothing of the interruption, for which Jane did apologise.

"How marvellous, I am glad, Jane, I told you so," he said with enthusiasm. "You wait, in a few years you'll feel quite blasé about such a thing!"

"Oh, never, Jimmy! Promise whatever happens you'll never let me get blasé. Hit me on the head or something," she begged.

He laughed. "Don't worry. I'll remind you of your young days when you panicked in the Burlington Arcade," he chuckled.

"I'd better ring off, you must be terribly busy, Jim, but I did want to catch you before you went out," she said.

"I've got to pass your house this morning," Jimmy said. "Can I come and drink a toast to Mrs. Barton in some of your coffee or are you dashing out at once to buy another hat?"

"Do come, Jimmy, how lovely. I'll be here all day. I feel too excited to get a thing done."

"See you later, then." Jimmy hung up and turned away from the telephone. He washed his hands, whistling under his breath, and returned to his waiting patient.

He found Jane and Mrs. Barton sitting in the garden on the terrace discussing their imminent fame.

"Hullo, Jimmy. We're too excited to do any work," said Jane, getting up.

"Congratulations, Jane," he said. "It's marvellous, but you know, Mrs. Barton, I always told Mrs. Rutherford they'd take it."

"I didn't see as how they could fail," agreed Mrs. Barton complacently. "I'm ever so thrilled about it, doctor. Just fancy all those gentlemen choosing my picture."

She went off to fetch the coffee, and Jim and Jane sat down again upon the terrace wall that was warm in the rare sun.

"Mrs. Barton seems to think as much credit is due to her beauty as your skill,

Janey," he remarked.

"So it is," said Jane promptly. "If she hadn't had such an interesting face I shouldn't have found so much in it to paint."

Jimmy said with an effort, "Isn't Michael delighted?"

"He doesn't know yet," she answered. "The letter didn't come till after he'd gone, and I rang you up at once."

"Haven't you rung Michael up?"

"No. He doesn't like being rung up at the office," she explained hastily. "It will keep till tonight. I'll be calmer then." She smiled at Jimmy. "I had to tell you at once though, Jim. I'd have burst if you'd been out." She did not seem to think her reasoning odd.

She showed him the letter and they both read it several times, while their coffee steamed forgotten beside them.

Jane said, "I cried a bit, from being so pleased, like when you've had a baby. Isn't it stupid?" Her eyes were very bright now, as if she might weep again.

He could not say anything for the longing to take her in his arms.

Jane looked at his hand which gripped

the terrace wall where they sat. It was square, scrubbed-looking, strong. She felt an uncontrollable impulse all of a sudden to put her own over it; so strong was the desire that it seemed impossible, as she quickly got to her feet, that she had not done it.

"Your coffee will be cold," she said shakily, handing him the cup. He looked at her as though nothing out of the ordinary had happened, so she presumed she had not after all touched him, but she dared not risk it again and held her own cup and saucer tightly with both hands to make sure.

When he had gone she took a hoe out into the garden and pretended to be weeding, but she could not settle. She kept stopping, thinking a bit about her picture, but more about Jimmy and how nearly she had touched him.

Michael, when he came home, showed emotion at last. He was delighted at her success, kissed her with warmth and promised to come with her to the Private View. Instead of being glad, Jane felt miserable, for she had arranged with herself that if he could not come Jimmy

286

should take his place.

It was fine enough to sit out for a while after dinner, and Jane, in a deckchair beside Michael on the terrace, was shocked at her own thoughts while her husband sat reading and smoking. It was Jimmy she wanted beside her now, not Michael. This was the sort of dreadful thing that she had been so swift to condemn when she had seen it happen in the war. Married people just did not fall in love with other people, even if they had grown bored with their partners. She had decided then, arrogantly, that it was a matter of will power. But it wasn't. It was a matter of suddenly meeting someone tuned in to your own wavelength.

If it hadn't been for the war we'd have gone on meeting at Rhosarddur, she thought sadly, and then in the fullness of time we might have married. She remembered how sincerely on her wedding day she had vowed to love Michael, and how there had been nothing that was too much effort for her to do for him. So you felt when you were young, gallantly throwing the years ahead into a blindly ignorant gamble. Perhaps if she had married Jim she would feel as stale in his company as she did with Michael; you did grow used to someone when you lived with them for so long and excitement had left your relationship. But she knew that if she had been free she would have risked it all again for Jim. She could not believe that they would ever fail to complement each other, and Jim made her feel she mattered.

She took a grip on herself. It was wrong and dreadful to think like this. She must put the whole thing out of her mind. Jim was simply an old and valued friend, just like Molly, and loved in the same way; the love which she knew Jimmy felt for her was just the same sort of deep affection. The flutter in her heart whenever they met was simply her imagination over-working as usual. The best thing that could happen would be for Jimmy to find himself a nice little wife, or marry Molly, and settle down to his own happiness.

★ ★ ★

Varnishing Day came and went; so did the Private View. Jane's picture hung upon the line in a favoured position; the critics praised it gently; famous artists praised her when they met. She wore her flowery hat to the Private View and looked very nice, "Not like an artist at all," said Michael approvingly. He strolled round the galleries, looking at a few of the paintings, spotting celebrities, and being scandalised by the bohemians. He was gratified beyond measure to be present, and as Jane was the instrument he was unusually affable to her. As they moved through the throng a tall, slim young woman with long ash-blonde hair came up to them, and greeted Michael with warmth. She glanced at Jane with some amusement when Michael introduced her.

"Who's Mrs. Belmont?" asked Jane, when she moved away on her very high heels.

"Oh, just a business friend," said Michael airily.

But Jane was not really curious. She did not notice that for a few moments Michael had lost his composure.

She did not enjoy the Private View nearly as much as the later outing with Mrs. Barton, which perforce included the two little boys. They were ecstatic at a train journey, and fascinated at seeing Mummy's painting hanging in what they felt must be a shop. It was on this visit that Jane saw fixed to her picture the red star that meant it had been sold. She felt a queer thrill; she could only discover that a dealer had bought it for a private buyer, and she was glad now that she had painted a smaller copy for Mrs. Barton to hang in her parlour. They had a tremendous tea to celebrate, and Jane bought presents for everybody out of the money she would get for her picture. She got a large handbag for Mrs. Barton, a model yacht for Peter and an electrically operated racing car for Bill. As an afterthought she bought Michael a silk tie.

It was not until two years later that she discovered it was Jimmy who had bought the painting and given her her first success.

6

MICHAEL that autumn was full of new ideas for campaigns to sell vacuum cleaners to miners' wives and electric mixers to duchesses. He was home later in the evenings and often went away on business trips. At weekends his golf was still his main occupation. Jane was content. Her days were busy, with plenty of time now to study her work and to practise. She found a technique for talking to Michael in the evening, listening with only half her mind while the rest of her thoughts were busy with plans for new paintings, or worry because Bill would not learn to count, or pride that Peter had inherited some of her artistic skill. She dreamed that he would become a famous architect and build immortal cathedrals. She tried not to think about Jim, but if, as often happened, he came unbidden into her mind, she told herself that she was as foolish as she had been as a girl, building impossible dreams in her head.

But when they met she knew it was not all dreams. Once she said, fearfully, "You won't ever go away from here, Jim, will you? You won't go somewhere busier, more squalid?"

He understood what she meant.

"I've a full job here, Janey," he said. "There's a lot of squalor in the town, you know. I'm as useful here as I'd be anywhere. I won't go away unless I'm sent."

She knew now by the catch in her heart how much it meant just to see Jim in his car driving to the hospital, to meet him at a cocktail party, even to be in the same part of England. She was like two people; one part a sedate, middle-class matron, the other as deeply in love as any young girl, in fact more so, for it was because she loved his gentle, humorous nature so much that Jane wanted all the rest of love as well.

Little do you know, she would think to herself, sitting on the opposite side of the fireplace from Michael in the evenings, busily knitting while he read business papers, little do you know that I am sitting here, longing to leave you and be with another man, only kept on the rails by duty and the boys. I, who was always so high-minded! Probably Jimmy is too good, even if he wanted to, to run off with me, and what about the medical council, but I would go with him if I wasn't afraid. I'm afraid of leaving my boys, I'm afraid of the wrath of God. What hypocrites we are! How much is fear, and not duty, responsible for our actions! Dear Jimmy, whom I've never even kissed. I'd be afraid even to do that. At least, she thought, I've danced with him, the one intimate contact that convention allows, but that was so long ago that it doesn't count. It had no meaning then.

She began to long to dance with him again. If that could only happen she would know whether or not he loved her too in the way that she loved him, as in her heart she was sure he did, without either of them stepping aside from the path of propriety.

Like an answer to prayer came an invitation from the Manor to a private ball before Christmas. Mrs. Wilkinshaw, who rarely entertained, every few years made up the arrears by a party of such excellence that everyone forgave the length of the intervals.

Michael was quite eager to accept the invitation. Mrs. Wilkinshaw moved in the county circles he aimed to reach one day and he might meet important people in her house. He had just got a new suit of tails, too, for in his position he did not think his old prewar ones adequate, and this would be his first chance to wear them. They had been made in Savile Row and the cut was exquisite.

Jane wished she could have had a new dress for tonight; just a fraction of what Michael's tails had cost would have paid for one. He had a new dinner jacket too, for he went to so many dinners that it was necessary. She sighed a little, but she realised that though her old midnight blue was well known in the district it was new to Jimmy.

That night she dressed for him. She was convinced he would be there though she had had no opportunity to find out for certain. She took infinite pains with her face and hair; she used some of the scent her mother-in-law had given her for her birthday, and she gave not a thought to Michael, now with many groans and contortions inserting himself into his stiff shirt and collar.

When she was ready she waited for Michael in the drawing-room, standing by the fireplace, very calm, a little pale. She looked much taller than usual in her high heels and the long, flaring dress. She wore her old beaver coat that looked quite smart in electric light, and her one beautiful ring sparkled on her thin little hand. She looked to Michael pale and remote.

Before, if they were going out in the evening, she would have hoped for comment on her looks, though he had never been known to say more than, "I like that dress," or more usually, "I don't care for that dress."

Now he looked at her in some surprise. So long unused to compliments, he could not find one. "That dress always suited you," he said at last.

But Jane barely heard.

The party was getting under way when they arrived. Michael dropped Jane at the door and went to park the car, and she left her coat in Mrs. Wilkinshaw's surprisingly pale pink satin bedroom.

The big ballroom was filling up. The band was playing a tango, and a dozen couples of varying degrees of skill circled the floor. Michael came into the room, and with an expression of resignation swept her out to join them. Round his shoulder she looked for Jim, but she could not see him. Her chin was opposite Michael's elbow, just as it had been on the night that they met, but she forgot that now.

Her next partner was Charlie Hunt, who had had several drinks and told her she looked stupendous. Jane saw Michael, who still looked as if he suffered acutely, as perhaps he did in his too tight collar, sailing majestically round with Hesther. As she and Charlie dizzily rotated, Jane kept one eye on the doorway, but even so she did not see Jim enter. When the dance ended and she left the floor with her partner, she saw him on the other side of the room, standing by the fireplace talking to his hostess who was splendid in crimson lace.

Jane relaxed; she accepted Charlie's

offer of a drink and began to pay attention to his talk.

It was an hour before she danced with Jimmy. She could hardly bear to watch him come towards her across the room. Amongst all that crowd of mutual friends they might have been alone. Afterwards she could not remember whether he murmured some formality or not, she could only remember that there they were, on the floor together, and it was as she had dreamed of it. Perfectly in step, as though they had danced with one another every night for a year, they went around the room with wings on their heels. Like innocent young lovers they wished the clock would stop. Jim could smell the perfume she had used, and the fragrance of her skin. Her hair was soft and silky by his face. Her body seemed so little in the circle of his arm.

They did not speak. She thought the pounding of her heart was louder than the band. His breath tickled her ear. If she turned her head half an inch she would kiss his cheek.

After a few minutes they felt calmer; Jane's heart slowed; she relaxed against his arm; he tightened it about her and they moved more surely. Jane had never danced like this with anyone, every step matching, every move spontaneous. Presently Jim began to talk.

"I thought I wasn't going to get a look in with you tonight, Mrs. Rutherford," he said.

Jane said demurely, "It is for you to ask me, you know."

"Every time I tried someone swept you off under my nose," he said.

"Well, here we are now," she said.

"Yes, here we are," said Jim. "Oh, Jane!" He held her away from him for a moment to look at her, then drew her close again. "Has anyone ever told you how lovely you are?" he said then, trying to keep his voice light.

"No," she said softly.

Jimmy said no more for a turn or two. He swept her round in a series of complicated steps which she followed perfectly. Finally he said gruffly, "Well, I wish I could only tell you properly just what I think about it," and then he whirled her round again so that she could not answer. After that he started to talk hard about trivialities, and then the music stopped.

They danced together twice more that night, once in an old-fashioned waltz when they spun round and round in a daze till both of them were dizzy, and the second time in the Gay Gordons, which was almost better, for though you had to let your partner go for a moment, there was still to come the instant when after you had spun giddily round on your own you could cast yourself again into his arms. Jane thought primly that it was not a dance to take part in with someone you did not know well.

"Quite a good party, but what an hour to go to bed," said Michael at four o'clock.

★ ★ ★

The months passed.

Christmas came and went. It seemed even more tiring than usual, and in the morning Jane was very sick. When another week had passed she realised that what she had thought just a false alarm again was this time true. She was pregnant.

At first she was filled with a terrible despair. She wept because to conceive a child now seemed in a way a betrayal of Jim; she wept because not to welcome it was a betrayal of all she had once felt for Michael; she wept from what she recognised as pure selfishness, because she must again be tied, though two years ago she would have rejoiced at the prospect of another child.

But when she had wept, and acknowledged all her fears, she accepted the inevitable and was able to be glad. Now she would have the daughter who would be with her when the boys went off to school; a daughter who would cling to home more than the boys ever could; a daughter to dress in pretty frocks and take to dancing class; a daughter whom Michael might learn to enjoy, and spoil a little, as he never could his sons.

She did not tell him at once; she was too much ashamed of her own reluctance, and wanted to be wholly glad before she faced the task of making him be pleased, and before she could break the news to him the little boys developed measles, which they must have contracted over Christmas at a party. For a week they were both very ill, lying limply in their darkened room. Jimmy came every day to see them, and Jane reckoned time from day to day. At last the children began to get better; they grew demanding and petulant, needing constant amusement, till finally they were up and palely leading convalescent lives. Jim prescribed strong tonics, and on his last visit said to Jane:

"You must take it easy now, Jane. You've had a rotten fortnight with those two, it couldn't have come at a worse time."

"You know about the baby, Jimmy!" she exclaimed. "But I haven't told anyone," she added naïvely.

Jimmy said lightly, "People get a certain look about the eyes; I can often spot it before they know themselves. It's about July, isn't it?"

"Yes," she nodded.

"Better let me take your blood pressure," said Jimmy. He got out his apparatus in a business-like way, tied it round her arm and pumped the mercury up the dial.

Jane sat meekly while he did it.

"Well, that's all right," he said.

Jane said, "I wasn't going to bother about it yet, I haven't even told Michael."

"He'll be glad," said Jim stoutly. "You are, aren't you, Jane?" He looked at her intently.

Jane said honestly, "It's come too late, Jimmy. I'd passed beyond wanting another. I was appalled at first, but I am glad now, very glad."

"Of course you are," said Jimmy. He patted her shoulder gently. He had faced this possibility in his imagination many times. "How do you feel? Much sickness?"

"No, not much. My back aches rather, but it's having the boys ill. I'll be all right now," she said with a smile.

Jimmy looked at her pale, large-eyed face.

"Well, rest all you can," he said. "We won't go into arrangements now, you'd rather wait till you've told Michael, there's plenty of time for all that; but you must have some iron, and I'll come again in a month to have a look at you."

"Yes, Jimmy," said Jane meekly.

Jimmy went away, and Jane returned to the nursery where the boys were sadly painting. If only the weather would clear up so that they could get out they would soon feel stronger. Jane picked up a drawing book and began to draw pictures of racing cars for them to colour.

A week later Michael came back from the office aching in every limb and with a sore throat. His head throbbed, his nose burned, and he was clearly in for 'flu.

Jim came the next morning.

"Sure it isn't measles?" he asked Jane, chuckling.

"He's had it," she said with a smile.

"Poor you, Janey. Everything comes at once," said Jimmy. "You must send those rascals back to school."

"They aren't well enough," she protested.

"It won't hurt them, even if they are a bit pale," said Jimmy hard-heartedly. "Put them to bed a bit earlier. You'll be the one who'll suffer if you don't."

"I'll see," said Jane, prevaricating.

Jim said, "Well, I'd better see the patient; we'll argue over coffee as usual."

He followed her up the stairs. Michael was lying, eyes shut, tucked under the blankets. He managed to look handsome even with 'flu, Jimmy thought irritably. Only chickenpox had made him lose his looks.

"Ha, you've come," he growled rudely. "How soon can you get me on my feet? I've work to do."

"Let's have a look at you first," said Jimmy, refusing to be hurried. He tapped Michael's chest and back, peered down his throat, took his pulse and temperature, all watched by a pair of baleful brown eyes from the invalid.

"Well, you've certainly got 'flu," Jimmy said at last. "You'll be lucky if you're up in a week. There's a particularly nasty sort about."

"Can't you give me something to put me right?" Michael demanded. To him his body was a machine; if it went wrong, which was seldom, he called in a doctor as he would a mechanic, for an instant repair.

Jim longed to say "Nothing short of a miracle could put you right." He controlled himself and said mildly, "I'll

304

give you some pills that will keep your temperature down, and something for your cough, but I'm afraid it must take its course."

Michael glared. "I've work to do," he said again.

"They'd have to manage without you if you were run over," said Jim. "You must look upon this the same way." He packed up his things slowly.

"I'll call in tomorrow," he said at the door.

Michael watched the door close behind him. Through his throbbing fever, he had gained a distinct impression that Jimmy did not like him. Such a thing was most fantastic, why, everyone liked and admired handsome Michael Rutherford! "Well, I don't like you either, you silly little man," he muttered childishly, and turned his face away from the door.

Jane and Jimmy drank their coffee in the nursery by the fire. The little boys were out in the garden in the thin winter sunlight playing on the swing, a lull before their next quarrel.

"It is 'flu, isn't it?" said Jane.

"Yes, and nasty 'flu," said Jimmy.

"You must keep out of that room, Jane. You don't want to catch it."

"The harm's done, I expect," said Jane with a smile. "I'm sleeping in the spare room now, I won't go in more than I must."

"Have you told him about the baby?"

"Not yet, and this hardly seems the moment," she said.

Jim said gently, "Won't every day you put it off make it harder?"

Jane had already discovered this.

"A few more won't make much difference," she said. "I'll wait till he's over the worst."

"Well, don't go running up and down stairs all day," said Jimmy. "Think of yourself for a change; and send those boys back to school tomorrow."

"You're sure it won't hurt them?"

"Jane, you trust me, don't you? Believe me, I'm as anxious for their welfare as you are, but you're my patient too now. Of course it won't hurt them. Half the school has had measles, and the rest are incubating it. Let them all convalesce together."

"All right, Jimmy. It will be a relief.

They seem to squabble all day and I don't want them to disturb Michael."

Michael be blowed, thought Jimmy. God, what jealousy can do to the mildest nature! Though by no means a lover of all men, Jimmy had never disliked anyone as much in his life as he disliked Michael, and now he was worried about Jane, who looked so very pale. Michael must be blind himself not to have noticed that something was the matter with her. How dreadful to be too much afraid of your husband to tell him you were pregnant.

Jimmy swallowed his coffee quickly and got up. "I must fly," he said. "Lots more people with 'flu to see." He hurried away before he gave voice to his thoughts.

Michael was a trying patient. He never wanted his bed made when Jane was ready to do it. He grumbled at steamed fish though he had no appetite for more. He wanted books from downstairs, the papers, tots of whisky, all at times when Jane had just come up with something else. Jane got Mrs. Barton to carry the coal up for his fire, but otherwise she did not let the little woman enter his room, for she knew that if Mrs. Barton got 'flu it would be even worse than if she did herself.

After two days back at school the boys seemed to pick up, and Jane realised that being occupied had done them good. She put them to bed early every night, and went to bed herself as soon as Michael had had his supper. She could not get enough sleep, and her back ached all day, but the sickness was passing, and was at worst only slight. She realised that Jimmy was right, and that if she did not soon tell Michael about the baby she would never find the words, and it would be clear to everyone else before he knew.

When he got up for the first time, and was sitting, pale and interesting to himself, by the fire, she told him.

Michael was even more dismayed than she had feared. He spent some time in wondering how such a thing could be possible. Then he said, "Well, you must get rid of it, Jane. You must move the furniture, or jump down the stairs. You must bring it on."

Jane took a deep breath. Losing her

temper would help no one.

"Michael, you don't know what you're saying," she said coldly. "I am glad about the baby. It will be lovely. Of course it will upset our lives, mine more than yours, but it will bring us so much happiness if you will only let it. It will be a girl this time, I'm sure. If the Hunts can afford six children we can afford three. Mrs. Barton will help me with it, so we won't be tied like we were with the boys. You'll love to have a pretty little daughter to show off."

Michael did not think so. He grumbled on, still wondering why it had happened.

Jane got up and left the room. She could not stay there, she was trembling all over. Though she was unsure about so much, unhappy and confused, one thing she knew beyond doubt, and that was that purposely to lose her child would make her guilty of a frightful crime. She turned her mind resolutely towards the new life, and vowed that when it was born she would more than make up to it for all the apathy of its conception.

But the next day she was shivery and her head ached; by evening she had a temperature. She had developed Michael's 'flu. She said there was no need to call the doctor, but after two night's sleep Michael, though still not reconciled to the prospect of being again a father, had a slight conscience about Jane; after all, she would have the trouble of the child. Bar paying for it, another more or less would make little difference to him, as long as Jane did not let it interfere with the smooth running of the rest of the household. He made her stay in bed, boiled the breakfast eggs himself, sent the boys to school and summoned Mrs. Barton early.

Jimmy came as soon as surgery was over. He had expected this. He told Jane some jokes to make her laugh and said, "I'm going to see Mrs. Barton to discuss how you can manage. I'll come and tell you afterwards."

Jane said, "Jimmy, it's all right. I'll be well in a day or two."

"Now look, Jane," he said gently. "I'm your doctor now, and you are staying in bed till I say you can get up. Michael will have to stay at home for a few more days, too. Mrs. Barton and he between

310

them will have to see to everything."

He went away, and soon returned. It was all arranged. Mrs. Barton would come in time to get breakfast, prepare lunch and return again every evening until further notice.

"I'll ring up Hesther and ask her to have the boys to tea on Sunday, then it won't be so much for Michael," said Jane.

Jimmy thought it would do Michael good to have to cook, clean the house, and look after the boys for two weeks, but it would perhaps not be very soothing for Jane.

"All right, you do that, Jane," he said. "Now, you won't worry about anything, will you? It's a pity you had to catch 'flu to have a rest, but it will do you a lot of good to be in bed just now. How's the back?"

"How did you know it still ached?" she asked ingenuously.

"Dr. Dick with his X-ray eyes knows everything," said Jim with a smile.

"It's not so bad, lying down," said Jane.

"Try putting a pillow under it. Have

311

you got a little one somewhere?" said Jim. He was still smiling at her, but a little anxiously, for she should be getting over the backache by this time.

"There's one in the nursery cupboard," said Jane. "I found it when I was going through the baby things the other day."

"I'll get it," said Jimmy. He went downstairs and searched in the cupboard, where he soon found the small pram pillow in a case covered with embroidered ducks. He brought it upstairs, plumped up Jane's other pillows and tucked it neatly under her spine.

"Thank you, Jimmy. That's better already," she said. He patted her hand, gently, matter-of-factly. "You always do me good," she added drowsily.

Jimmy said gruffly, "That's what I'm for. But now you look as if a good sleep would do you more good, so I'll go."

The 'flu took a lot of Jane's strength, and left its usual depression behind, but now she concentrated most of her thoughts on the child. She began to feel better; the weeks passed; she became happy enough. Michael grew resigned to the inevitable, but they did not discuss it much.

At the end of April Michael had to go to Liverpool for an exhibition in which his firm was to display its latest products. Far from feeling lonely, Jane was looking forward to what she could only describe to herself as a holiday. Standards all round could be lowered in his absence; if the weather was good she would take the boys for a picnic to hunt for primroses; she could get up a little later in the mornings, and go to bed as early as she liked each night. She could forget about him.

The day before he went she noticed that the stair carpet needed tacking down on the landing, and she asked him if he would do it for her.

"Surely that's a job you can do yourself, Jane, you know where the hammer is, but mind you put it back," said Michael, busy with thoughts of how his feet were going to ache after standing all the week, and wondering if he had enough clean collars.

"All right, Michael, I'll do it," she said. It was never worth arguing. At that moment she was on her way to fetch his clean shirts and pyjamas, and when his packing was done she forgot about the carpet.

On Monday he left, and Jane and Mrs. Barton spent the morning straightening the house after the weekend. In the afternoon she wrote to Molly and to her mother, to whom she owed letters, with the pleasant feeling that she could sit at her desk as long as she liked. When she put the boys to bed, and again later when she went to bed herself, she noticed the carpet, and thought, oh dear I must nail that down tomorrow.

On Tuesday Hesther telephoned and invited Peter and Bill to spend the day. Jane accepted gladly, and spent a lazy day herself. She did a little gentle gardening; then she had lunch on a tray and spent the afternoon sewing at the little smocks she was making for her daughter and listening to the wireless. She thought how nice it would be to escape from Michael into hospital; he would only visit her very briefly, she knew. She would have a good rest and read a lot of books.

She closed her eyes for a moment,

listening to the quietness of the house around her. The clock on the mantelpiece ticked softly; outside the nesting birds twittered and rustled; daffodils would soon be peeping. Rory the dog lay asleep in a patch of sun on the terrace, dreaming blissfully of rabbits. Jane let her sewing drop and went into a dream: she was married to Jim; his was the coming baby. At any minute he might come in from a case, wanting his tea, kissing her, laughing and tender. Perhaps things were worrying him, and he would tell her about them, but unlike the amps and voltages they would be things she could understand and share with him. He would fuss over her gently, joke a little, read stories to the boys. He would look after her and be kind.

This dreaming was a game she often played now. She thought if no one knew, no one was harmed, and she escaped into make-believe as she had done as a child when she could not face reality. Wouldn't it be lovely if Jim did come to see me this afternoon, she thought, coming back to the present. He might; sometimes, but not often, he dropped in unexpectedly.

Jane sighed and sat up. No, he wouldn't come, but never mind. She had three more whole days to herself when she need not think of Michael. Tomorrow they would go for a picnic. Now it was time to think about going to fetch the boys; there was something she had intended to do today, something urgent. What could it have been? She had ordered the groceries, so it wasn't that. She had done the ironing. No, she couldn't remember. Never mind, it couldn't have been so important after all.

The next morning was not so fine; it rained a little, but cleared about eleven, so after lunch they went off to the woods to look for primroses, for it might be worse the following day. The little boys ran happily about, picking flowers, and Jane sat on a log watching them, wondering whether Gillian Mary would have dark straight hair like Peter and Michael, or be plump and curly like Bill. Probably she would be completely different from either of them, blonde even, like cousin Julia, who now had four blonde babies. They would bring

Gillian Mary here next spring in her carry-cot, and she could watch them primrose-hunting.

It began to get cold, and a mist started to rise from the ground. Jane called the boys, and they ate their picnic tea in the car, for now it seemed too damp and cold outside. But the boys enjoyed it all the same, putting sticky fingermarks on the upholstery and dropping hard-boiled egg — to them an essential of every picnic meal — down the seats and on the floor.

On the way home they ran into quite thick patches of fog, rising up in layers from the ground. The air had the stillness that comes with fog; like a grey blanket it hung among the trees and by the hedges near the river. Jane was glad to get home before it was any worse. She put the car away, and the boys ran into the house with their primroses to find vases. Soon they were busily arranging them in paste pots. Jane washed up the picnic things and went upstairs to turn down their beds. The carpet! That was what she had meant to do yesterday, nail it down. Mrs. Barton had commented on it this morning, it was getting worse; she would have done it but she could find no nails. Jane went out to Michael's shed where a few tools lived among the garden implements. She hunted about but could only find some tiny tacks, not long enough to go through the pile of the carpet. She took the hammer upstairs and tapped in one of the old nails that still stuck to it; that was better than nothing. She would buy some nails tomorrow. She put the hammer back in the shed; fog swirled round her, it was dense now and most unpleasant.

She put the boys to bed and read them an extra long story as a treat. Then Bill asked her to bring up his precious jar of primroses from where he had left it in the hall. She went off to fetch it, and as she came to the top of the stairs the telephone began to ring. She turned, for it was nearer to answer it in her bedroom, but before she had taken two steps the bell stopped, so she shrugged and turned again. She thought it might have been Michael, he had promised to telephone tonight. Then the bell began again. Jane thought, I may as well go on downstairs now I've started. But she quickened her pace; she caught her foot in the loose edge of carpet, stumbled, tried to save herself by clutching the banisters but missed, and fell heavily down the first short flight of stairs.

She lay for a moment, sprawled on the little landing; the blood pounded in her ears, but above it she heard the insistent ringing of the telephone. She got up unsteadily; her ankle hurt. She went slowly down the rest of the stairs to speak to Michael.

He was very tired; his feet ached; tonight he had to go out to a banquet; he was not interested to hear the boys had picked some primroses; he would see her on Friday. Goodbye.

Very carefully Jane replaced the receiver. She turned and went slowly back upstairs, limping a little. On the landing she remembered the cause of her journey; turned again and fetched the primroses.

Peter said, "I thought I heard a crash, Mummy."

"Yes, darling, I slipped over that bit of loose carpet and fell down the stairs," she said.

"Poor Mummy. Did you hurt yourself?" asked Bill.

"Just my ankle a little. It's getting better," she said.

"Go to bed early," advised Peter.

"Yes, I will," said Jane.

"I'll mend the carpet in the morning, Mummy," said Bill. "I've got some nails in my hammering set."

"Thank you, darling," said Jane carefully. She kissed them both, opened the window, closed it again because of the fog which at once curled clammily in, went out of the room, closed the door, and walked very slowly downstairs again. She sat on the sofa.

I must keep very calm, she told herself. It wasn't such a very big tumble. Those stairs are only shallow flights. I haven't got a pain. Shall I go and fetch Mrs. Barton? No, I ought to go straight to bed, just in case. Suppose something has gone wrong, though? I'm alone in the house with two small children. If I go to bed, it will be all right. Peter could fetch Mrs. Barton early in the morning, if the fog has lifted enough for him to see the way. I won't ring up Jim. The fog is too thick to bring him here on a wild-goose chase; he would only put me to bed, and I can do that myself.

First I must make up the boiler. Now I must let Rory out.

Upstairs now, slowly, don't rush, but something is wrong, haven't you noticed it?

Nonsense, that wasn't a pain, it's imagination.

Undress; never mind your teeth; skip washing. Lie very still and breathe deeply. You aren't cold, so why do you shiver? Gillian Mary, don't die, don't die.

Jane lay rigid for an hour, but then she knew she must get help. She raised herself to reach the telephone and dialled Dr. Brown.

Mrs. Brown answered. Jane told her shakily what had happened.

"Are you in bed?" the older woman asked at once.

"Yes," Jane said in a trembling voice.

"Stay just where you are, my dear. Someone will come as quickly as possible. It will take longer than usual because of the fog, so try not to worry. My husband is over at a case in Wolverstoke. I'll ring him there at once." She rang off and asked the exchange for the Wolverstoke number, while Jane lay back against the pillow. It would be at least half an hour before anyone could possibly arrive, allowing the minimum delay for the fog. She looked at her watch; it was only nine o'clock.

"Oh God," she began urgently, and while she prayed remembered sharply how once she had bargained with Him for Michael's safety, thinking she need never ask for more.

The minutes passed. Five past nine: nine-fifteen: nine-twenty.

At twenty-five past nine Jim came running up the stairs.

Much later, Jane said, "But why not Dr. Brown?"

"Mrs. Brown couldn't get hold of him. I was nearer." He stood at the window, looking out at the black fog beyond the curtains.

Jane said with feverish irrelevance, "She's dead, isn't she?"

And Jimmy said, "I'm afraid so, Janey." He turned then, and came to sit beside her, gently holding her hand. She was better off here than if he had tried to get her to hospital through the fog; he had driven here like a blind man along the blanket lanes, praying to arrive with speed and safety.

Jane said, "You must have driven much too fast, Jimmy."

"Much too fast, Jane," he said with a smile.

"Do you need anything? Have you had any supper?" she asked once, rousing a little.

"Yes, I have," Jimmy answered, "and Mrs. Barton is here. I stopped to tell her on the way, and she walked up. I heard her arrive a little while ago. Everything's under control, Janey."

"I know," she smiled faintly. "In a way, though I'm worse, I feel better, Jim. You know you always do me good."

"This is a rotten thing to happen, especially when you're here on your own," said Jimmy with some bitterness.

"I think it's just as well Michael is away," said Jane. "He can't do with illness. We needn't tell him yet, Jimmy. Anyway he's out banqueting tonight and he can't possibly leave Liverpool unless

I die. I won't die, will I, Jimmy?"

"Of course you won't die, Jane, don't be a goose," said Jimmy robustly. "In a few months you can start another one; it would be the best thing you could do."

Jane said, "I wouldn't like to leave my boys."

"You aren't going to leave them," said Jimmy firmly. "We'll ring Michael up in the morning, and I expect he'll come straight home."

"He won't," said Jane, smiling wanly.

They were silent. Jimmy had done all he could for her. Now they could only wait.

"You won't go away till it's over, will you, Jimmy?" she asked once, fearfully.

"I won't, Janey," he said grimly, smoothing her hair back from her damp forehead.

She looked at him. "I'm afraid I'm not very brave," she said, "but there's only you to know."

It ended with the dawn.

Jimmy thought it would have been easier for Jane to bear if the tiny bloodied thing had been another boy, but it was the Gillian Mary she had wanted.

Jane cried then, great gulping sobs, her face pressed into the pillow. Jimmy sat beside her, stroking her hair gently and holding her hand, not speaking. She seized his gentle hand and gripped it hard, beside her cheek, wetting it with her tears, clutching it as though she would never let it go.

Jim thought that after so much weeping she would sleep, and crying eased the soul. As he watched her, he felt like crying, too.

Presently her sobs lessened and he helped her to recover by finding her a clean handkerchief and sponging her face.

"I'm sorry," she said at last.

"That's all right, Janey," he said gently. "You'll be better for a cry."

She attempted a smile. "That's what Nanny always said."

"And wasn't she right?" Jimmy said. "Now I'm going to give you something to make you sleep. Mrs. Barton will stay here till you're better. She'll see to the boys, don't worry." He knew that to send the children away to friends now would deprive Jane of her best help to recovery.

"I must go now, dear Jane, but I'll come back for a cup of coffee later and we'll have a nice gossip." He patted her gently on the shoulder. "Tuck down, Janey. See, you're nearly asleep already." And before he had packed away his things she was sleeping. Then, because she would never know, and only God could see, Jimmy bent and kissed her pale smooth brow.

He went to the window and drew the curtains back a little. All the fog had gone and it would be a brilliantly lovely day.

At eleven o'clock, when he had satisfied himself that Jane was as well as she could be, Jimmy telephoned Michael. He had a great deal of trouble in having him located at the exhibition, and then he was minutes coming to the telephone. He was greatly surprised to learn that Dr. Fraser wished to speak to him.

Jimmy told him crisply and matter-of-factly what had happened. As soon as he had been assured that Jane was all right, Michael said, "Oh well, it's just one of those things. How did it happen?"

Jim told him she had tripped over the carpet.

"I suppose she forgot to nail it down. It

was her own fault, then," said Michael.

Jim nearly blew up, but he remembered that Jane might possibly be listening on the upstairs telephone. When Michael returned Jim promised himself the pleasure of a straight talk.

He waited to hear that Michael would catch the first train home, but no such offer came. Michael simply said, "There's nothing I can do, is there? Get everything you need, Fraser, spare no expense."

"No, you can't really do anything," said Jim quietly. He described the arrangements he had made, for Michael had a right to know them. Then he rang off.

Upstairs, he told Jane falsely that Michael had sent her his love.

Jane looked at him steadily over the sheet.

"Jim, that's the first time in our lives that you've told me a lie," she said at last. "I was listening."

Fool that I am, thought Jim.

Jane said, "He was right, you know. It was my own fault."

Jimmy said, "Jane, your tumble was nobody's fault. It wouldn't have hurt

Michael to have nailed that carpet down himself. Anyway, you might have slipped in the garden, or over the dog. As a matter of fact you surprised me by carrying that child so long. I must admit that as you'd got so far I thought you'd get to the end, but you had so much backache and so much bad luck in the early stages that every time the phone rang I thought it was to say you'd lost it. So don't blame yourself. Perhaps she was never meant to live."

Jane said slowly, "Perhaps she's better where she is. A boy can fend for himself, one feels, but it would be awful to watch a daughter making the same mistakes as oneself, and not be able to stop her." She plucked at the sheet, crumpling it a little in her long thin fingers. Then she said, "Jimmy, you must be exhausted, you had no sleep last night."

"I'm tough," said Jimmy with a smile.

Jane said shyly, "I wanted Dr. Brown to come, but I'm awfully glad it was you, Jim."

"I always do you good," said Jimmy briskly. "Testimonial from a satisfied patient — very gratifying."

Jane said, "You know what I mean, Jimmy."

"Yes, I know, Jane," he said gently. "Promise me," he went on, and then stopped.

"Yes?" she said.

He changed it. "Promise to ring up at once if you want me."

She nodded.

He had nearly said, "Promise to tell me if ever I can help you," recognising her unhappiness with Michael; but he remembered her words in the night, "I don't want to leave my boys." She had found a way of managing her life. In fifteen years the boys would be grown men; then there might be a chance that they would spare her to him for just a while.

★ ★ ★

At first Jane made a good physical recovery. Michael was surprised on Friday night to find her sitting up in bed playing dominoes on a tray with the boys who were waiting in their dressing-gowns for his return. He kissed her and gave her some carnations he had sent a messenger to buy. Jane's eyes flew to the daffodils and tulips that, Jim, against his conscience, had himself bought in Wolverstoke's one unambitious florist's. Beside them were arranged paste pots of now wilting primroses. The boys, who luckily had not been told about the coming baby, thought she was in bed because she had twisted her ankle.

Michael thought it was an ill wind that blew no one any good. Now there would be no unexpected school fees, and such a slip would not occur again.

Jim came in on Saturday morning and knew at once that these were Michael's thoughts. He reported on Jane's progress and ended, "The best thing that could happen would be another baby, in a little while, when she is strong again."

Michael laughed. "Oh no, my dear chap. I shan't get caught again."

Jim counted ten. Then he gave Michael a lecture about the emotional upset to Jane and all she had been through.

"She'll get over it. It isn't as if she hadn't other children," said Michael. "Have a glass of sherry."

Jim recognised a blank wall when he met it. Michael could not always have been like this, or Jane, foolish young girl though she must have been, would surely not have failed to see it. He must have been getting gradually more and more self-centred as he grew more successful.

Jim said, "I'm giving her a tonic, but she must take things very quietly and not overtax her strength."

"I'll see she doesn't overdo things," said Michael impatiently, and then, in exasperation at the implied criticism of himself, "Dammit, man, she is my wife, after all."

Jim said nothing. Yes, he thought, she's your wife, as that's your chair, and this your house, a possession, not a treasure.

He refused the sherry and left.

Jane was up in time to go with Michael to take Peter to his new school at the beginning of the term, but Jim only allowed it because he thought it would be more harmful for her to stay behind brooding about the parting than to go and get over-tired. Peter's face fell slightly when he said goodbye, but he did not cry. Jane tried to convince herself that he would soon settle down.

She and Michael barely spoke on the way home. They agreed that the company of other boys was desirable at the age of nearly eight; that games would develop the team spirit; that stern masters instead of susceptible women would induce discipline. Jane wondered how much of a wrench it was to Michael to part with his first-born.

She was very tired and rather miserable next day. The house seemed very still after Bill had left for school. She collected up Peter's clothes to wash, stripped his bed, tidied his toys away, and had a little weep. Then she bundled up a parcel of all the baby things she had collected for Gillian Mary and addressed it to Dr. Barnardo's. When she had done all that her back ached, her head ached, and she felt utterly wretched. She was thankful when Bill came back from school, also rather sad and missing his brother, but very well behaved now that he was the only pebble. Jane knew she must guard against spoiling him, but postponed the time to begin as she curled up with him on the sofa to read about Little Grey Rabbit.

When he was in bed she decided that she could not face Michael, so she got his supper ready, put it in the oven, and went to bed.

After this she seemed to get no better. The least effort tired her; she was ready to cry at the slightest thing, even if she broke a plate or could not get kidneys from the butcher. She gave herself brisk lectures, and would not admit to fatigue in her effort to overcome it, but she could not. Even Michael realised how very pale and thin she was. Jim sent her to a specialist, who said there was nothing wrong physically, and advised a holiday, but Jane could not face the complications of arranging one. Michael went so far as rather unwillingly to offer to take her to Bournemouth, but the thought of seven days in his company amid the sleepy pines was too much for Jane, and the thought of a week by herself was as bad, for she found herself poor company. Jim suggested asking Molly to go with her somewhere, but she had just started a new job and Jane knew she would not be able to take time off so soon. She would not go home to her mother, for she did not want her mother's penetrating eyes to see the depths of her despair.

"I'll be all right, Jim, you give me another bottle of that beastly stuff of yours, and I'll soon pick up," she said with an attempt at a smile. Indeed, when Jim came to see her she felt sure she would soon be strong again, but as soon as he left her apathy came down like another fog.

"What about starting another painting," said Jim. "You want to have something ready for the Academy next year, don't you, and you'll be giving your own exhibition too before long." He spoke bracingly.

Jane said, "I just don't feel in the mood, Jim. There's nothing I want to paint, I have no inspiration."

"What you need is a fortnight at Rhosarddur," said Jim stoutly. "Bournemouth's not the place to be pepped up in, you need strong bracing air. If you won't go alone, which I can quite understand, wouldn't your mother go too?"

Jane said, "I don't want her just now, Jim. No, I'll be all right. I despise myself for giving way like this. Look at the people who lose baby after baby and never give in."

But Jimmy knew the baby was only the last straw.

After that Jane attempted to paint a new portrait of Bill, but he hated to sit still, and she felt so restless, that the work was doomed and she put her paints away again.

But a few days later a letter came which altered things. It was from Julia, who with her gay nature and large family was a rather spasmodic correspondent.

Dearest Jane (said the letter)

I have just heard from my mamma via your mamma about your wretched mishap. What bad luck; I believe you feel awful after such a thing, full of frustrations. Wouldn't a holiday do you good?

As you see by the address I am back at Rhosarddur with the kids. We've taken this house for three months as London is so ghastly at this time of the year, specially with infants, and we were very lucky to let our own house to some Americans for the whole summer, so in the end we make a profit. Poor Phil is camping out in his club, and he comes up here when he can for weekends. I wondered if you'd like to come up for a bit, you always loved it here, and it's certainly bracing. It would be nice to have some company, so do try. I hear Peter has begun boarding school, so bring Bill, if you like. It surely won't hurt him to miss a bit of school at his age. He can muck in with the twins so you needn't see him unless you want to. I have a nanny(!) but not one of those terrifying posh ones like yours used to be, she's most human and won't mind one extra a bit, in fact she is always eyeing me hopefully to see if there is more fuel for her energy on the way!

Don't say Michael can't manage without you. It does all husbands good to be left sometimes and he'll appreciate you all the more!

Come as soon as you can. In haste,
Yours with love,
Julia.

Jane read this artless, typical missive through three times. Then she thought, of course I can't go, it's impossible, but all day she kept thinking about it and by tea-time her mind was made up. Perhaps the ozone would brace her up and give her the strength she needed to cope with her life again. In any case she had always longed to go back one day to Rhosarddur, and here was her chance.

Before she could change her mind she wired Julia to expect her next week.

Michael was dismayed at first when he heard that after all Jane was going away; and shattered, though he did not reveal it, that she could take a decision like that without first consulting him; but already she showed more animation than she had for nearly two months so for once he kept his views to himself.

He contented himself by saying, "Very well, Jane, you go. I expect I can manage," in a martyred voice.

Jane said firmly, "Mrs. Barton will

come in every evening to see to your supper. I expect it will be rather plain as she's not much of a cook, but you won't starve."

Michael was silent. Then he said, "I had some good news for you, Jane, but it can wait now, I suppose."

"Oh?" Jane was not much interested.

"I don't think you are aware that old Norton is to have his portrait painted to hang in the boardroom — all the chairmen do, eventually. We were discussing it today and wondering who should do it."

"Really?"

"It was decided to give you the job," said Michael.

Jane gaped. This had penetrated her self-absorption, even if nothing Michael had said earlier had been able to do so.

"I said, it was decided to get you to do it," repeated Michael distinctly when she did not answer. He could not now, after so many years, find the words to tell her that in some obscure way he had felt giving her a task like this and showing confidence in her ability to do it might give her the necessary impetus to come to terms again with life. Neither did he say how delighted Mr. Norton, who had greatly admired the little he had seen of her work, had been with the idea. Instead, somewhat ungraciously, Michael said, "It won't cost nearly as much as getting a proper artist to do it, and I expect yours will be almost as good."

But this unfortunate speech had the effect of firing Jane. A proper artist, indeed! She'd do a masterpiece of Mr. Norton's pale, ascetic face.

"I assume it doesn't have to be done at once?" she said. "I could do it in the autumn, when we come back from Milton." Then belatedly, she added, "It was nice of you to think of it, Michael. Thank you. I won't let you down."

Placated, Michael said, "That's all right, Jane, I know you won't. I'll let Norton know and we can arrange the sittings later. There's a small room at the works that isn't used much, we thought you could use it as a temporary studio. It's got a good north light."

"I see," said Jane. She began to feel that one day after all she might paint again, and decided to take her equipment with her to Rhosarddur. Julia had four children whom she might paint, and there were the rocky scenes she had painted long ago. Already she felt the future might be faced.

Michael opened his diary and leafed through its pages. A vision of Norah Belmont's long blonde hair and wide inviting mouth swam before him.

"Er, Jane, I have got one or two commitments in the next few weeks," he said. "Tell Mrs. Barton I shan't want her every night. I'll let her know when I'll be in."

7

AT dinner Mrs. Brown said to Jim, "How is little Mrs. Rutherford getting on? I saw her in Wolverstoke a week or so ago and was shocked at the change in her. I meant to ask you before, Jim."

Jim considered for a moment.

"She needs to get away," he said at last. "There's nothing wrong physically, I sent her to Wilson to make sure — she's anaemic, of course — she's still badly upset in her mind."

"Poor child. I shall never forget that dreadful night," said Mrs. Brown, shuddering again. "That pea-soup fog, and both of you out, and me telling her calmly that someone would be there directly!"

"The only thing you could do, my dear," said her husband with a smile.

"Poor girl, all alone with those babies, and that to happen," said gentle Mrs. Brown. "I'm sure a thing like that does take a lot of getting over. Won't she go away, Jim?"

"Says she'll be going to the sea in August anyway," said Jim flatly.

"Yes, but that isn't much of a holiday for her. They take a house, don't they, every year? She still has to cook and house-keep."

"I know. I've done everything I could to persuade her to go away, but she won't, not even to her mother's," said Jim. "I am worried about her. She can't seem to snap out of it, somehow, though I know she tries."

"That husband of hers ought to take her off to Monte Carlo for a fortnight," said Dr. Brown.

"I expect she needs a holiday from him, too," said Mrs. Brown shrewdly. "He's a nice enough young man, I suppose, in his way, but not a comfortable person. I never feel at ease with those film star sort of men. Thank goodness Jim here isn't one." She smiled at her husband. "I couldn't have let you bring someone like that into the practice, Geoffrey."

"Doing well for himself, young Rutherford, I hear," said Dr. Brown.

"He's his boss's idol — he's on to a good thing, too, a growing business and no one to take it on when the old man goes. He'll be his own boss one day."

"Perhaps he's too ambitious for his wife," said Mrs. Brown. "What do you think, Jim? You know them better than we do."

Jim said awkwardly, "Jane's no climber; I get the impression he definitely is."

"Funny girl," said Dr. Brown musingly. "Until this happened, she seemed to have come on suddenly, burst into flower as you might say. She was so quiet and mousey when they first came here, never a word to say for herself and never left the fellow's side. Then all of a sudden she found herself — full of chat, and got quite pretty."

Jim was silent.

Mrs. Brown said, "I expect the success of her painting gave her confidence."

Dr. Brown nodded. "It will be a help to her now, to get over this bad patch. She's very clever, too. Wonder what she'd charge to do you, my dear."

Mrs. Brown blushed delightfully.

"What nonsense you talk, Geoffrey,"

she said. "I'm far too old to get my picture painted."

"You're prettier than ever, my dear," said her husband gallantly.

Jim said, "If only Jane would start painting again I'm sure it would help her, but she says she can't. Perhaps if you did ask her to paint you, Mrs. Brown, it would give her some encouragement to begin. She wouldn't expect to be paid, though perhaps you should ask her about a fee just for a formality." He thought for a moment of the amazement with which Jane would hear such a question, then realised that at the moment poor Jane was beyond even feeling amazement.

"Very well, then, I'll drop in tomorrow and see about it," said Dr. Brown promptly. "You agree, Jim? She's well enough to take it on if she can be talked into it?"

"Oh yes," said Jim. "You'd do her good, too, Mrs. Brown. You're always so calm, you might soothe her." He smiled at the elderly woman, of whom he was so fond. She smiled back, looking at him with affection, wiser than he knew but equally discreet.

Next day, however, when Dr. Brown called at Rose House, the bird had flown.

Jim was surprised that Jane had gone away without telling him, but glad.

"Where's she gone?" he wanted to know.

"I never asked," said Dr. Brown, who had only seen Mrs. Barton. "To her mother's, I imagine. It's a good thing."

"Yes," Jimmy agreed.

"We'll ask her to do the portrait when she comes back," said Dr. Brown.

That evening Jim had just seen the last patient in the surgery, which was attached to the side of Dr. Brown's house, when Mrs. Brown came in.

"Finished, Jim? Come and have a glass of sherry with me," she invited. "Geoffrey's out at that silly dinner in Wolverstoke and I'm bored with my own company."

Jim thanked her, and when he had locked up he went through the door that led into the senior partner's house, and on into Mrs. Brown's drawing-room. It was a dull, chill day, although it was the middle of June, and a fire crackled in the grate.

"Very wicked in June, but we need it," said Mrs. Brown.

Jim accepted his sherry gratefully, and when she was sitting in her chintz-covered chair he too sat down, with a sigh.

"You're tired, Jim," she scolded gently.

"Just a bit," he admitted.

"What about that trip to Italy, you've been planning? I thought you were going last year?"

Jim said, "It didn't seem worth all the trouble, somehow."

"You only had a couple of long weekends. No one can go on working like that," said Mrs. Brown. "Now why don't you go away next week?"

"Next week? But I couldn't possibly," said Jim.

"Yes, you can. Geoffrey can manage. There's no one likely to die, and only one baby due, which he can quite well see to even if it is in the middle of the night. You go, Jim. If not to Italy, then to Scotland or somewhere."

Jim said, because he was tired and did not think before the words burst from him, "She's gone for a fortnight, hasn't

346

she?" Then he realised what he had said and went very white.

But Mrs. Brown only said very calmly, "Yes, so I understand. I quite see that you felt you must stay whilst she was so unwell, poor girl, but now you are free to go away. You'll be better for it, Jim, believe me."

"I'll have to speak to Dr. Brown," he said slowly.

"It will be all right," said Mrs. Brown. "You'll find you'll be able to carry on much better if you just go away for a little while."

Jim looked at her kind face. She was either incredibly blind or she was the most understanding woman he had met.

"Help yourself to some more sherry, Jim," was all she said, "and tell me what to say when I open the hospital fete next month."

★ ★ ★

Jane and Bill motored all the way to Rhosarddur in the old Ford. They had to put in a pint of oil every hundred miles, but they never had a puncture

347

and they got safely to the top of every hill. They started after breakfast, and they arrived when it was nearly dark. Bill was sleeping in his seat, and Jane was almost dropping at the wheel, but they had been good company for each other, singing as they often did when Michael wasn't there — he thought it most peculiar that his family sang so much — and playing 'I Spy.'

She had gone by car rather than by train partly from obstinacy, since Michael had decreed the train would be best, partly from a silly wish to save a few pounds, partly because it was easier to chuck everything into the back of the car than to compress gumboots, sou'westers, painting things, Bill's bucket, spade and shrimping net all into a few suitcases.

The last few miles were full of memories. She crossed the Menai Bridge in the dusk; little boats rocked below as they had always done, but the water was dark now in the evening light, not Mediterranean blue as she had seen it long ago in her first glimpse from the train.

She found Julia's house; it was near

where they had stayed every year as children. Bill stirred when the car stopped, grumbled a little when Julia's Nanny picked him out of his seat, but dropped off again against her shoulder as she carried him away. Soon he was tucked, unwashed but undressed, into a camp bed beside the twins, hardly having roused at all.

Jane had to wait till the next day to see the bay again. Julia took one look at her white, drawn face, and said, "Off you go to bed. We'll unload the car in the morning. Which case has got your nightie in? I'll go up to the phone box and ring up Michael to say you've arrived safely."

Jane was glad to obey these instructions. She was reminded of how she had been similarly sent to bed by Aunt Madge when she arrived to stay after her appendicitis. Julia now looked just like Aunt Madge had looked then; she must too be only a few years younger than her mother had been on that earlier occasion, the fateful visit in which Jane had met Michael.

The bay was tiny. Where was that huge expanse of yellow sand? It had shrunk to a fraction of its remembered size, but it was just as lovely as she had always thought it. Jane spent the morning walking slowly round, showing Bill the little sandy coves and the rocks where shrimps lurked at low tide. He was ecstatic: a sociable child, the company of Julia's twins, not to mention their elder brother and younger sister, was enough to make him happy.

The first days were dull, but then the unpromising summer changed its mind and the sun shone. The children bathed, and Jane plunged tentatively in and out of the crystal clear water, promising herself a proper swim next day. The twins took to Bill, who was a little older than they, and so able to impose himself authoritatively upon their united front. He enjoyed this after years of being bossed by Peter. The children dug endless pits and castles on the sands where Jane remembered Julia's brother doing the same thing. She sat and watched them, chatting to Nanny about simple things like baby teeth, and growing feet, and cod-liver oil in the winter. It was soothing. She wrote to Peter with details of the journey. She sent Michael a picture postcard, and another to Mrs. Barton. After four days she was sleeping better and had an appetite. She thought of nothing, she let each day unfold and looked no further.

Julia had hired a boat for the summer, and when the sea dropped they went sailing. Jane had almost forgotten what it was like to scud along with the wind and water singing past. She could not even remember how to handle a boat, and made Julia laugh with her landlubberly remarks. But after a day or two it all began to come back, and she felt more competent to take the tiller.

Julia was an excellent companion. She asked nothing, and did not fuss. She thought if Jane wanted to pour out her soul she would do it when she was ready; if she preferred to keep her own counsel it was her own affair. Sometimes getting things off your chest did you good, but sometimes you later regretted confidences given. It was for the individual to decide. Meanwhile Julia took everything at its surface value. She assumed that Jane and Michael were not as happy as she and Philip. No letters passed between them, and Michael was a stern sort of a person. Philip had told her how keen on discipline and efficiency he had been in the war. But after all, Jane had chosen him, and stuck to him for a long time; probably she was fond of him, but it did all couples good to have a rest from one another. It did not seriously occur to Julia that there could be more to it than that.

One afternoon, when Julia had gone shopping and Nanny was playing french cricket with the children, Jane took the boat and venturesomely sailed alone out to the Bay Rock where she had been marooned twenty years before. The thought of the length of time that had passed was frightening; what had happened to those lost years of youth? The war, for which there had been so little preparation, had swallowed them, and when it was over light-heartedness had gone.

She got in a muddle sailing in against the rock, anxious not to ram it and yet to stop, but no one was about to see her failure for at this time of the year there were few visitors; it was not till August that the place filled up. In any case, Jane did not mind now who thought her foolish; that was one consolation the twenty years had brought.

She stopped somehow, jumped out of the boat and pulled it along till she found a jutting piece of rock to tie the painter to and make fast. Then, slowly, she walked over the rocks to the tunnel she had discovered so long ago. It was still there, but like the whole bay shrunken to doll size. It was still fascinating, though; red sea anemones still clung like jellied rubies to the stones over which the clear water rippled gently. She went on, up over a ridge of rock till she looked down on the hollow where she had sat painting the day that she had drawn the caricature of Jim. Slowly she began to climb down over the rocks till she could see up the miniature ravine which divided them to the ledge where he had sat reading that day. Then she stopped, for someone was before her.

Head on hand, pipe in mouth, same lock of thick brown hair hanging forward, Jimmy sat gazing out at the blue sea.

For a moment Jane panicked; how or why did not occur to her till later. She turned, to escape quickly before she was seen, but at that moment Jimmy looked round and saw her, and it was too late. For an instant they stared at one another. Jimmy was the first to recover himself. He got up and said, "Jane! I thought you were staying with your mother!"

She began to go down the rock towards him.

"I thought you were in Wolverstoke," she said.

"I'm having a holiday," he said.

Jane asked, naïvely, "All alone?"

"All alone," he answered gravely. "I'm staying at the hotel."

Jane said quickly, "I'm staying with Julia. She's got a house here for the summer. Bill's with me. Julia's Nanny is looking after him."

"Oh."

What could they say, when there was so much to say and none of it could be uttered? They sat down instead, and were quiet, looking at the sea.

"It's still the same," said Jimmy at length.

"But smaller," answered Jane.

"I always loved the clearness of the sea. It's the rocks below, I suppose," he said, conversationally.

"Yes. Like the Mediterranean. Not that I've ever been there," Jane said.

At last Jimmy said, painfully, "Jane, shall I go away?"

She answered swiftly, "Oh, no," before she had thought.

He said, because it was a possibility that ought to be faced, "Michael might think I'd followed you here."

"But you didn't even know I'd gone away."

"I did." He told her about Mrs. Brown and the painting.

Jane said, "I ought to have told you I was going, Jimmy, but it was arranged so quickly. It seemed best just to go."

"There was no reason why you should tell me," he said gently. "You knew I was keen on the idea of a holiday for you."

"It would have been more polite to let you know," she said primly.

He laughed then. "You and I don't have to fence about being polite to each other," he said, chuckling.

She smiled too, and the tension began to ease.

Jane said, "Come back to tea, Jimmy," and he thought, why not? It is a coincidence, both of us being here. No need to make a mystery.

"I will," he said, "and thank you."

Bill was delighted to see Jim again, and if Julia was surprised she made it seem as if she thought it was the most natural thing in the world, and asked him to stay to supper.

Afterwards they played Canasta, and grew hilarious as the scores rose. It was eleven o'clock when Jimmy finally walked down the road to the hotel.

After that neither Jane nor Jimmy was strong enough to avoid spending most of every day together. According to the weather, they spent the mornings walking or sailing, while Julia cooked the lunch, a task she would not in any case let Jane share. In the afternoons they sometimes took the children shrimping; once, when it rained, they went to the cinema, taking

Julia with them. Once the two young women dined with Jim at the hotel, and once again he came to supper with them. On the fifth afternoon Jane and Bill went to meet him on the shore as a mackerel fishing trip was planned for young Bill's benefit. Jim too had hired a boat, and he waited for them sitting on the gunwale, bare legs in the water, smoking his pipe and checking the lines.

When Jane saw him she called out gaily and waved; Jimmy took his pipe out of his mouth and waved back, then stood up in the shallow water, the little boat rocking behind him as his weight left it.

Then the words burst from Jane: "Oh Jimmy, that's how I must paint you, sitting on the boat like that!"

He looked at her. Her eyes were shining, her face tanned brown; she moved swiftly in her old grey skirt and faded blue aertex shirt. Beside her Bill, in bathing trunks, capered about.

"I mean," she began to explain, "I've never been able to think of the right pose for you, Jimmy. All pompous in a suit wouldn't be right, somehow, too boardroomy. Like that is right, sitting on the gunwale, with your pipe in your hand. Will you let me do it, Jimmy?"

"Madam, you have only to command," said Jimmy, sweeping her a low bow. His eyes twinkled. "When do we start?"

"I suppose we can't now, as we've fixed this trip for Bill. Never mind, there are five more days left. Are you sure you don't mind, Jimmy? I've been wanting to paint you for ages but as I say I've never seen you in the most paintable position till now."

"I shall be honoured, Jane," said Jim, grinning. "What's this one to be? 'An old salt ruminates?'"

She laughed. "No nothing whimsy. Just 'Jim,'" she said.

For a moment their eyes met, then abruptly Jimmy picked up Bill. "All aboard, young man," he said briskly, and popped him into the boat. He pushed her out a little way, and Jane got in; then another push, Jim followed and they were away.

Next day the painting began. The weather was kind, and they took the boat to a deserted cove where only an occasional longshoreman passed incuriously by. Under the warm sun Jane worked, and Jimmy sat and looked at her, and thought that if this was all they ever shared for the rest of their lives, it was still more than many people had.

Jane's canvas was not as large as she would have liked, but it was the biggest she had brought, so it must do. With love she painted him, every line of face and feature, putting into her work all that she could not say. She showed not just his round, faintly smiling face with its short snub nose and clear grey eyes; she also caught the essence of his humour and his kindliness. Tenderness and wit, intelligence and strength, all were in his expression and faithfully she transcribed them.

At intervals they stopped for rest; they swam sometimes, or merely sat and talked. Neither dared to look ahead, both lived entirely in the present.

On the fourth day the painting was finished. It was the first that Jane had done since her illness, and she knew now that she could begin again, could return and paint Mr. Norton, could look for further subjects, but could never hope to paint another picture such as this. Even Julia, who was the least sensitive of people, thought it was a masterpiece.

Jimmy hardly liked to say what he thought about it.

"The world must judge it, Janey," he said lightly. "I only see myself back to front in the mirror when I shave." He grinned at her, but he felt awed and very humble at all she had found to transfer to her canvas.

In the evening Jane said, trying to speak casually, "Julia, would you mind if I went for a picnic with Jimmy tomorrow, if the weather's good? We thought of going to Silver Cove."

"Good idea, Jane, you go," said Julia matter-of-factly. She was sewing a button on one of the twin's pyjamas, and now bit the thread off sharply, glancing across at Jane as she did so. Then she said:

"You look marvellous, Jane. The holiday's done you a world of good."

"I feel fine," said Jane quickly. "It was sweet of you to have me, Julia."

"Not at all. Any time," said Julia. "I expect we'll be here again next year.

360

It was lucky Jim coming; he's been company for you, for us both, come to that. Nice to be dined and wined in the evening. I like men."

Jane had to laugh at this frank statement.

"And he was always keen on you, Jane. Rather nice to have a faithful swain to dance attendance on you all your days. Keeps your husband guessing. I shall have to acquire one."

"Oh, but — " Jane began.

"Oh, I know you're both as pure as the lily, but he dotes on you, my dear," said Julia. "Poor Jim, he did when you were a kid. I expect you've blighted his life by marrying another, but now he gets some recompense by a platonic friendship in your middle age."

Jane did not know how much of this was serious. She looked doubtfully at Julia, who laughed.

"Go on, Jane, you enjoy your little romance," she said. "It isn't doing anyone any harm. You owe the poor chap a picnic after making him sit still all those hours while you painted him. If that hasn't killed his devotion nothing will."

Jane said, prissily, "We're just good friends, Julia."

"I know," said Julia, nodding. "You're a respectable and godly matron like me. Don't worry, Jane, I'm only teasing. After all, you wouldn't be so open about it if there was anything to hide. A little male company is good for one's ego," she went on. "Makes one feel youth hasn't entirely gone with the advance of one's awkward years."

Jane burst into laughter at this, for Julia was only thirty-two. "I think you could still break a heart or two," she said weakly, wiping her eyes.

"I wonder if I shall?" mused Julia. "I believe people do suddenly tend to go off the rails when they've been soberly married for about twelve years. I can't imagine wanting to, but you never know. Whatever would Philip say?" She began to giggle too. "I sometimes wonder if I'd marry again if he died, always supposing someone offered, of course. I rather need a man about the place. Being on my own for too long gets me down. But another one wouldn't be the same; it might be too much bother to train him to one's ways. Would you, Jane? Marry again, I mean, if Michael fell under a bus or ran off with a redhead?"

Jane said lightly, "I'd probably be a good-time girl instead."

"Yes, of course. With all your painting friends you could have a lot of bohemian fun," said Julia. "Or shut yourself happily up in a studio all day, I suppose." She mused. "Ah well, one can't tell what lies in store; and perhaps it's just as well."

★ ★ ★

The morning was beautiful, fine and sunny, with the promise of heat to come. Only a few tiny woolly wisps dotted the early sky, and later even they disappeared as the blue deepened. Jim was waiting for her at the mooring, as he had waited for their last picnic fourteen years before. The sails were up and flapping idly, all ready to move out of the bay in the small breeze.

Jane said, "What a lovely day, Jim. Do you think it will last?"

He looked up at the sky and smiled. "It looks as if it's come to stay, but you can't tell in our climate," he said, and gave her a hand to climb on board.

Jane went forward at once to the bow of the little boat, and Jimmy pushed the tiller round so that gradually the sail filled with wind. Jane let the rope go, and they began to move noiselessly over the calm water, very slowly, on their way to the open sea. The jib fluttered loose in the little wind, and Jane caught the sheet and tied it down to the cleat. Then she perched on the centre thwart looking out under the boom to the way ahead.

Jim trimmed his sail, and they slid gently past their Bay Rock through the channel and out of the little bay. The breeze was stronger here, and the boat moved more swiftly on her new course. Jane gave a sigh of happiness and turned to smile at Jim.

"How perfect," she said simply. "Nothing to do all day but just be idle."

"You won't be idle all day," said Jim with a grin. "You'll sail the boat in a minute."

"Do you trust me not to wreck us?" she asked lazily.

"On a day like this, yes," he said.

She dipped her hand in the water and splashed him lightly. They both laughed, and Jim said, "Did Bill think he should be included in this trip?"

Jane shook her head. "No, he has plans for a special prawning expedition. He thinks we can take a bucket of live prawns home. What a horrid journey we shall have with a cargo of dying prawns. I've persuaded him not to post any to Peter. He's developed a passion for them himself."

Jim asked, "Are you going to do the whole trip in a day?"

"No, we're going to stay at Molly's house tomorrow night. It isn't far off our route, and she'll be home for a long weekend. It will be nice to see her."

"Give her my love," said Jim, chuckling.

"I will," said Jane. She smiled. "I still hope for something to come of that," she said cheerfully.

"Hope on," said Jim. "A beautiful friendship is all there will ever be between Molly and me."

Jane said no more. She sat dreaming for a time, until presently Jim suggested she should take the tiller and she moved aft. She perched on the gunwale, holding the tiller in her right hand and the mainsheet in her left, frowning slightly as the boat veered a little and had to be brought back on its course. Jim filled his pipe and watched her, smiling at the earnest expression on her face. Her short hair blew in the breeze, and her face was tanned by the sun and the sea air. She was still thin, but she looked well now, clear-eyed, and the tension had gone from her.

Jane was conscious of his gaze; she looked at him for a moment and smiled.

"Your old pipe," she said with tenderness, as he lit it, puffing hard.

Jim said, "This is what keeps me so good-tempered. Have you ever seen an angry man smoking a pipe?"

Jane did not think she had. They speculated about it, till at last they came level with Silver Cove and turned for the run-in. Jane sailed the boat in, and Jim crouched in the bow to watch for the submerged rocks that lay just under the surface. Soon the bows scrunched on the sand; Jane let the sheet fly and Jimmy jumped out to pull the boat up the beach. Jane pulled the rudder out and got out herself. Then Jimmy ran the anchor up the beach so that they could still reach the boat when she floated on the incoming tide.

They took their picnic basket and bathing things and the thick spare jerseys they had brought out of the boat, and carried them up the shore to a corner by the rocks where the sand was like clean silver dust.

Jim said: "No paints?"

She shook her head. "Not today."

"But the painting's all right again now, Isn't it, Janey? You can go on with it now?" He looked at her anxiously.

"Oh yes, Jimmy. I know now I must go on with it, whatever happens." She met his eyes steadily. "I won't pack it in again."

"That's all right then," he said, reassured.

Jane sat down on the soft sand and hugged her knees with her arms.

"I was so afraid it would blow great guns today and stop us from coming," she said softly.

Jim sat on a smooth rock a yard or two away from her.

"I had an alternative programme planned," he said. "A cultural trip round the old castles of Anglesey and North Wales."

"Oh dear," said Jane. "It sounds a bit restless if you meant us to see them all."

"With suitable stops for refreshment," he grinned.

"This is cosier," said Jane. "We ought to bathe, I suppose, if we're going to before lunch." She got to her feet again and wandered off to change behind a jutting rock.

Jim was soon ready. He waited for her, thinking cynically that if he were the hero of a novel now he would rush immediately behind her rock.

When Jane emerged, wearing her red bathing-dress, he was chuckling to himself.

"What's the joke, Jimmy?" she asked.

"I was thinking of 'The Blue Lagoon,'" he answered at once. Jane began to laugh too.

"'Innocents Abroad,'" she said, putting

her cap on and tucking her short curls under it. "Come on, Jim. We must take the plunge."

They walked into the water, shivering a little, then at last with breath suspended dived forward and swam, gasping till their bodies grew used to the cold water. They swam slowly out to the slippery, seaweed-covered rock they had raced to before, side-by-side, keeping level. They clambered on to it and rested for a while to get their breath back.

"We used to dash in and get wet at once, and swim like mad and never puff," marvelled Jane. She pushed the flap of her bathing cap up from one ear, explaining, "I must do this or I shan't hear what you say."

Jim said, "I was never the fish you were, Jane. I always puffed."

"I don't believe it," she said with a smile. "But I never used to think the water cold. Did you?"

"Not specially," he admitted. "It seems Arctic now, though."

"It's all right when you've been in a little while," said Jane. "I have to count three before I can get wet. It's better if you dive in from a rock. You get it over in one, then. You can't do that at Milton, there aren't any rocks, and you wade out for miles. But the most chill-making of all is to stand supporting one's darling children and encouraging their efforts whilst you congeal slowly from the feet up."

Jim said, "Bill will swim soon. If he'd only keep on with his arms, he'd be away, but he forgets about them and so he sinks."

Jane said, "He'll do it in August, I expect, if we get some reasonable weather. This fortnight has given him a little boost."

Jim said, "Will you always go to Milton, Jane? It's not a very restful holiday for you, with all the chores."

"Someone else's sink is a holiday for me," said Jane lightly. "It makes a change. But perhaps when the boys are bigger we might go somewhere different. Michael's golf is the big draw. I thought if I made some money from my painting I might take us all abroad. The Italian Lakes and the Leonardos, as you said, Jimmy."

"That's a good idea," he said. "You'll be paid for doing Mr. Norton, of course. How much?"

"Michael told them I'd do it for nothing — save the shareholders money — but old Norton insisted on fifty pounds," said Jane. "Isn't it marvellous! What a lot! Of course I spend a bit on canvases and things, but still."

"You ought to charge two hundred," said Jim. "That's what anyone else would charge, without doing half such a good portrait."

"It may not be any good," said Jane gloomily.

"Of course it will be," said Jim.

"I like him well enough. I expect I'll catch something," said Jane. "I don't think you could paint a good portrait if you didn't feel something about the person — admiration, interest, even acute dislike. But if your sitter holds no interest for you, if you're quite indifferent to him, you could only paint a hollow mask." She was silent for a minute, and then went on more softly, "Of course, if you're really fond of people, that's the easiest. Mrs. Barton is a dear, for instance, and the children; and I'm sure I could do justice to Mrs. Brown, I think she's charming." She pulled a piece of seaweed off the rock and threw it into the water with a tiny splash. By a natural association of ideas she went on: "Jim, I never asked you what you would like to do with your portrait?"

Jim said, "I haven't anyone to give it to, Janey. My parents are both dead, as you know. Will you keep it for me for the moment?"

Jane sighed with relief.

"Yes, I will, Jim," she said thankfully. "I'll keep it till you have a house of your own to hang it in." She pulled down the flap of her cap again and fastened it.

"Now let's have another race," she challenged.

They dived in again, and swam in a flurry of splashing water to the shore, and this time it was a dead-heat.

As they unpacked their picnic lunch Jim said: "I'm afraid this doesn't compare with last time."

"Never mind, it looks very good," said Jane, unwrapping the ham sandwiches and sausage rolls Jim had got the hotel

372

to provide for them.

"We had hardboiled eggs, and chicken, last time," said Jim reminiscently.

"Peter and Bill don't think it is a picnic unless there are hardboiled eggs, even if it's tea," said Jane.

Jim took a bite of sausage roll. "Rather weighty, these," he said. "Hunt the sausage."

Jane said, "Picnics always are filling."

Jim unwrapped something he had got done up in a table napkin. "I brought this to make up for the dull food," he said. It was a bottle of hock. "I hope it's all right. It looked the best on their list."

"Oh, Jim, how lovely. What good ideas you do have," cried Jane.

"I ought to have got it out before and chilled it in the sea," said Jim.

"Never mind, I expect it's cold enough," said Jane. "I think the chilling can be overdone."

Jim laughed and opened the bottle. He had brought two glasses and now poured out the wine.

Jane picked up her glass and sipped. "It's delicious," she said.

Jimmy smiled and lifted his glass in a

silent toast. They drank solemnly. Then Jane said, "Jimmy, do you remember when we were here before, just before the war; we talked about the war. We wondered if we'd ever come back again."

"And we have," he said with a smile.

She sighed a little. "Yes, but it hasn't put the clock back. We aren't like we were then."

Jim said, "Our circumstances have changed, but we haven't, Jane, except that we are older and not so lighthearted, perhaps."

Jane thought for a moment. "Perhaps that's true," she said at last. "If we have changed, we've both changed the same sort of way, so that we still — still like each other."

"Yes, Jane," he said gently.

They had finished their meal, and now packed away the remnants of it, still with their wine to finish. Jane settled herself with her back leaning more comfortably against a rock.

At last she said, "I tried to change once, Jim. Be more flashy, you know, and poised. It didn't work, so I gave up — I had to anyway when the boys arrived,

374

but I didn't feel real, I wasn't me."

Jim said, "One is different with other people, sometimes — all things to all men, you know."

"Yes, perhaps that's it. It's with just a few people that one is really oneself, with no pretence." She sighed. "With other people you're just a machine walking round saying what you think they want to hear, and with different people again you're a sort of jumble, a bit of each." She thought for a moment. "But you aren't like that, Jim. You're always you, I mean the same with everyone. That's why you're such a good doctor."

Jim said, "I think all our different selves fuse together after a time. We learn to overcome things like shyness, though they may still be there. We don't show fear so transparently, we control anger. But underneath we're still the same. And we reveal more of our true selves, without that control, to some people than to others."

Jane said, "I never pretend anything with you, Jimmy. If I tried it you'd catch me out at once." She smiled as she spoke.

Jimmy picked up a knife left from the picnic basket and began drawing queer patterns in the sand. "The same things make us tick," he said at last.

"Yes." She was quiet then, but content, watching him draw squatting cats in the sand, then rub them out with his foot and begin again.

"It's a nice, safe sort of feeling," she said after a time. " I get scared, sometimes."

Jim looked at her. "What of, Janey?" he asked.

"Oh, all sorts of things. Death, you know, and all that, but I'm rather afraid of living too. It's so difficult." She sighed. "You want to do what's right all the time, and bring the children up to be good and unselfish, but how are you to know if you are right in what you think? How are you to know what difficulties your own children will have to face? They won't be the same things as you meet yourself."

This was a long speech for Jane. Jimmy remembered what she had said after she had lost her baby, about watching a daughter make her own mistakes.

"Environment counts for a lot, Jane," he said. "You must keep faith and hope. There's nothing without that. Your boys will form their standards by you. You won't fail them, and I'm sure they won't fail you."

Jane said, "Sometimes one does the silliest things from the best of motives."

"Isn't that more honest than doing the better things from wrong motives?" suggested Jimmy.

"I don't know." Jane looked at him, and sighed. "I think the boys trust me," she said at last, "but they're still so young. Their lives are ahead of them."

"They'll be all right," said Jimmy. "You must have faith in the future, Janey."

She knew that he was right. Without the bright future of her boys to plan for she would be lost; now a candle of hope for her painting burned as well. Beyond these things she could not look. The day would come when the boys would be adult and no longer need her; Michael would be president and chairman of his firm, married to his work, and might not miss her if she could no longer bear to live with him. Under those circumstances anything might be possible. She glanced at Jim, half fearfully, wondering if he knew what was going on in her head, but he only smiled and went on drawing cats. She thought then of Julia's remarks the previous evening and their discussion about second husbands in the event of Michael running off with a redhead. She began to laugh.

"What's the joke, Janey?" asked Jim.

"Oh, it was some nonsense Julia and I were talking last night," she said. "We were planning what we would do if our husbands ran off with redheads. Can you imagine Michael doing such an unconventional thing? Even if he wanted to, he'd never have the nerve."

Jim smiled. He could not see Michael casting propriety to the winds, but one never knew.

"It doesn't seem likely," he agreed mildly.

Jane said, "Sometimes I think he'd be happier if he did find himself a more glamorous companion. I've no doubt he'd weather the attendant scandal."

Jim said, "He's fond of you, Jane."

"He's fond of his idea of me, you mean," she amended. "The dutiful little woman, with no other idea in her head than to serve him. It took him a time to swallow the painting, but now he's been able to put it into its proper place in relation to himself — a sort of distinction by proxy. He'd never have accepted it if it hadn't been for my small success."

Jim knew that what she said described the situation exactly.

"We never talk like this, you know," Jane went on. "Michael wouldn't understand a word we've said." She sighed. "When I married him I thought I was getting a friend. It's wrong of me to criticise him to you, Jim, I shouldn't do it."

He said gently, "There are things between us, Janey, that don't have to be put into words. Things we both know are there, without us ever mentioning them."

They looked steadily at one another for a long moment, the blue eyes and the grey.

Jane said, on a long-drawn breath, "Yes, we do both know," and coloured a little.

This time it was Jim who looked away. He began to scribble furiously in the sand, and said in a gruff voice. "When you plunge into a swift flowing river, it's hard to swim against the stream. You have to give in, either go with it or go under. So unless you want to go on with the current it's best not to take the plunge. But the river is still flowing there, waiting for you, if the things that chain you to the land are ever altered."

He looked at her again when he had finished speaking, and for an instant it was all there, hovering between them in the stillness of the air. Then Jane smiled. For a moment she rested her thin fingers lightly on the back of his strong, square hand.

"Bless you, dear Jimmy," she said softly, and got to her feet. She walked swiftly away from him over the sand and down to the water's edge, where she picked up a stone and skimmed it over the surface of the sea, pretending not to have heard his muttered "Jane, oh Janey."

She picked up a second stone, and another, and another, moving about looking for smooth, flat ones.

Jim stayed where he was, frowning to himself, busily writing in the sand, "I love you, Jane, I love you," the words he could not say.

Presently she came back up the beach towards him, whistling cheerfully, saying she wanted another swim, and he rubbed out his messages and said in a bright voice, "Very well, Mrs. Energy. This time I really will swim faster than you."

8

IT was good to be home again. Rose House looked lovely in its midsummer glory. The roses bloomed to welcome them; the little willow that had grown so much waved graceful green hair in the summer wind. The flower-beds needed weeding; Peter's holiday clothes must be sorted; there were plums to bottle and jam to make. For all these tasks Jane was ready and reinvigorated.

Michael was touchingly glad to see her back, but whether because a wife's place was in her home or because he had genuinely missed her Jane was cynically unable to decide. He had fresh advertising and administrative glories to relate; was not much interested in the seaside doings of Jane and Bill; was dismayed at the bucket of prawn corpses produced by Bill.

The first evening Jane told him about Jim being at Rhosarddur, for if she did not tackle it at once she would lose

382

her nerve. She told him in a calm, matter-of-fact voice, remarking upon it as a curious coincidence.

"Oh, indeed," said Michael. "See much of him?"

"I painted him," said Jane, in what seemed to her a very queer voice.

"Oh, that's good. I'm glad you've begun to paint again," said Michael. "Doesn't do to brood," he added, not unkindly,. "Now we must plan for Norton's portrait. I suppose there isn't time this term. Better leave it till the autumn, eh?"

The danger was over. In her relief Jane wondered if he would notice if she had told him she was leaving him. She felt a little guilt to think he was so trusting, but still, as Jim had so neatly put it, they had not leaped into the river. Perhaps she should feel guilty because her heart had gone from Michael, but that had happened before Jim's coming, though it had taken Jim to make her realise all that she had missed.

Now she was calm; to Michael's relief she was clearly in efficient working order. She slept well, she ate well, she cooked delicious meals. She met Jimmy at a tennis party and thought, calmly, how fortunate they were thus to see one another sometimes and be able to talk. Now she knew that this could be enough. She would manage like this, without jumping into the river, happy just to gaze at it. She felt it must be much harder for Jimmy than for herself to accept their circumstances with philosophy; he had no home or children to deflect him but she knew too that he had so much more inner courage than she had herself, and he had his work.

Autumn came, and Jane began her painting of Mr. Norton. Twice a week she went up to London with Michael, and spent the morning working in the little room at the factory. She enjoyed these sittings. She had never been to the works before, and was amazed at the magnificence of the office where Michael spent his days, a large, close-carpeted room with a huge mahogany desk covered in telephones, and an internal loudspeaker system, just like an American tycoon in a film. She was amused at the slight condescension displayed to her by his raven-haired secretary, with her sheer nylon stockings and stilt-high heels, aggressive bust and long scarlet-tipped fingers. Miss Wilks took care to show that Mr. Rutherford was very much a piece of her property.

Mr. Norton chatted gently during the sittings. He was naïvely delighted to watch his likeness gradually appearing on the canvas, and interested in the way Jane achieved her effects. He talked about Michael, praising his conscientiousness and application, his calm and level-headed way of planning sales campaigns and swifter methods of production, his efficiency.

Usually Jane lunched splendidly in the directors' private dining-room, but once, when Michael and Mr. Norton had to entertain an important customer, she met Jim, who happened to be in London that day for another conference. They lunched in a small French restaurant, talked of everything that came into their heads, and laughed a little. Jane went happily home on the three o'clock train and blessed such islands in her life. She was content.

Bonfire night came round again. By now, Bill was blasé, boasting that he would set off rockets and whizz-bangs, and being firmly squashed by Jane.

Before it was time to go, she washed up their tea things, and put the supper ready. The wireless was on, playing gay and lilting dance music. Jane hummed to it, all the time thinking that later she would see Jim, for he was certain to be there. The night, like the day, was fine, though cold.

She finished what she had to do, caught Bill by the hands and danced round the kitchen with him, singing.

"Will you dance with me, Bill, when you're a man?" she asked.

Bill said gravely, "I'm going to be a policeman in a Jaguar and take you shopping."

She laughed and caught him to her, spinning him round. He beamed up at her, little merry face and twinkling blue eyes. Sometimes she feared Peter might grow a little pompous, but Bill would never do that. They waltzed wildly round the kitchen.

"What fun, Bill," she gasped at

last, and he winked at her wickedly. "You're too lovely, Mummy," he told her, "Supersonic."

She picked him up and kissed him, laughing, then she said they must get ready.

Jim came up to her in the firelit darkness, as she knew he would. They stood together, watching the fireworks, not talking; Jane thought that next year Bill would be away at school and she would have no pretext for coming to the bonfire unless kind Maud invited her alone. She sniffed the fumy smell of the exploded fireworks, which she loved, acrid and fragrant, like no other odour. Then Bill came running up with a bundle of sparklers, wanting them lighted, and they became involved in a circle of children clasping sparklers, and trying to keep them burning continuously.

Afterwards, over drinks in the house while the children tucked in to Maud's annual buffet, Dr. Brown came to talk to Jane.

"You see we're both here," he said, nodding at Jim. "No one can be ill tonight."

He asked Jane then if she would paint his wife. "Later, in the spring," he added. "She's going away after Christmas to stay with her sister in Switzerland. It will do her good to get away from all the fogs we have in January."

Jane gladly agreed to take on the job, and when with some embarrassment he suggested fixing a price, she said practically. "The cost of the canvas only, Dr. Brown. I'm not starting to charge until the New Year, and this has been commissioned before that," and he laughed and thanked her.

Michael, arriving late, was glad to see Jane looking so bright. She seemed to have settled down perfectly after that upset in the spring. She would be all right now and give him no more trouble.

After Christmas, surprisingly at Michael's suggestion, they made up a party and went to the Hunt Ball. Michael would have liked to hunt, if he could have afforded it, but more for prestige than for pleasure. They invited the Hunts and the Fellowes to join them, and as Molly was staying for a few days it was obvious that Jim must be included.

So they danced again. This time Jane had a new dress, blue again, but cornflower coloured, and it made her eyes look like sapphires, Jimmy thought, dutifully circling round with Molly.

"She looks lovely, doesn't she?" said Molly, following his look.

Jimmy looked confused, but recovered himself and said "Yes, she does," in a calm voice.

Molly said, "Poor Jane. Michael's such a stick."

"Yes," said Jim.

"What a difference it's made to her, having you near," Molly went on. "She used to be a bag of nerves, but you've got her right, even after that awful business last spring. I used to worry about her, but I don't now. She seems to have found a way to live."

They danced on in silence, Jimmy for once at a loss for words. He did not know quite how much Molly meant. Presently she told him she was going to be married.

"To a solicitor of forty," she said lightly. "It's quite a businesslike arrangement. I've known him for some time. He's a widower with a small daughter. We're very fond of one another and I'm sure we shall be happy. Neither of us has any romantic delusions." She smiled. "It's a secret at the moment. We want to get married without a cattlemarket of fuss. Jane knows, but no one else. I wanted to tell you, though, Jim." She looked at him, a little sadly, as he wished her happiness; he never knew that she would have been only too ready to fall in with Jane's plans for them both.

Later, Jim danced with Jane.

"Lovely frock, Janey," he said brightly.

"New," she said. "Part of Mr. Norton's portrait."

"Well done," said Jim. "Are you pleased with the picture?"

"Moderately," she said. "It isn't like yours, of course, but that wasn't to be expected. I thought of trying yours on the Academy. Would you mind? Not to sell, of course."

"Of course I wouldn't mind," said Jimmy. "What else are you doing?"

"I've done a few landscapes. Some down by the river, where the willows grow," she said.

"Oh. By the river."

"Yes." They danced on, both silent for a time. Then Jimmy said, "Molly told me her news. I'm glad."

"Yes, it's splendid," said Jane. "I believe he's very nice, and he'll be kind to her. I used to think it was a cold-blooded way to get married, but now I'm not so sure that it hasn't a better chance of lasting happiness than the other way. They must be real friends."

"He's a lucky chap," said Jim.

"No regrets?" asked Jane mischievously.

He shook his head and smiled, tightening his arm a little round her. "No regrets, ever, Janey," he said.

In the end it happened so suddenly.

One morning, two weeks after the Hunt Ball, Jane was busy pouring kettles of water over the drainpipe from the bathroom which had frozen during the night. A bitter east wind had been blowing for days, and it bit through her old coat as it whistled round the side of the house. At last, with a cracking noise, the ice gave and a trickle of water began to flow from the pipe. Soon it strengthened, and with a rush all the waste water gushed out.

She took her kettle inside and went up to the water tank in the loft to break the ice that had formed during the night on its surface, a daily task during the bitter spell of icy weather.

Then she climbed down the ladder, dusty and chilly, and went into the kitchen. Bill was at school, and so of course was Peter. Jane made up the boiler and washed her hands in the sink.

Mrs. Barton arrived now, borne in through the back door on a gust of icy wind.

"Good morning, Mrs. Barton. It's as cold as ever," said Jane cheerfully. "Are your pipes all right?"

"So far," said Mrs. Barton. "It's when the thaw comes we must watch them."

"Yes," said Jane. "Brrrr, I'm cold. I've just been up in the loft."

Mrs. Barton said, "Oh, Mrs. Rutherford, isn't it dreadful about Dr. Fraser? Have you heard how he is today?"

Jane stared.

"Dr. Fraser? What's the matter with him?" she gasped.

"Haven't you heard about it? Oh, I was

sure you'd know, being as how you were such friends," said Mrs. Barton.

Jane's heart began to thud.

"What's wrong? Has he had an accident?" she asked.

"Oh no, Mrs. Rutherford. He's very ill, pneumonia, I believe it is. He's in Wolverstoke hospital. Took bad some days ago, he was. The postman said he's very bad."

Jane said, gaspingly, "Do you mean he's dangerously ill?"

"I believe so, Mrs. Rutherford," said Mrs. Barton. "But there, they can do marvellous things nowadays. He'll pull through, I'm sure."

Jane said, "But you don't *die* of pneumonia nowadays." She was numb with shock. How could such a thing happen so suddenly?

Mrs. Barton said, "I don't expect so."

"I must ring up," said Jane. Movement came back to her limbs, and she flew to the telephone to dial the exchange. But the instrument was dead. Strong winds in the night had blown a branch on to the line and the whole village was cut off.

She could think of nothing but that

she must go to Jim.

"I must go and see how he is," she said to Mrs. Barton. She tried to pull herself into calmness. "The telephone's out of order. I'm sure he's all right, but I must go and see."

"Yes, you go," agreed Mrs. Barton.

Jane dashed out. Her car did not want to start, spluttering in the icy air, but at last she got it to go, and tore off down the road with scant regard for the icy surface.

She had been to the hospital once or twice, when she had taken people from the village to the outpatients' department on a few occasions. It was a gaunt, barrack-like grey building, quite large, for it served a wide rural area.

She burst into the hallway as if all the hounds of hell were after her, as indeed they were. A smell of floor polish and ether greeted her; the atmosphere was one of breathless silence. There was not a soul in sight. She banged on a door marked 'Enquiries.' No reply. A young nurse, starchily rustled through the hall, and Jane said urgently, "Nurse, can you tell me how Dr. Fraser is?"

"Better ask sister on the ward," said the nurse.

"Which ward?" begged Jane desperately.

"Look, there's the porter, ask him." The nurse, in a hurry to get on with her work, pointed down the long corridor to where an ancient man in a beige overall could be seen slowly approaching.

Jane ran down the passage towards him.

"Ah now, let me see. I shall have to look at my list," said the old man, when appealed to. Jane had to curb her impatience and walk beside him back to his office, where very slowly he consulted pages of typed names. Then, when he had tracked down Jim's whereabouts he ambled off again down endless corridors, with Jane fuming beside him, praying for him to hurry.

* * *

Jim's room was very dark. He thought it was morning, for that blonde nurse was surely the one who usually came on in the morning, but perhaps they had forgotten to draw the curtains. There

395

was a queer rasping noise, like someone fighting for breath, in the room. He did not realise it was himself. The pain was better, he would soon recover now. Jim smiled a little. He felt very swimmy, as if he was floating away on a river. You could look at a river. You need not jump in. Rivers were lovely to look at, calm in patches, sometimes raging torrents. They took twigs that fell into them down to the sea. Fish swam in them. Boats sailed on them.

Boats sailed on the sea too.

The sea was like blue silk, crystal clear when you peered into it. The sand was like silver dust, a fine powder that slipped through your fingers. Jane's fingers were so thin and supple.

Bill had little starfish hands, plump and round. He was a merry lad, good company. Peter could draw. Peter looked like Michael.

The whited sepulchre.

Why didn't Jane come?

But he hadn't asked for her. He had nearly called her name, but he had stopped in time. People would think it strange.

Perhaps she didn't know he was ill. She would come if she knew. They weren't letting him have visitors, but he would tell the blonde nurse that Jane wasn't a visitor. She must be allowed in.

But he would be better soon, anyway. Dr. Brown had been so angry when he arrived back from Switzerland and found him coughing and shivering. It was only 'flu, what a fuss. Pills and injections. It was the night call to the farm at Picton Hill that had done it. The car had got stuck, and he had had to walk; then after the birth in the chill dawn, shivering with his own fever, he had walked back to the car, a mile away near the foot of the hill. It wouldn't start. The wind had been icy. At last he had pushed the car round and got the engine to go by running down the hill. Then the pain in his chest had begun. He had thought it was a pulled muscle.

There wasn't time to worry about it. Too many people were ill and Dr. Brown had gone to Switzerland for three days to take his wife out to spend the rest of the winter with her sister. He had kept going till Dr. Brown got back, then he had collapsed. When he was better he would go to Switzerland for three days. Jane would like Switzerland. She could paint the mountains. Dame Jane.

Why didn't she come? If she didn't hurry she would be too late. He must tell them to fetch her quickly.

No, he mustn't do anything that could cause speculation. He was getting better, the pain had gone. The wild dreams in which day and night had strung together in a delirious maze had stopped. He would be weak, of course, for a bit, but soon he would be strong.

Strong. Jane was strong now, calm and courageous. She would manage.

A bleeding knee; a little girl in grey shorts and a blue shirt, with a grubby, tear-stained face.

Jane in her blue evening dress, eyes like cornflowers, coming into his arms at the Ball. What a long time ago. How long had he been ill? A month? Six months? He must find out the date.

Jane was lying ill in the fog. That was why she hadn't come. He must get to her quickly. He half raised himself.

Hands, invisible to Jim, pushed him back, but he had scarcely moved an inch. The fog was very thick; he screwed up his eyes. There was a corner now, where was it? It's all right, Jane, I'm coming.

The fog blew away. The sun was shining brightly. Jane's blue eyes were looking at him tenderly. Suddenly she got to her feet and began to walk swiftly away from him over the silver sand.

"Jane, don't go, don't go," he called after her, struggling forward again from his propped pillows. She turned, and he saw that she was weeping. "The river," she was calling, "we can't jump in, it's gone away."

"Wait, Janey, wait," he called again; but no sound came to those who watched.

She had stopped. She was coming towards him. Now he need not hasten after her, she was on her way. Jim fell back again against his pile of pillows, smiling. "Jane," he said, quite clearly.

Then he died.

★ ★ ★

Matron said soothingly, "He was in a coma at the end. He didn't know anything."

Jane said, "But no one was with him, no one at all. Why didn't you send for someone?"

"Dr. Brown knew of no close relations, only a sister in Australia," said Matron.

"He didn't — he didn't ask for anyone?" whispered Jane.

"No. At the end he called out clearly, a name it was, nurse said, Joan, Jane, something like that, smiled, then he was gone. His sister perhaps."

"Perhaps," Jane said dully.

"It's a tragedy," said Matron more briskly. "We shall all miss him. Everyone liked Dr. Fraser."

"Yes," said Jane. She braced herself. Matron was looking at her enquiringly, but Jane did not notice.

"I — he — we were old friends," she said at last.

"I'm so sorry," said Matron, inadequately.

A probationer entered, bearing a tray with two cups and saucers and a brown teapot. Matron thanked her as she set it down on the table where a sprig of

400

mimosa sagged in a too-small vase. She poured out busily. Tea was the only remedy at such times.

"Typical of a doctor, of course," said Matron. "He got a bad cold, 'flu probably, and neglected it. It turned to pneumonia and by the time he took notice of it, it was too late."

"I see." Jane could not think, could not register. There was no future. There was no life. Only Jim was dead, lying silent a few yards away, dying as she entered the building half an hour earlier.

She gulped down the hot sweet tea Matron offered, not knowing what she did. There was nothing she could do. She could only go home, back to her frozen pipes.

★ ★ ★

Michael came in stamping his feet, rubbing his cold hands together, saying, "Brrr, ugh! What a cold night."

Jane was sitting by the fire, dry eyed, very still. She looked at him as if she had never seen him before.

"Beastly cold on the train," said

Michael, quite unnoticing. "The heating never seems to warm it properly." He went to the cupboard and poured himself out a large whisky and soda. "Enough to give anyone pneumonia," he went on.

Jane said: "Jim Fraser died of pneumonia this morning."

The words fell into the warm room like drops of ice. They seemed remote, detached, not about Jim at all.

Even Michael was shaken.

"What did you say?" he asked, putting down the syphon.

She repeated the seven words.

"What a dreadful thing," said Michael. "Come to think of it, I did hear he was ill the other day, someone on the train mentioned it. I don't think I told you."

It was too late for anger now. Jane sat still, staring at the fire.

"Bit of a shock, I suppose, since you'd known him as a kid," said Michael, with surprising consideration. "You always liked the little chap."

"Yes," said Jane. "Yes, it was a bit of a shock."

"When's the funeral? I suppose we'd better send a wreath," said Michael. "Is he being taken home?"

"He's being buried in Wolverstoke on Friday," said Jane. "His only relation is his sister in Australia."

"Oh, Friday. Well, I can't go. Got a very important meeting," said Michael with relief. "I don't really approve of women at funerals, but as he was a friend of yours you'd better go, I suppose. It will look bad if one of us isn't there. And order a decent wreath, won't you?"

He sat down and took a sip of his drink.

"Ah, that's better," he said. "Well, well, it's a reminder to us all about the uncertainty of life, isn't it?" He shook his head. "Poor fellow. A dreadful thing. Still, he's got no worries where he is now, I suppose. Ah, well." Michael picked up his paper, shook it open, and holding it at arm's length began to read where he had left off in the train.

★ ★ ★

Jane went to the funeral on Friday.

When she came back, she went up to the spare room where in a big cupboard she kept all her old canvases. She took out the portrait of Jim, set it on the easel, and looked at it steadily. She could not believe that the memory of him would ever fade.

She had never been to a funeral before, too young to go to her father's; he had died as she played, and Jim had died as she hastened to him.

It had been frightening to think of his sturdy body lying in that awful box. His clear grey eyes were closed for ever, his gentle mouth was still. She would not think of him like that; she would remember him as he was in this picture, half-smiling, warm and tender, unfailingly kind.

"There are things between us, Janey, that don't have to be put into words," he had said, "Things we both know."

He must have wondered why she never came. He knew that she loved him, she must always believe that he knew. But it was left to a stranger to hold his hand at the end as he uttered her name.

At last Jane wept.

Presently she dried her eyes. She put a cloth carefully over the canvas and put it back in the cupboard. Then she put on her old coat and went outside. She walked through the garden and climbed over the fence at the end. The first snowdrops lifted white drooping heads under the hedge, and the young weeping willow was already yellow with the promise of spring. Jane walked across the field; it was hard from the long frost. Jim's grave must have been dug with a pick, she thought vaguely. What a lot of daffodils and tulips had covered the stark mound of earth by that raw, gaping hole. They would shrivel and wilt in the frost tonight.

She shivered, and walked on, not caring where she went. A flock of ewes looked up at her approach; already several lambs, white like cotton wool, stood on spindle legs beside their shaggy mothers. When the frost broke it would be spring.

Presently she came to the path that led down by the river. She must have walked three miles without realising how far she had come. The river flowed black and mysterious between the rimed banks, like murky ink. Jane thought of Jim's river, the one that would have borne them both away. They could never jump into it now.

She remembered the morning. The church had been packed; Jim in three years had made himself the friend of all. Everyone was shocked and stunned by what had happened; but to Jane it seemed the end of all things.

She stood looking at the water as it swirled gently along; the frozen grasses at the brink stood stiff like small green spears. She would get over this, of course; you did, in time, everyone knew that. One day Jim would be only a distant tender memory of clear grey eyes and gentleness, eternally young as she grew old.

"Oh Jim, Jim, where are you? Where have you gone?" she cried aloud in her despair, staring at the pale blue sky as if to see him there.

It wasn't the end, of course. Life still went on; she would go back to her home and her children. She still could paint, she had promised Jim once that she would never give it up again. She would force herself to work, until she had grown used to this forsaking. All her life she had run away from her problems; she had shrunk into dreams as a child; when she grew up she had sought refuge with Michael, the first haven who appeared to offer shelter from the difficulties of adult life. Then, when the disappointment of her marriage had reached a climax, Jim had come to show her another way of escape, even though it must always have remained a dream. She had fought against its limitations at first, then she had learned to accept the fact of perfect friendship and make it enough. Now there was nothing left, only the bitterness of knowing that the years would blur the memory of the little they had shared.

But though time would blur the memories, it could not blur the fact. Jim had lived, and had loved her; he had given her confidence to live as an individual; that was not lost. One day she might, if she endured, find a serenity to equal his; this time she could not escape.

Jane picked up a stone that lay on the river bank. It was heavy, smooth and round, cold in her bare hand. She threw it far out into the dark water. It disappeared with a splash, sending widening circles of disturbance rippling over the surface of the river. Presently the circles began to diminish, getting smaller and smaller until there were no more. The river flowed on, secret, serene, as though nothing had happened to disturb its calm, and the stone lay hidden for ever in the heart of the cold water.

THE END

CLOUD OVER MALVERTON
Nancy Buckingham

Dulcie soon realises that something is seriously wrong at Malverton, and when violence strikes she is horrified to find herself under suspicion of murder.

AFTER THOUGHTS
Max Bygraves

The Cockney entertainer tells stories of his East End childhood, of his RAF days, and his post-war showbusiness successes and friendships with fellow comedians.

MOONLIGHT
AND MARCH ROSES
D. Y. Cameron

Lynn's search to trace a missing girl takes her to Spain, where she meets Clive Hendon. While untangling the situation, she untangles her emotions and decides on her own future.

NURSE ALICE IN LOVE
Theresa Charles

Accepting the post of nurse to little Fernie Sherrod, Alice Everton could not guess at the romance, suspense and danger which lay ahead at the Sherrod's isolated estate.

POIROT INVESTIGATES
Agatha Christie

Two things bind these eleven stories together — the brilliance and uncanny skill of the diminutive Belgian detective, and the stupidity of his Watson-like partner, Captain Hastings.

LET LOOSE THE TIGERS
Josephine Cox

Queenie promised to find the long-lost son of the frail, elderly murderess, Hannah Jason. But her enquiries threatened to unlock the cage where crucial secrets had long been held captive.

THE TWILIGHT MAN
Frank Gruber

Jim Rand lives alone in the California desert awaiting death. Into his hermit existence comes a teenage girl who blows both his past and his brief future wide open.

DOG IN THE DARK
Gerald Hammond

Jim Cunningham breeds and trains gun dogs, and his antagonism towards the devotees of show spaniels earns him many enemies. So when one of them is found murdered, the police are on his doorstep within hours.

THE RED KNIGHT
Geoffrey Moxon

When he finds himself a pawn on the chessboard of international espionage with his family in constant danger, Guy Trent becomes embroiled in moves and countermoves which may mean life or death for Western scientists.

TIGER TIGER
Frank Ryan

A young man involved in drugs is found murdered. This is the first event which will draw Detective Inspector Sandy Woodings into a whirlpool of murder and deceit.

CAROLINE MINUSCULE
Andrew Taylor

Caroline Minuscule, a medieval script, is the first clue to the whereabouts of a cache of diamonds. The search becomes a deadly kind of fairy story in which several murders have an other-worldly quality.

LONG CHAIN OF DEATH
Sarah Wolf

During the Second World War four American teenagers from the same town join the Army together. Forty-two years later, the son of one of the soldiers realises that someone is systematically wiping out the families of the four men.

THE LISTERDALE MYSTERY
Agatha Christie

Twelve short stories ranging from the light-hearted to the macabre, diverse mysteries ingeniously and plausibly contrived and convincingly unravelled.

TO BE LOVED
Lynne Collins

Andrew married the woman he had always loved despite the knowledge that Sarah married him for reasons of her own. So much heartache could have been avoided if only he had known how vital it was to be loved.

ACCUSED NURSE
Jane Converse

Paula found herself accused of a crime which could cost her her job, her nurse's reputation, and even the man she loved, unless the truth came to light.

A GREAT DELIVERANCE
Elizabeth George

Into the web of old houses and secrets of Keldale Valley comes Scotland Yard Inspector Thomas Lynley and his assistant to solve a particularly savage murder.

'E' IS FOR EVIDENCE
Sue Grafton

Kinsey Millhone was bogged down on a warehouse fire claim. It came as something of a shock when she was accused of being on the take. She'd been set up. Now she had a new client — herself.

A FAMILY OUTING IN AFRICA
Charles Hampton and Janie Hampton

A tale of a young family's journey through Central Africa by bus, train, river boat, lorry, wooden bicycle and foot.

THE PLEASURES OF AGE
Robert Morley

The author, British stage and screen star, now eighty, is enjoying the pleasures of age. He has drawn on his experiences to write this witty, entertaining and informative book.

THE VINEGAR SEED
Maureen Peters

The first book in a trilogy which follows the exploits of two sisters who leave Ireland in 1861 to seek their fortune in England.

A VERY PAROCHIAL MURDER
John Wainwright

A mugging in the genteel seaside town turned to murder when the victim died. Then the body of a young tearaway is washed ashore and Detective Inspector Lyle is determined that a second killing will not go unpunished.

DEATH ON A HOT SUMMER NIGHT
Anne Infante

Micky Douglas is either accident-prone or someone is trying to kill him. He finds himself caught in a desperate race to save his ex-wife and others from a ruthless gang.

HOLD DOWN A SHADOW
Geoffrey Jenkins

Maluti Rider, with the help of four of the world's most wanted men, is determined to destroy the Katse Dam and release a killer flood.

THAT NICE MISS SMITH
Nigel Morland

A reconstruction and reassessment of the trial in 1857 of Madeleine Smith, who was acquitted by a verdict of Not Proven of poisoning her lover, Emile L'Angelier.

SEASONS OF MY LIFE
Hannah Hauxwell
and Barry Cockcroft

The story of Hannah Hauxwell's struggle to survive on a desolate farm in the Yorkshire Dales with little money, no electricity and no running water.

TAKING OVER
Shirley Lowe and Angela Ince

A witty insight into what happens when women take over in the boardroom and their husbands take over chores, children and chickenpox.

AFTER MIDNIGHT STORIES,
The Fourth Book Of

A collection of sixteen of the best of today's ghost stories, all different in style and approach but all combining to give the reader that special midnight shiver.

DEATH TRAIN
Robert Byrne

The tale of a freight train out of control and leaking a paralytic nerve gas that turns America's West into a scene of chemical catastrophe in which whole towns are rendered helpless.

THE ADVENTURE OF THE CHRISTMAS PUDDING
Agatha Christie

In the introduction to this short story collection the author wrote "This book of Christmas fare may be described as 'The Chef's Selection'. I am the Chef!"

RETURN TO BALANDRA
Grace Driver

Returning to her Caribbean island home, Suzanne looks forward to being with her parents again, but most of all she longs to see Wim van Branden, a coffee planter she has known all her life.

SKINWALKERS
Tony Hillerman

The peace of the land between the sacred mountains is shattered by three murders. Is a 'skinwalker', one who has rejected the harmony of the Navajo way, the murderer?

A PARTICULAR PLACE
Mary Hocking

How is Michael Hoath, newly arrived vicar of St. Hilary's, to meet the demands of his flock and his strained marriage? Further complications follow when he falls hopelessly in love with a married parishioner.

A MATTER OF MISCHIEF
Evelyn Hood

A saga of the weaving folk in 18th century Scotland. Physician Gavin Knox was desperately seeking a cure for the pox that ravaged the slums of Glasgow and Paisley, but his adored wife, Margaret, stood in the way.

DEAD SPIT
Janet Edmonds

Government vet Linus Rintoul attempts to solve a mystery which plunges him into the esoteric world of pedigree dogs, murder and terrorism, and Crufts Dog Show proves to be far more exciting than he had bargained for . . .

A BARROW IN THE BROADWAY
Pamela Evans

Adopted by the Gordillo family, Rosie Goodson watched their business grow from a street barrow to a chain of supermarkets. But passion, bitterness and her unhappy marriage aliented her from them.

THE GOLD AND THE DROSS
Eleanor Farnes

Lorna found it hard to make ends meet for herself and her mother and then by chance she met two men — one a famous author and one a rich banker. But could she really expect to be happy with either man?

THE SONG OF THE PINES
Christina Green

Taken to a Greek island as substitute for David Nicholas's secretary, Annie quickly falls prey to the island's charms and to the charms of both Marcus, the Greek, and David himself.

GOODBYE DOCTOR GARLAND
Marjorie Harte

The story of a woman doctor who gave too much to her profession and almost lost her personal happiness.

DIGBY
Pamela Hill

Welcomed at courts throughout Europe, Kenelm Digby was the particular favourite of the Queen of France, who wanted him to be her lover, but the beautiful Venetia was the mainspring of his life.